──────────────── ★ ────────────────

I heard noises. A scream. Shuffling. A loudly barked order.

Someone yelled in English, "Get back! Get back!"

Marco left me leaning on thin air and ran to the nearest alley, one that ran downhill and to the right. He stopped.

"Oh, Dio!"

Lettie and I hurried along to join him. The alley opened out to bright sky at the other end, but I could go no farther than the entrance because Marco stopped me with his outstretched arm. He didn't stop Lettie, who, being a bit shy of five foot one, ducked under his arm.

Afternoon sun poured into the far end of the alley, highlighting red-streaked walls, red puddles on the cobblestones. It must have been a horrible battle. From a dark mound at the base of one wall, a bare arm stretched out and up at an awkward angle.

"It's our photographer!"

──────────────── ★ ────────────────

Death
on the
Aegean Queen

Maria Hudgins

WORLDWIDE®

TORONTO • NEW YORK • LONDON
AMSTERDAM • PARIS • SYDNEY • HAMBURG
STOCKHOLM • ATHENS • TOKYO • MILAN
MADRID • WARSAW • BUDAPEST • AUCKLAND

For Nelson and Aquilla Bible

Recycling programs
for this product may
not exist in your area.

DEATH ON THE AEGEAN QUEEN

A Worldwide Mystery/June 2011

First published by Five Star Publishing

ISBN-13: 978-0-373-26754-5

Copyright © 2010 by Maria Hudgins

Printed in U.S.A.

CAST OF CHARACTERS
(in order of their appearance)

Dotsy Lamb—Ancient history professor and an archaeology buff.

Lettie Osgood—Librarian from Virginia.

Ollie Osgood—Lettie's husband.

Marco Quattrocchi—Carabinieri captain from Florence.

George Gaskill—Car salesman from Indiana.

Kathryn Gaskill—George's wife.

Luc Girard—Famous archaeologist and resident lecturer on the *Aegean Queen*.

Malcolm Stone—Antiques dealer from England.

Willem Leclercq—Belgian home designer/architect.

Demopoulos—Junior officer in ship security.

Letsos—Chief of ship security.

Constantinos Tzedakis—Captain of the ship.

David Bondurant—FBI agent.

Brittany Benson—Member of ship's dance troupe.

Sophie Antonakos—Member of the dance troupe.

Nikos Papadakos—The ship's photographer.

Lieutenant Dimitris Villas—Policeman from Mykonos.

Nigel Endicott—Mysterious passenger from Vermont.

Ernestine and Heather Ziegler—Mother and daughter from Chicago.

Goatman—Hygienically challenged man.

Robert Segal—Brittany Benson's boyfriend.

ONE

"WHY DO WE HAVE TO go to that voodoo island?"

Lettie Osgood glared at me as if I were in charge of the itinerary. In a few minutes a tugboat would pull our ship, the *Aegean Queen,* out of Piraeus Harbor on the south side of Athens. The Greek sun glanced off my sunglasses, warmed the top of my head.

Lettie, her husband Ollie, and I leaned over the rail of the Poseidon Deck and looked down on the heads of late-arriving passengers as they tugged their wheeled carry-ons up the gangway. We were waiting for Marco, a friend of mine from Italy. I had starved off seven pounds and bought new clothes in preparation for this cruise, inspired daily by my "Greek Islands" desk calendar and the photo Marco had stuck into a Christmas card. A picture of himself and me at the Coliseum in Rome.

"What voodoo island?" My brain returned to the present.

"The brochure says 'day seven, Santeria.' Didn't you read your brochure, Dotsy?"

"Santeria?"

"Santeria is just another word for voodoo, and I don't care what you say, zombies are real!" Lettie scowled at me.

"It's Santorini, Lettie," Ollie said. "Not Santeria."

I bit my lip.

"Santorini used to be Atlantis, scientists believe." Ollie's voice had taken on a scholarly tone. "Then it disappeared beneath the waves."

"So what's for us to visit?"

It promised, I thought, to be a great trip.

Lettie leaned over the rail and pointed. "That man is going the wrong way."

I found the man she was pointing to, a rather bow-legged guy in a red-and-yellow sport shirt and Bermuda shorts. He was weaving aggressively through the oncoming foot traffic. Bumping shoulders and dodging suitcases like a tight end with the football. "He's probably been seeing someone off and he's trying to get back ashore before they pull up the gangway."

"They weren't letting anyone but ticketed passengers through security," Ollie said. "If he isn't going with us, how did he get past the guards?"

On the deck behind us, a three-piece musical combo fiddled with their microphones and speakers. Waiters lined up scores of blue drinks in tall glasses on the bar, inserting a little Greek flag and a white flower into each glass. Passengers whisked the drinks off the bar as quickly as the servers could put them out.

"Here's Marco!"

"Where?"

Lettie clapped her hands and pointed over the rail toward two women, one overweight and one overloaded, who were obviously traveling together. Behind them was a man in a blue shirt and tan shorts. But that couldn't be Marco. Marco wore a beard.

Marco Quattrocchi, a Carabinieri captain from Florence, was the friend I expected to join us. Lettie and I had met him two years ago when we were on a tour of Italy and a member of our tour group got murdered at our Florence hotel. I had graciously made my observational and analytical talents available to the ensuing investigation, and thereby had become Marco's friend, then enemy, then friend again. We'd kept in touch, and it was he who had suggested this cruise. Ollie, who normally isn't interested in the foreign tours Lettie and I love to take, had been persuaded to come along this time because, as he put it, "On a ship, nobody tells you when to get up and get on the bus."

The man who turned at the top of the ramp and waved to me was Marco without a beard, and I didn't like it at all. He looked shorter. His upper lip was too thin. I'd never seen his upper lip before. Oh, dear. He disappeared into the side of the ship where the stairs to our deck were located.

"Dotsy! And Lettie!" Marco appeared at the top of the stairs and hurried across the deck. He took Lettie's left hand, my right, and gave us air kisses on both sides. "Your hair, Dotsy," he said in his thick Italian accent. "You have…"

"Let it go natural." I finished his sentence for him. I'd forgotten that, in addition to losing seven pounds, I'd let my hair grow out to its natural auburn and gray. It didn't occur to me he might not like the changes in my appearance as much as I didn't like the change in his.

We introduced him to Ollie and sent the men to the bar for drinks while Lettie and I grabbed a vacant table. Marco returned with two of those blue cocktails, Ollie, with a blue thing and a Heineken.

A building contractor at their home in Fredericksburg, Virginia, Ollie was known as "The Snowman" to his workers, but they didn't call him that to his face. Big, barrel-chested, and bald as a trailer hitch, he had no neck at all and a rather button-like nose. I lived in fear of accidentally calling him "Frosty."

After we were all seated, Lettie said, "When did you get here, Marco? Did you fly straight from Florence?"

"No." He swigged the blue liquid and poked himself in

the eye with the Greek flag. "Unfortunately I could not find a flight straight from Florence to Athens. I had to drive first to Milano. Alitalia has a straight, no-stopping flight from Milano to here."

I had to become reaccustomed to Marco's refusal to use contractions. His English was pretty good, but I supposed he thought the use of contractions would be pushing the linguistic envelope. He also had a way of putting the same stress on all his syllables, which made the rhythm of his speech awkward. I had to listen intently when he talked.

The band's spirited rendition of "Never on Sunday" wound down, and a piped-in announcement broke into our chatter. It was delivered in Greek, then repeated in French, English, Italian, German, and Japanese. "We will depart Piraeus in five minutes. All visitors should now be ashore. If you are onboard and are not sailing with us, you must disembark immediately."

Ollie slipped a pair of sunglasses out of his shirt pocket, stretched the earpieces over his temples, and looked toward the stairs leading up from the gangway.

"There's that wrong-way guy again."

I followed Ollie's gaze. The man in the yellow-and-red shirt, now toting a duffle bag, was back on board.

SOON AFTER THE SHIP LEFT the dock, we had the mandatory lifeboat drill, which Marco suggested was actually a trick to give the crew a chance to slip our luggage into our rooms. It was the only time until the end of the cruise, he pointed out, that the halls would be clear of passengers. We each had to don the life jacket we found on the bed in our room and wait for the announcement to dash to our designated lifeboat station on deck. Marco and I were assigned the same station because our rooms were on the same level and a mere four doors apart. I waited for him in the foyer at the foot of the stairs leading up to the next level where a long row of lifeboats hung suspended above the promenade deck.

It startled me to see a small Cycladic figure in a display case at the base of the stairs. A female figure carved out of marble with a sloping head and arms folded above the belly, its abstract form hinted at an eerie link between the prehistoric and the modern. I'd seen similar sculptures in the textbooks I used in my ancient history classes and I knew they could be found in Greek museums, but I would never have expected to find one on a cruise ship. I read the descriptive plaque. They claimed it was genuine and from Naxos, an island in the Cyclades, 2500 B.C.

Marco slipped up behind me and blew in my ear. I jerked around, prepared to slap somebody, then smiled when I saw him, but I didn't like the way he looked in a life jacket. My virile, fearless Florentine cop looked a bit silly in an orange jacket and with no beard.

"Can you believe they have an actual Cycladic fertility figure on a cruise ship? Isn't this dangerous?"

"Dangerous?" Marco looked baffled. "Do you think it is going to promote too much conception among the passengers?"

"No, silly. I mean this is so valuable. Priceless! Irreplaceable! How can a cruise line afford to buy such things? Who would let them buy such a thing? The ship might sink! The figure might get swiped or broken."

"Dotsy, if you knew the conditions thousands of these—what you call them?—priceless objects are in right now, you would realize this little woman is very lucky. There are Etruscan antiquities hidden in warehouses that are firetraps. There is Minoan pottery painted black by smugglers who try to pass it off as cheap souvenirs at border crossings." Marco's eyes took on an intensity I'd only seen in him once or twice before, as if a dentist's drill had struck a nerve.

We climbed the stairs together, joining the throng of passengers heading for the deck. At the top of the stairs, Lettie and Ollie passed us, and I had to choke back a laugh. A puffy orange life jacket, its straps let out to the fullest extent, on Frosty the Snowman was like water wings on a blimp. Ollie looked as if he'd certainly float without any help. In fact, he looked as if you could unstack him and save several smaller, denser folk.

"The lifeboat drill is required by law," Marco told me, "but they have another reason to do this. It helps them find stowaways."

"Stowaways?"

"Certainly. Anyone who is still inside or who does not have a properly numbered jacket is not supposed to be here."

"What would they do with a stowaway?"

"They would make him walk off the plank. Have you not seen the pirate movies?"

I WASN'T SURE HOW dressed-up to get for dinner. The men would be wearing suits, or at least ties, I thought. I settled on my black dress with red poppies and, since the dress had a scoop neck, a black onyx necklace and earrings.

We four had elected the first seating for dinner and were joined at our large, round table by George and Kathryn Gaskill, of Elkhart, Indiana. After introductions all around, we exchanged the basic information: what do you do, how many children, is this your first cruise, and so on. As usual, I took top honors for most children. Ollie and Lettie had two, Marco, two, the Gaskills, none—they had apparently married late—and me, five. Our children, grown now, we were all empty-nesters including, I suppose, the Gaskills, whose nest had never been full.

The Gaskills made an unassuming little pair. Kathryn was a small, round woman with short black hair and a rather vacant face. George had a goatee and wore his hair slicked straight back. A round, flesh-colored Band-aid bobbed on the curve of his jawbone below his left ear as he talked.

"He cut himself shaving this morning," Kathryn said. I must have been staring at his jaw.

"I sell cars," Gaskill said, in response to Ollie's question. "Used cars."

George talked with a slight whistle. His prominent front teeth made him look like a beaver. His dark hair plastered to his skull, his goatee twitched as he talked. Make that a wet beaver. When he reached for his wine glass, I noticed the sleeves and collar of his white shirt were frayed.

He asked Marco about the Carabinieri. "What is it? Is it like our police?"

"It is the military police in Italy. We also have police. La polizia. But we, the Carabinieri, we have nicer uniforms," Marco said, glancing around the table as he said it.

I knew he was testing to see who had a sense of humor.

"If someone gets mugged," Kathryn asked in a small, squeaky voice, "does he call the Carabinieri or the police?"

"He can call either one. Our duties, unfortunately, are not clearly...different. In spite of the fact that our government has tried to unite the two and to spell out the responsibilities of each, we still do many of the same things." Marco paused and glanced around the table again. "But the Carabinieri do it better."

Lettie giggled and put her napkin up to her mouth.

Ollie said, "How's the car business, Gaskill?"

"Slow. Very slow. Normally, I wouldn't take a vacation

in June like this, but sales are so slow it didn't seem to make any difference whether I left or not."

"It's the economy," Lettie said. "Money is so tight."

"Speaking of money ..." George Gaskill turned to acknowledge the waiter who was attempting to maneuver a lobster cocktail between George's and Kathryn's shoulders. "I see they have a casino on the Poseidon deck. Anyone for a wager or two after dinner?"

"I'll join you," Ollie said and looked at Marco.

"No, thank you. I want to see the show," Marco said. "The Greek dancers. Dotsy, will you come with me?"

I nodded.

"Does anyone else want to go with us?" he asked.

Lettie indicated she'd rather see the show than gamble, but Kathryn said she needed to go to their room and finish settling in.

THE SHOW LOUNGE WAS on the Dionysus deck. The *Aegean Queen*'s decks were all named after Greek gods. The top one was called the Zeus deck, an appropriate name since Zeus was the king of the gods, and below it, the Hera deck where we had just eaten. Then in descending order, the Apollo, Poseidon, Dionysus, Ares, Athena, and Demeter. My stateroom was on the Athena deck.

Marco, Lettie, and I grabbed a table for four near the round stage. A waiter took our order immediately, but we had no more than sampled our drinks when Kathryn Gaskill slipped in and joined us.

"Settling in didn't take as long as I thought it would." She gave the waiter her order and looked around. As the lounge filled up, we checked out our fellow passengers. "That's a lonely looking man over there," Kathryn said.

She nodded toward a lean, angular man with chin-length hair, a goatee, and black-rimmed glasses. At a table in the corner, he sat, slouched, with his chair pushed back against the wall, one finger running idly around the rim of his glass.

I knew him.

"What is it, Dotsy?" Marco asked.

"I know that man, but I can't place him. Oh, who is he?" By whatever process the mind goes through when it tries to recall a person, a particular face, I realized he wasn't anyone I'd ever actually met. He was someone whose picture I'd seen. Surrounded by dirt. Pith helmet. Khaki shirt. Trowel.

"Got it!" I said. "That's Luc Girard. He's a famous archaeologist. French, I think. I saw him in a documentary about Minoan civilization I showed to my students last year."

Lettie faced Kathryn. "Dotsy teaches ancient and medieval history at a junior college back in Virginia. She knows all sorts of stuff about times past."

It was as good a summary of me and my current life as I could have done myself. "What's he doing here?" I said. "This is excavation season; why isn't he out digging or something?" The four of us looked at Luc Girard until he glanced up and we all turned our heads, guiltily, in one direction or another.

The lights dimmed and the dancers, in traditional Greek rural costumes, entered and ran down the aisle. One of the girls tripped on the edge of the stage and began her performance with a three-point landing.

TWO

OLLIE OSGOOD PUNCHED the button on a slot machine for a few minutes, won the token equivalent of $20, then attempted to join George Gaskill at the blackjack table. Smoke swirled thickly through the casino, the clinks and the rinky-dink carnival sounds of the machines assailed the ears, flashing lights dazzled the eyes. The blackjack table was full, and several onlookers stood behind the players, waiting for their own chance to play.

Ollie drifted to the bar, ordered a beer, and struck up a conversation with two men who soon introduced themselves.

"Malcolm Stone, London," said the gray-haired one with black eyebrows, extending his right hand to Ollie.

"Willem Leclercq, Antwerp," said the other. Younger, probably in his early thirties, he was dressed casually in a knit shirt and jeans. He greeted Ollie with an intense stare from his pale blue eyes.

The three men exchanged small talk while they scanned the action at the blackjack table. Stone and Leclercq told Ollie they were on a reconnaissance/buying trip for a wealthy client of Leclercq's, a client who wished to remain anonymous and for whom Leclercq was designing and furnishing "one helluva house," the Belgian said, in a French-sounding accent.

He explained further. "I have asked Malcolm to come with me on this trip because he's an antiques appraiser in London. An expert in classical Greek and Mediterranean artifacts."

"I take it your client wants his helluva house furnished with real antiques," Ollie said.

"No fakes."

"Not for this bloke."

The two men mentioned they had a suite on the Apollo deck, where it was quiet and the air was clean. Ollie, Leclercq suggested, might like to join them there for a few hands of poker.

"I'm here with a friend." Ollie indicated the blackjack table with a jerk of his head. "I'll check with him."

Ollie lumbered across the room and delivered the invitation. George Gaskill raked his chips off the table and all four men bought a supply of chips from the cashier after mutually agreeing that a pot with dollars, pounds, and Euros would exceed their combined mathematical skill. Before they left the casino, George phoned his stateroom and got no answer. "Kathryn may have gone to the show after all," he said.

Stone and Leclercq led them up one deck to a suite Ollie imagined might be the largest and most luxurious on the ship. Two bedrooms, a bath, and a kitchenette surrounded a large living room with a conversation area, a round dining table with four chairs, a fully stocked bar, and a wall of glass doors opening onto a softly lit balcony.

"Being American, I suppose you blokes are familiar with Texas hold 'em poker," Malcolm Stone said, slapping a new deck of cards on the round table.

Ollie gave a little start at the sound of that down-home phrase rendered in a British accent. "Absolutely! Gaskill? Okay with you? Leclercq?"

"Belgium is not on Mars," Leclercq answered. "Isn't it called world-class poker?" On hands and knees, he dragged a white dealer button out from under the table and handed it to Stone. "We have television in Antwerp."

Malcolm Stone slipped off his tie and dinner jacket and tossed his cuff links onto the glass-topped coffee table. Ollie and George followed suit, making themselves comfortable, while Leclercq pulled a beer from the small refrigerator under the bar.

"Who wants beer?" Leclercq asked.

"I'll take one," Ollie said. "Do I see a Heineken in there? That'll work."

"Not for me. I'll have a gin and tonic," said Stone, rolling up his starched sleeves. "Can't abide this American custom of serving beer ice-cold. Gaskill?"

"Thank you. I'll have a gin and tonic, too."

While Stone assembled the drinks, the other three chose places at the round table. Leclercq took the chair nearest the bar, George to his right, and Ollie opposite Leclercq, with his back to the balcony doors. Stone brought George his drink and took the empty seat to Leclercq's left.

Stone dealt the first hand. No limit, Texas hold 'em. A type of poker in which each player makes his best five-card hand from the two in his hand and the five cards, which, interspersed with several rounds of betting, are dealt, face up, in the center of the table. Of the four players, only George needed a refresher course in how the betting went. Stone explained it.

The play moved along pleasantly enough, with no one winning or losing a substantial sum, until George looked at his watch and, his S's whistling through his front teeth, said, "Uh-oh. Kathryn's going to kill me. She doesn't know where I am and if she checks the casino she'll be out of luck."

Ollie leaned back in his chair and stretched. "Lettie won't be looking for me. She'll be in bed already, with that God-awful green goo she slaps all over her face every night."

Leclercq laughed. "Last hand, then?" It was Gaskill's turn to deal. He dealt two cards (called hole cards, because they're seen only by the holder) to each man. At this point, a fly buzzing around the table could have seen:

Gaskill with 8♠,9♠.

Leclercq with 10♣,10♦.

Stone with K♠,A♠.

Ollie with A♣,A♥.

Ollie and Leclercq were each looking at a pair before the first round of betting. In the majority of hands played so far, a pair, especially a pair of aces like Ollie's, would have had a good chance of winning regardless of what cards were subsequently dealt. But for the first round of betting, Leclercq and Stone, the first two players to the left of the dealer, were in the blind positions, required to ante a standard starter for the pot. Ollie, keeping a perfectly straight face, placed a small bet of 10, and Leclercq raised it by 10 and called. The others matched his bet. This put a total of about eighty dollars' worth of chips in the pot. The exact value of the chips could only be determined by using the currency conversion rates and none of the players, at this point in the evening, were at all prone to do the math.

Gaskill discarded the top card, as the dealer was required to do, and slapped the next three cards down, face up, in the middle of the table: 7♠,10♠,A♦.

Leclercq bet 50. The other three matched it and called.

Gaskill revealed the fourth card: J♠.

Leclercq checked, that is, bet no additional chips. Stone bet an additional 300, precipitating coughs and sputters from the other three, but they all matched his bet and stayed in the game.

Gaskill flipped the fifth and final card onto the table: 10♥.

A perfectly ordinary card but in this case it gave Ollie a

full house, Stone, a flush, and Leclercq, four 10's. Gaskill already had a straight flush before the last card was played, so all four went flat out to win this last hand, betting madly with all the chips they had.

With about $9,000 worth of chips on the table, George Gaskill and his straight flush scooped up the whole pot.

THREE

WHEN THE LIGHTS IN the show lounge went up, I looked across the room and noticed Luc Girard had apparently slipped out. Marco rose and helped me with my chair. "I was planning to ask your famous archaeologist for his autograph, Dotsy, but he appears to have left."

"It's okay. If he's here for the whole cruise, I'll have other chances to meet him," I said.

Still *la-la*-ing the folk dance music as she pushed through the lounge doors, Lettie tried to link arms with Kathryn and me, to start an impromptu, slightly tipsy, Greek circle dance, but she slipped backward off the top step of the staircase. Kathryn and I tightened our grips and saved her a nasty fall. I felt grateful and somewhat guilty for feeling I'd been saved from making a spectacle of myself.

The grand staircase, dazzling with chandeliers and polished brass rails, peeled off left and right at each landing then reemerged into a flight of double-wide central steps leading up or down to the next level. One could go all the way from the top to the bottom of the ship on this stairway, or one could take the elevator running parallel to it, a few yards aft of the stairs. Lettie left us on the next lower level, the Ares deck, assuring us she had her room card and knew her room number. She kissed us all good night and la-la-ed her way, fingers snapping and feet kicking, through the swinging doors that led to a long hall and her stateroom.

The Ares deck was what some call a promenade deck. With teak planks running completely around the ship on this level only, it was the place for joggers and strollers to get their exercise and, lined with deck chairs, it also attracted writers, readers, loungers, and nappers.

Marco, Kathryn, and I continued down one more level to the Athena deck. "Which room is yours, Dotsy?" Kathryn asked. "Ours is number three seventy-eight."

"Number three sixty-five," I said. "Like the days in a year."

"Good way to remember it."

Marco stopped with me at my door while Kathryn walked on by. An awkward moment. Did he expect me to invite him in? I hoped not. It had been two years since we'd seen each other and he felt rather like a stranger to me.

But Marco, bless his little Latin heart, made a better suggestion. "I noticed a nice walking place up on the deck where Lettie's room is. Would you like to take a walk with me?"

We hiked back up the stairs and out through a set of double doors to the wooden rail on the starboard side of the ship. The breeze from the movement of the ship blowing my hair across my face, I looked over the side and down, way down, to the water. The lights from portholes below us reflected off the black surface, reminding me we were at sea. If there was a moon out tonight, it was on the other side of the ship.

"I'm turned around," I said, running my hands along the polished wooden rail. "Are we going north, south, east, or west?"

"We are going to Mykonos. It is east of Athens."

"So right now, we're looking—what—southward?"

Marco placed his hand on top of one of mine and

glanced toward me, studying my face. I felt my own hand tense up. As if he had read my mind through the palm of his hand, he slowly withdrew it and laced his fingers together, his forearms against the railing.

He cleared his throat self-consciously and said, "You will like Mykonos."

"You've been there, have you?"

"I was there once. It attracts artists, writers, and jet-setters because it is very pretty. Windmills. Little streets and churches with blue or red domes. Many fishermen."

"Ah. Then Ollie will like it. He loves anything to do with fishing."

"They have a very strange pelican there. I hope we will get to see it. Big bird." Marco folded his arms into bird wings.

"What's strange about it?"

"I think there are several of them, actually. They are white, but their faces are pink and yellow and blue. You will have to see them for yourself."

After a few more minutes in the warm night air, Marco walked me back to my room, smiled, and ruffled my hair. "Goodnight, Dotsy."

Marco Quattrocchi is a class act, I thought.

"DOTSY! I CAN'T FIND my husband! Is he with you?"

It had been a long time since I'd been rousted out of bed with such a question. It took me a minute to remember I was on a ship in the Aegean Sea. I rolled myself up to a sitting position, swung my legs off the side of my little bed, and shook my head, feeling the thud of a slight hangover at the base of my skull. I searched the vicinity for something that would give me a clue about what time it was.

Giving it up as a lost cause in the dark and having no

memory of where any light switches were, I stumbled to the door and opened it a crack.

"I'm so, so sorry to wake you up at this hour, Dotsy, but I can't find George anywhere." Kathryn Gaskill appeared to be fully dressed and desperate. Rubbing a bit more sleep out of my eyes, I looked at her again. She was dressed in cropped pants and cotton shirt, but wore no makeup and her hair was uncombed.

I waved her into my room and flipped a light switch I found near the door. She didn't want to sit down, but I plopped myself on the side of my bed and yawned. "He and Ollie Osgood were going to the casino, weren't they?"

"Yes, but that was about nine o'clock. It's after three now, and neither he nor Ollie is in the casino. I've already been up there and checked." Kathryn's tiny voice sounded strained.

"Is the casino still open?"

"I think it stays open all night. I asked a dealer and the bartender and the girl at the place where they change the money. The dealer remembered him and he remembered Ollie, too, because he's so big, you know. He said George played blackjack at his table for a while, but he and the big man left a long time ago! About ten o'clock, he thought."

"Have you checked with Ollie?"

"I don't know what room they're in. I remembered your room number because you said it was the number of days in a year."

"I've written their room number down somewhere." I stumbled around, fumbled through my evening purse, and finally found the number on a note pad beside my phone.

I called their room and Lettie answered in a sleepy sort of croak. Ollie didn't know where George was. In the background, I heard Ollie's gravelly voice saying, "He went back to his room. Same time I did."

Lettie and I put Ollie and Kathryn on the phone so they could communicate directly. Kathryn pumped him for more information but it appeared that he wasn't much help. She hung up and said, "They went up to some guys' room and played poker for a couple of hours. A couple of guys they met in the casino. But Ollie says they left about midnight. He says he got back to his own room at twelve-fifteen."

"And George was on his way back to your room then?"

"Oh, golly! Where can he be? George isn't a big drinker. He wouldn't have gone to the bar, I'm sure."

"There's a disco lounge on one of the upper decks, I heard. We could check there. If you'll give me a minute to dress, I'll go with you." I could think of little I'd like to do less than get dressed and go hiking around the ship, but Kathryn was clearly in need of a companion. I pulled on a pair of Bermuda shorts and a big shirt while Kathryn stood near the door, her hands clasped prayerfully in front of her face.

"Wait," I said. "Didn't I see some deck plans of the ship in the booklet they gave us when we boarded? Let's take it with us." I found my envelope full of shipboard information under my bed and pulled out the booklet I wanted. The first diagram showed the disco bar on the Zeus deck at the very top of the ship.

"Before we hike up there, Kathryn, I think we should try the promenade deck first. He might simply be getting a little fresh air."

"For three hours? Well, at least it's a place to start."

We climbed up one flight and out the same doors Marco and I had used earlier in the evening. The deck was deserted now except for two women at the rail about forty yards to my left.

"If he's out here, we'll miss him completely if we walk

around the ship together and he's walking the same direction we are," I said, imagining us and George Gaskill, like carousel horses on opposite sides, circling eternally and never meeting each other. "You go that way," I said, pointing to the right as I pivoted to my left. I passed the two women. One, I recognized from the show as the dancer who had spent much of her performance on the wrong foot, circling the wrong way, and a half beat behind the music. Poor thing. I glanced back again and realized the second woman was also from the dance troupe. One of the better coordinated ones.

On the other side, the port side, Kathryn and I met, having now covered the whole circuit. Except for the two of us, this whole stretch was deserted. One of the portholes on this side, I reasoned, must be Lettie and Ollie's window, but all of them were dark. We decided to make double sure by continuing around in the directions we were already heading. As I rounded the aft end of the ship, I paused. The deep burble of the engine vibrated the deck under my feet, the twin propellers churning the water below into an iridescent ribbonlike trail behind us. I felt a bit queasy, looking down.

Kathryn and I met up again at the same place we'd parted and decided to go straight to the shipboard security office, wherever that was. It stood to reason it would be in the vicinity of the purser's office and the main desk, which were on the next deck up. We passed through the side doors and along a corridor until we found the grand staircase Lettie had nearly tumbled down earlier. Up one deck and around to our left, we walked past the photo shop where the embarkation pictures they had taken of each group as they boarded were displayed on felt-covered panels. Beyond the photo shop was the main desk where we found a grizzled, gray-haired attendant playing a hand-held video game. We explained our situation in slow, deliberate English.

"One minute, please." The man punched a button on the desk phone and paused, then began talking in Greek to whomever had answered.

"Kathryn, I'm going to call Marco. I hate to wake him up, but he'll know what to do. He's a policeman." I looked around for another phone. Marco's room number was 373. I remembered it was four doors down from my own and on the same side of the hall.

"I have talked to security," the attendant told us as he hung up the phone. "They want you to wait right here. They will be here in a minute."

Kathryn pointed to a phone on a low table in the center of the arc of counters that included the main desk and land excursion sales cubicles. I took a deep breath and punched in Marco's room number. Four rings, no answer.

Kathryn nudged me and pointed toward a baby-faced young man approaching us. He wore a short-sleeved white shirt with a security patch on one sleeve and a gold name-plate that read, "Demopoulos." I assumed it was his last name.

I hung up the phone and listened as Kathryn explained her plight to the security kid. He paid close attention but didn't appear to be all that shocked. It dawned on me this might be a fairly common occurrence on a cruise ship, and the lost spouse would frequently turn out to have been indulging in a little tête a tête in the wrong room.

Kathryn launched into a description of George and what he was wearing the last time she saw him, but Demopoulos stopped her with an upraised finger. "I have better idea," he said, taking her by the arm. "The photo shop has already posted the embarkation pictures. The shop is locked but I have a key. There should be a photo of your husband that will help us find him much more easily."

He unlocked and slid open the glass door of the shop and let us walk around among the panels displaying hundreds of photos, all taken in the same spot at the bottom of the gangway the day before. I couldn't figure out how they were posted: alphabetically, in order of arrival, or what. We wandered around until we finally found it. George and Kathryn Gaskill, embarking on their dream vacation, hand luggage in hand, arms around each other's waists.

Demopoulos lifted the photo off the board and said, "I'll bring this back after we've found him." We stepped out and he relocked the photo shop door. "We have security cameras located almost everywhere on the ship, except in individual staterooms, of course. I will first call the two bars that are still open, the cabin stewards' storerooms, and so on. And I will check all the monitors in our office. If you find anything, you can dial seven on any phone and get me or whoever is in the office." He paused and looked at his watch. "The Chief of Security and the day shift will go on duty in about two hours. If we have not found Mr. Gaskill by then, although I'm sure we will have, Chief Letsos will take over."

Kathryn nodded and repeated, "Dial seven for security."

"May I have your room numbers?" he asked.

We gave them to him.

Backing away from us, the photo of George and Kathryn in his hand, he added, "I would suggest you return to your rooms and wait for my call. And don't worry. We will find him."

This was a problem. I couldn't imagine Kathryn going back to her room and simply sitting, waiting for the phone to ring. It would be torture for her. But on the other hand, if we weren't in our rooms, how would we know when

George had been found? There were a couple of other places I thought we could check first. I fished the deck plans out of my shorts pocket and studied them again.

"There's a big, open deck and pool area on the back end of this deck," I said. "Let's look out there before we go downstairs." We tried, but the doors to that part of the deck were locked. Through the etched glass doors, I could see starlight dancing on the pool water. "There's also a small deck at the back of the level where our rooms are."

Returning to our own floor, we scooted past our rooms and on to a polished wood door that opened onto the stern deck. This deck, directly beneath the spot where I had paused and looked down at the propeller-churned water a half hour ago, was lit by two carriage lanterns on the wall. The teak floor was dry and empty except for a large, dark-red pool in the middle.

FOUR

FROM THE RED POOL A wide smear feathered out toward the stern rail, and I saw a few streaks on the white-painted iron of the rail itself. Another spot or two near the red puddle could, I thought, be shoe prints. A few seconds later I heard a sort of *swoosh-thud* sound, which turned out to be Kathryn sliding down the door frame and hitting the deck.

I knelt beside her, tapping her face lightly with my hand. "Kathryn. Kathryn." Luckily, a door marked ΤΌΥΑΛΕΤΑ, which I had already learned meant toilet, stood just inside the exterior door. I dashed in, wet a paper towel, and used it to bathe Kathryn's face. Her eyelids fluttered, then opened.

"Oh, no! No, no! What was that stuff?" Kathryn shook her head and looked at me as if she couldn't remember who I was. Pulling her arm across my shoulder, I let her lean on me while I maneuvered her back to her room. She stared blankly at her stateroom door while I fumbled through her pocket, found her room card, and opened her door.

I laid her out on her bed and said, "You stay right here. I'll be back in a few minutes. Don't leave! Do you understand me, Kathryn?"

She mumbled something vaguely affirmative. I dashed to my own room, a few yards farther down the hall, lunged for the phone, and dialed seven.

"Demopoulos."

I told him what we'd found, hung up, then dialed Marco's room. He answered on the fourth ring, his voice dusty with sleep.

"Pronto. Chi è?"

"It's Dotsy, Marco. I'm sorry to wake you up, but it's important. Kathryn has lost George and we've found a big red puddle at the end of the hall. I think it may be blood."

"Who?" Marco's sleep-addled brain had forgotten who Kathryn and George were. Quite understandable, I thought. After I reminded him and filled in a few other blanks, he said, "I will get dressed and come out."

I grabbed my little travel light and ran back to the stern deck. Demopoulos was already there with a big flashlight. He played the cone of light back and forth across the teak deck, pausing and crouching down near a smudge a foot or so away from the main part of the dark pool.

"Is it blood?"

"It smells like it," he said, touching it with one finger and then sniffing it. I wondered how much training Demopoulos had had in this sort of investigation. He looked so young; he couldn't be more than nineteen or twenty.

Marco pushed through the door. He motioned me back, looked at the puddle, then at Demopoulos. To me, he said, "Do not touch anything. And watch where you step."

Demopoulos rose from his squatting position and looked curiously at Marco.

Marco introduced himself, in English, and added that he was Carabinieri from Italy. They continued to converse in English, the universal language. "We have two footprints in blood right here. I assume it is blood. Do you see?" Demopoulos shone his light on the dark smudges I had noticed earlier.

"And a streak running almost the whole way to the rail," Marco said. "Did you notice it already? Two streaks, actually." He squatted and his knees popped. Careful to let only one foot and the toe of the other shoe contact the teak deck, he wobbled and was forced to put one knuckle down to steady himself. "These could be drag marks."

I was in the way so I decided to go and check on Kathryn, but, the tension bringing on a call from Mother Nature, slipped into the "toyaleta" first. The overhead light inside showed me a shiny, clean bathroom, an empty trash can, and a small, round, shiny object on the side of the sink. It looked like clear plastic. For no reason other than the fact that it looked curiously out of place, I stuck it in my pocket. I examined the little room for blood spots or anything else out of place, but it was spic and span.

A minute later, when Kathryn answered my knock and opened her door, her face begged for an update.

"Marco and Demopoulos are out there now, doing what investigators do," I said.

"Who?"

"Marco Quattrocchi. Remember him? He saw the show with us tonight, and he was at our dinner table."

"Oh, yes." Kathryn padded back to her bed and sat on its corner, her gaze fixed vacantly on the opposite wall.

Their room was exactly like mine, except everything was reversed left to right. Their beds lay against opposite walls with two small nightstands between them. Dressing table, mirror, and a row of closets to the left. Sofa, upholstered chair, and coffee table on the right. As I sat in the chair facing the bed, the bathroom was behind me. In my room the bath stood on the left with the dressing table and closets on the right. Their color scheme—cream, russet, and periwinkle blue—was the same as mine.

The only other difference I could see was that, this being an interior room, the curtain behind their beds covered a long fluorescent light whereas mine had a real window behind it. Having checked out Lettie and Ollie's room earlier, I knew the twin beds could easily be slid together to make a double. The cabin steward could make the change in a couple of minutes by sticking the nightstands on the outsides of the beds instead of between them. Did the separation of the beds say anything about the Gaskills' relationship or were they simply unaware of their options?

"Is it possible George did come in for a while after the poker game and then leave again? He could have slipped in quietly, couldn't he? And not wakened you?"

"No. When he left to go to the casino, he was still wearing his suit and tie." Kathryn turned sideways and looked at me. "If he came in late, he certainly would've at least shed his tie and jacket, and they aren't here now. If he went to bed at all, he wouldn't have put his dressy clothes back on again, would he? And his bed would be messed up."

"Of course."

I looked over my shoulder at the closets in the narrow hall across from their bathroom. Through one open door I saw a couple of pairs of men's shoes aligned neatly beneath hanging shirts and trousers. "Kathryn, do you or George know anyone else on the cruise?"

"You mean did we know anyone before we got on the ship? No. Nobody." She picked up the hem of her bedspread and crumpled it in her hand. "Dotsy, what's happened to George? I can't stand not knowing!"

I rose and slipped over to sit beside her on the bed. I patted her fist, still clenched around the blue-and-russet bedspread. "There's no reason for us to assume that…that whatever-it-is out there has anything to do with George. This is a big ship. Eight or nine hundred passengers, I heard. And there are lots of possible explanations for what we saw."

"Like what?"

"Like, it might not be blood. It might be paint somebody spilled. Or maybe there was a fight out there sometime tonight between a couple of folks we don't even know. Maybe somebody had a hemorrhage from a bleeding ulcer. Maybe the chef's assistant tossed some bloody entrails out the galley porthole and the wind caught it. Whipped it around the back of the ship. Maybe a sea gull got in a fight with a pelican."

Kathryn giggled a little. "Dotsy, you're wonderful. I know you're doing your best, but it ain't working." She stood up, tottered to the bathroom, and came back out with a wet face cloth pressed against her eyes.

I waited silently.

"We've been planning this vacation for years," she finally said. "George has had such a horrible time at work. He's not meant to be a salesman. Certainly not a car salesman. He used to be a teacher when we lived in Pennsylvania. He taught social studies for years, and then they made him the principal of the whole high school. I was so proud of him, but really, he should have stayed in the classroom. He's not a natural-born administrator. So many conflicts. Discipline problems, irate parents, school board members analyzing your every move."

"I can imagine. I teach in a junior college and I see a certain amount of that, too. Not discipline problems generally, but, yes, all the rest of it."

"Let's go out there again, Dotsy. I have to know what's going on."

I convinced Kathryn to wait for me in her room while I dashed down to my own for a minute. Closing her door behind me, I turned to my left and spied Marco, rushing down the hall toward me.

"I need a what-do-you-call-it, cotton on a stick," he said. "A cotton swab. Do you have one? And a plastic bag I can seal up?"

"I have both." Leading the way to my room, I shoved

my key card into the little slot, got the green light, and ushered Marco in.

"Your room is exactly like mine," he said.

I pulled out my top dressing table drawer and located my cotton swabs and a small locking plastic bag. I must admit I pride myself on traveling light and still having everything one could possibly need. I'm waiting for someone to ask me for the moleskin I saw on some packing list or other and have carried on every trip I've taken in the last ten years. I'm not sure what it's for, but I have some. I also have an emergency clothesline but I've never seen a shower curtain rod that wasn't handier. I like to collect things in tiny travel sizes so my luggage remains quite small, even though I have everything including a currency converter, Greek-English phrase book, and tide tables for the whole Mediterranean Sea, including the Aegean branch.

"What do you think has happened, Marco?"

"I cannot say for sure, but it certainly looks as if someone has been attacked and thrown overboard. I can see what looks like heel drag-marks in the blood. You know? As if someone has been dragged through the blood." He demonstrated with his hands. "Maybe pulled by his armpits from the place of attack over to the rail."

"The blood. Is it still liquid?"

"Yes, and that's strange. The blood should dry quickly in this air. With the breeze from the ship's movement and all. Even though we are over water, still, the Mediterranean air is very dry. The blood has not been there long."

I gulped. Marco, I knew, was an expert in crime scene analysis. None better.

"Can I come out with you?" I asked. "Can Kathryn?"

He ran his fingers through his hair and exhaled loudly. "If you promise to stay at the door. Do not come out into the middle of the deck or approach the rail. Do you think Kathryn can follow this rule, also?"

"I'll make sure she does."

Marco tucked the cotton swab inside the plastic bag and waited for me to fetch Kathryn from her room. We trekked back to the stern deck in single file because the hall was too narrow for three to walk abreast. When Marco opened the door to what I had begun to think of as the crime scene, I glimpsed a lightening sky. But before I could take in the breaking dawn, Marco let go of the door handle and took a flying leap at a man on the left side of the deck.

"Ma è pazzo?" Marco shouted, then roared an unintelligible jumble of Italian as he tackled a man who was holding a water hose. He wrapped the hose around the man's neck and shoved him up against the wall with a great splat. Within five seconds his prey, a poor, baffled cabin steward, was pinned to the wall with Marco's forearm across his chest.

Another man, not Demopoulos, yelled something and barreled across the deck toward them, yanking a walkie-talkie off his belt as he ran. This was a dark, bearded man, a good bit older than Demopoulos.

"He's a policeman!" It was the shortest, most succinct statement I could think of to get the message across quickly. The message that Marco was one of the good guys.

"What in the hell? You told him to wash the deck? Destroy the evidence? *Si è pevuto il cervello?*" Marco waved his arms wildly.

"We've taken pictures."

"Sure. All taken in the dark! You must wait until the sun comes up."

"We used a flash, of course," the man growled. "When the sun comes up, our passengers will start coming out here. We can't let them see this."

The new man, who I thought might be the Chief Letsos young Demopoulos had mentioned, yelled right in Marco's face. His spit sprayed out and glistened in the rosy pre-dawn light. Marco did not back off one millimeter but stood nose-to-nose, his chin rigidly set. Like an umpire and a first-base coach, all they needed was some caps to throw down and stomp on. Meanwhile, the cabin steward backed off and began coiling the hose into a stowage chamber within the bulkhead.

The argument between the two men degenerated into an olio of Greek and Italian. I turned to Kathryn and said, "We'd better leave."

As I grabbed the handle on the heavy exterior door, the morning light bounced off something white, stuck behind a wall-mounted life ring. I pointed toward it.

"I wonder if they've noticed that," Kathryn said. "We should tell them, Dotsy. It might be something important."

"Later. They aren't going to hear us now, anyway."

But Marco turned toward us, and I pointed to the orange life ring. He nodded slightly and returned to his argument.

Back in the hall, I said to Kathryn, "It's nearly six. I'm going back to my room for a shower, then I'll call Lettie and Ollie about breakfast. Would you like to go with us?"

"I couldn't eat a thing."

"You don't have to eat. The company might do you good." I promised to call her before I went to breakfast and left her at the door to her room.

From invisible, overhead speakers in the hall came the announcement, in English: "Will George Gaskill please call or come to the main desk?"

The announcement was repeated twice more.

FIVE

My eyes burned. I'd slept no more than three hours last night but now was no time to take a nap. Until they found George Gaskill or discovered what had happened to him, I felt as if I should be "on call." I picked up the flyer some-one had pushed under my door. Aptly named the "Oracle," it described the coming day's events. Three columns on a single sheet. Front and back.

After a shower and breakfast, I hoped I could slip back here for a nap. No, that wouldn't work because the ship was scheduled to dock in Mykonos at nine, and I was so looking forward to seeing the island. We'd be there until 4:00 p.m. but I had a week's worth of things I wanted to see.

So I could take my nap at four. Then my gaze fell on an item in the second column: World-renowned archaeologist, Luc Girard, will speak on "Links between Cycladic and Minoan Civilizations" in the ship's library at five o'clock. All interested passengers are invited to attend and to meet Dr. Girard.

I couldn't bear to miss hearing Luc Girard. I'll take my nap at six. *Maybe. Oh, forget it. By then it'll be time to change for cocktails and dinner. I'll try for a normal night's sleep tonight.*

I laid out a flowered shirt and yellow shorts, then slipped into the shower. The cruise line's little courtesy bottle of shower gel was made in England, I noticed. Wisteria-scented. Lovely. I took my time, luxuriating in the tiny shower, because it was too early to wake Lettie and Ollie and ask them about breakfast. I dried, powdered myself up, and slipped into the terry bathrobe the ship provided for all guests.

My phone rang. I dashed out of the steamy bathroom, stubbed my toe on the side of the dressing table, and answered the phone with "Ow!"

It was Marco. "The note you pointed to, Dotsy. It is a suicide note."

"From who?"

"From George. George Gaskill, I suppose, but it is just signed 'George.'"

"Wait a minute! Are you telling me George Gaskill killed himself? How? By jumping? Then why is the blood there? What about the drag marks?"

"I know. It does not make any sense. Letsos, the chief of security—"

And under his breath I'm pretty sure he added "the idiot."

"—thinks George went out to the deck, slashed his wrists, got tired of waiting to die, and speeded up the process by jumping overboard."

"And dragged himself to the rail by his own armpits?"

"I know. It is ridiculous."

"Does Kathryn know about the note?"

"Not yet. Letsos is looking for a plastic security bag to put it in. It must be dusted for fingerprints. If I had not stopped him, he would have handled it with his bare hands and got his own prints all over it."

"You know, Marco, shipboard security is not used to investigating crimes. They're mainly here for our safety, checking boarding passes and such. They've probably never dealt with anything worse than a belligerent drunk."

"That is why I have to watch their every step."

"What does the note say?"

"I only glanced at it, but it is very short. It is to his wife and it says something like 'I am sorry.'"

"Don't keep Kathryn in the dark too long, Marco. Show her the note soon as you can."

Marco promised he would and hung up.

I couldn't tell Kathryn about the note. It wasn't my place. So I dressed, blow-dried my hair, and did my makeup as slowly as possible, killing time until it was late enough to call Lettie and Ollie.

I needn't have waited. Lettie was up, dressed, and Ollie was already out when I called. We decided to meet in the big dining room, although the info packet said breakfast was also served around the pool on the Poseidon deck and at a couple of other locations. You could show up at your leisure since no seating times were assigned for breakfast. I called Kathryn as I had promised, but she said she didn't want to go with us.

THE SMELL OF COFFEE greeted me in the dining room. When the white-jacketed waiter had seated me and poured me a cup, Lettie bustled in, wide-eyed and wound up. She nodded at the waiter's upraised coffee pot and sat, her hands beating a quick tattoo on the linen tablecloth.

"What's the latest on George Gaskill? They still haven't found him?" She didn't wait for an answer, but jabbered on. "They took Ollie somewhere to question him about last night. He seems to be the last person who saw him."

"They played poker, you said." I poured a little cream into my coffee. "In the casino?"

"No, Ollie said they met two guys in the casino. One was from England and the other one was from Belgium. They invited him and George to their room to play Texas hold 'em. It's a kind of poker, I think. Ollie said their room was really posh with a balcony and a regular living room and two bedrooms and a bar with a refrigerator. They played for a couple of hours, and in the end George won everyone's money."

"How much did Ollie lose?"

"He wouldn't tell me, so it was probably a bundle."

"You're a lot more casual about it than I would be. Must be nice to be rolling in money."

"We're not rolling in money, Dotsy! It's just that Ollie needs this vacation so badly, and it's taken me so long to talk him into it. I don't want anything to spoil it." Lettie jammed her clenched fists into her lap.

"And these other guys. They also lost money to George?"

"Right. But I don't know if they were ticked off about it or anything. Ollie left before I had a chance to ask him."

I ordered a fruit plate, an omelet, and a basket of bread, then brought Lettie up to date on the scene at the stern deck and the discovery of the suicide note, which neither Kathryn nor I had yet seen. I told her about Marco's fight with Chief Letsos, which was funny, now, looking back on it.

"It's still possible George is somewhere on the ship, isn't it?"

"Possible," I said, "but looking less and less likely, especially since they found the note signed 'George.'" I tasted the honeydew melon on my fruit plate. "This fruit is fabulous, Lettie. I think it must be the hot Greek sun that does it."

I heard a distant fluttering sound. Lettie was discussing eggs with the waiter so I tuned her out and concentrated on the noise. I tried to decide if it was coming from inside or outside the room or if it was all my imagination.

It was real and it came from outside, growing louder into a *whump-whump-whump*. The diners on the other side of the room turned toward the windows, and one man pointed toward an object in the sky. The morning sun glinted off something silver. Lettie and I jumped up and dashed over, trying to get a better look over the heads of the people who had quickly crowded along the row of windows.

It was a helicopter. At first I couldn't tell if it was a military or a rescue-type chopper or what, but not far behind it, speeding across the water toward our ship, came a small power boat with, it looked like, three men aboard. On its side was the word ΜΥΚΟΝΟΣ and something else in Greek I couldn't read. The little boat careened around the left side of our ship and out of sight. The racket from the helicopter's rotors rattled the silverware and vibrated the water glasses as it banked right and disappeared overhead.

"I'll bet the authorities have been called in to help find George," I said.

"Can a helicopter land on this ship?"

"I don't know, Lettie. I forgot to ask them if they have a helipad."

As we returned to our table, I spotted Ollie coming toward us. His shirt was buttoned wrong. One buttonhole off, from top to bottom. He pulled out a chair, our waiter placed a menu in front of him, and Lettie reached over and grabbed the top of his shirt. She intended to fix his button problem but Ollie swatted her hands away. "Leave it, Lettie. We're in a restaurant, for God's sake."

He studied the menu for a minute, and gave his order to the waiter. He ran one beefy hand over his bald head down to the back of his neck, squeezed his neck muscles, and sighed loudly. "Great vacation, eh? Lose all your money to some guy you may never see again and first thing next morning, get accused of killing him!"

"Oh, but surely they didn't—"

"Yes, they did! The last time I saw the little wimp he

was heading down to his room with a pocketful of money. And that's the truth!"

"How much money did you lose, dear?" Lettie asked softly.

Ollie averted his eyes and looked toward the floor. "About two thousand."

"Ollie, no! Now we have no money for the rest of our trip!"

"We still have our cash. I got the poker chips with a credit card."

I said, "George traded in his chips and took it away in cash? That was dumb. How much did he leave with?"

"About nine thousand dollars. He insisted on cash. Just about cleaned them out of American money." Ollie snapped his napkin open and laid it across one knee. "At first the security guys seemed to think I killed him because I was pissed off about losing, and then, when they found out we'd gone back to the casino together and he'd taken his winnings in cash, they figured I'd killed him and taken the money. I told them, I said, 'Search me, search my room, search anything you like. Show me where I hid the nine thou!'" Ollie pressed all ten fingertips against his wonky-buttoned shirt.

"Well, of course. If you had the money, they ought to be able to find it," I said. "It would probably be in your room."

"If somebody did do him in and rob him, they don't need to look any farther than the casino for the culprit. There weren't more than three or four people in there when George left with his money, and they all saw the stack of hundred-dollar bills the cashier counted out." Ollie flipped his fork, tines down, on the linen cloth and pressed the back of it with his forefinger. Pressed it so hard I feared it was jamming holes into the surface beneath.

"Did you mention this to the security men?" Lettie laid one hand on Ollie's as if to soothe it and save the poor fork and table from further damage.

"They found a suicide note. Did they tell you?" I asked.

It was clear to me, Ollie had not been told about the note. The waiter brought his food, and Ollie stared at the plate as if he didn't recognize what it was. He tilted his head and looked at me. "A suicide note? From George Gaskill?"

"Apparently so."

He stared at his omelet another moment. "It's beginning to make sense, now. The officer left me for a bit and when he came back, his tone had changed. He started asking me about George's state of mind, like he'd forgotten about the money."

I WAS ON MY SECOND CUP of coffee when Marco breezed in and sat at our table. He appeared to have tidied himself up a bit since the last time I'd seen him, at six A.M., unshaven, uncombed, and wearing yesterday's shirt. He smelled of soap, now, and sported a fresh cotton shirt.

"We need you downstairs, Dotsy," he said, waving away the waiter holding the coffee pot. "They are ready to show Kathryn the suicide note, and I told them she might need a little—how do you say—"

"Moral support?"

"Yes. They have brought a nurse into the room to care for her, but Kathryn is not paying any attention to her. She said, 'I am not sick. I do not need a nurse.'"

As I pushed my chair back and fumbled around for my purse, Lettie said, "What's up with the helicopter and boat that came roaring up a few minutes ago?"

"Ah, yes. The boat brought police out from Mykonos, and the helicopter is from the FBI office at the U.S. Embassy in Athens. They need to plan their actions together, you see. The ship will dock in Mykonos in about an hour, and the passenger who is missing is a U.S. citizen. So the investigation, whether it turns out to be suicide, murder, accident, or whatever, will involve all of these."

"Oh, dear," I said. "I never dreamed it would be so complicated."

Marco, his hand at the back of my waist, ushered me out of the restaurant and down a short hall to a bank of elevators I hadn't seen before. So far, I'd only used the ones at the bow of the ship. These four were fronted by ornate brass doors reminding me of Ghiberti's Baptistry doors in Florence, but their panels depicted flowers instead of biblical scenes. The doors of one elevator slid open to reveal a dazzling rosewood-and-etched-glass-paneled car. Marco pushed a button on the panel inside, and the car dropped so suddenly my stomach did a little flip. He leaned back against a brass handrail that looked as if it had been polished within the last hour. I studied his face for a split second before he turned his gaze to me, forcing me to avert my own eyes to the row of winking lights beside the buttons. He was a handsome man, with his salt-and-pepper hair and his dark chocolate eyes. Noble nose. Pleasantly crooked teeth. I think slightly irregular teeth give a man's face character. My mind flashed back, unbidden, to that night on the roof of the hotel in Florence when Marco had kissed me. Now I felt myself gathering inward, like a bat hanging upside down in a clammy cave wraps itself in its leathery wings. For protection. His beard had felt soft, I remembered. Today, his beardless face looked a little better to me than it had yesterday. I might be getting used to it.

We exited the elevator on the Athena deck, and Marco corrected me when I turned left into the hall. "This way," he said, and headed right. Left, I then realized, would have taken me back to the stern deck. I glanced in that direction and saw the yellow caution tape that now criss-crossed the door. Beyond it, I knew, was the bloody deck.

Our timing was good, because Chief Letsos and a tall man in a light gray suit were already knocking at the Gaskills' door, a hundred feet ahead of us. Marco mumbled in my ear, "They have given permission for you to be with Kathryn when they show her the note, but they may ask me to leave because I have no official reason to be there. If they do, I will leave. I will not make a fuss."

"They should be glad for your help," I said.

"If I had not been here this morning, Dotsy—if you had not called me when you did—they would have ruined the whole case already." Marco's words trailed off at the end as Kathryn's door opened. A white-uniformed nurse admitted us, and we all introduced ourselves to each other in funereal tones. Marco introduced me to the captain of the ship, Constantinos Tzedakis, a short but commanding sort of man with gray hair and beard, white uniform, and lots of hardware on his shirt, who bowed stiffly and took my hand. Seven people now crowded the little room.

Kathryn Gaskill sat, looking terribly small and vulnerable, in a russet-upholstered armchair. I tripped over and sat near her on the foot of the bed. The nurse moved back, ceding the guardian angel position to me. Kathryn looked at me, confusion in her eyes.

"Why are you here, Dotsy?"

"Marco asked me to come down. They have something to show you, Kathryn."

Kathryn's mouth opened and quivered a bit as Chief Letsos stepped forward and held out the small white sheet of paper now encased in a clear plastic sleeve.

"We found this on the deck, Mrs. Gaskill."

Kathryn took the sheet and read it. Her eyebrows knitted and she said, "What's this?"

"It's a note, Kathryn. They think it's from your husband." I reached out and touched the arm of her chair.

Kathryn looked up at Letsos, then at me. Her eyes widened and she snorted. "Totally ridiculous! Of course, it's not from George. My name is misspelled! This says C-A-T-H-E-R-I-N-E. My name is K-A-T-H-R-Y-N. Don't you think George would know that, after seventeen years of marriage?"

"Uh, oh," I said. She handed me the sheet and I read:

Dear Catherine,

I'm so very sorry but I simply can't go on. Believe me, it's better this way.

Love,

George

"Ah ha. I told you. I knew it was a fake!" Marco spun around on one foot and threw both hands toward the ceiling.

Chief Letsos glowered.

The FBI man stepped forward and took the note from my hand. "What we have here is, quite likely, the handiwork of a murderer."

A hush, so heavy it felt as if it had pushed the air from the room, fell on all of us.

"This makes it all the more important for us to try to lift a fingerprint off of it," Marco said, glancing pointedly at Letsos as he said it. What he wanted to say, I knew, was, "And if it weren't for me, there would be dozens of other prints on top of the murderer's by now!"

SIX

OUR SHIP TIED UP at a dock in a desolate, treeless part of Mykonos Island from which we were to be taken by one of the waiting buses over a hill and around a bay to Mykonos Town. They wouldn't let us go ashore until, Marco told me, the various investigators put their ducks in a row and agreed on how to proceed. While we were ashore they would comb the entire ship, bow to stern, bilge to stacks, with the proverbial fine-tooth comb for any trace of George Gaskill. Mykonos police phoned the little island airport, the ferry dock, and the marinas warning them not to let anyone from our ship leave the island. The closed-circuit TV in every room informed us our rooms would be checked while we were ashore.

They couldn't force us to go ashore and, based on conversations I overheard in the hall, quite a few guests preferred to stay on board. I imagined some folks were still sleeping off last night's excesses in the disco, others were here for the cruise and had no interest in the island, and still others were honeymooning. However, when ship security, the FBI, and the Mykonos police came calling, DO NOT DISTURB signs would be disregarded.

Disembarking was a computerized affair. We had to show them the plastic boarding card they had given to each of us yesterday in Piraeus. The card would then flash our photo, name, stateroom, age, weight, and bra size up on a screen for all to see. To get back on the ship, we had to show the card again.

It had made me nervous that they required us to surrender our passports to the purser before we sailed, but Marco explained it was safer than letting us hold on to them. "On a cruise like this," he told me, "you can be certain at least ten people will lose their passports. Some will drop them overboard accidentally, some will leave theirs on an island and not realize it until the ship has left port, and someone will threaten to sue the cruise line if the ship does not wait for them to go back to shore and search the whole island. It would be chaos."

When he put it like that, I could see it was purely for our own safety. After all, what would a cruise line do with my passport? Sell my picture? Sell my passport number? I'd already surrendered those on several other documents. With our passports all safely tucked away in the ship's vault, our boarding cards became our passport to everything.

The line to disembark snaked around from the exit door across the foyer and down one hall. Marco, Ollie, Lettie, and I stood behind two girls I recognized as dancers in last night's show. They were also, I thought, the same two girls I'd run into on the promenade deck at 3:00 a.m. The shorter of the two, a perky girl with dark, curly hair, chattered away in Greek-accented English. The other girl answered her in a pure middle-America drawl. Ohio or Pennsylvania, I'd have guessed.

This second girl was beautiful in the sexy, full-lipped way that men seem to love. Long auburn curls, high cheekbones, and dimples. She turned toward us, looking back over our heads to the line of people behind us. "God, this is taking forever," she said. "By the time all these people get off, it'll be time to get back on."

"Forgive me," I said, "but I'll bet you and I are from the same part of the world. I'm going by your accent, of course. I'm Dotsy Lamb from Staunton, Virginia."

"Oh, hi. Brittany Benson," she answered, her smile broadening as her gaze turned to Marco. "And you're right. I'm from Pennsylvania originally, but I haven't been home for years. I work on the ship."

"I know. We saw your performance last evening. Lovely."

"Oh no," the smaller girl said, throwing both hands across her face. "You saw me fall onto the stage, didn't you? I was trying to forget about that."

And screwed up the whole circle dance by going the wrong way, I thought, but what I said was, "You fell beautifully."

"I'm Sophie Antonakos," she said, extending her hand. We completed the introductions all around and chatted while the line inched toward the security post. Ollie asked the girls where he might go to see fishermen bringing in their catch, and both agreed he could do that almost anywhere along the shoreline but a little bay south of Mykonos Town, a bay within walking distance, was a good bet.

To Marco, Lettie, and me, the girls strongly recommended we walk to a section of town called Little Venice. "Many nice bars and coffee houses, they have," Sophie told us.

"And a great place to take pictures," Brittany added, her eyes twinkling at Marco.

Lettie and I both spotted the man in the yellow-and-red flowered shirt at the same time, because as I was trying to remember why his shirt looked familiar, Lettie said, "There's that wrong-way man again. The one who was going down the ramp yesterday when everyone else was going up."

"Oh, right." As I said it, the man looked back, spun around to a display case on his immediate left, and began studying it intently. That particular case, I had noticed earlier, held another beautiful antiquity. A black-and-gold bull's head mounted on a wooden block. Raising five children has taught me a thing or two about acting nonchalant and attempting to blend into the scenery. Young boys will jam their hands in their pockets and whistle a nonsense tune, little girls will twirl their hair and look at the ceiling, and grown men will pretend to be interested in whatever is handy. This man, I thought, had seen something—or someone—he'd rather avoid.

When he handed his card to the security man, I slipped around Brittany and Sophie, trying to see his name as his vital statistics flashed up on the screen. It said "Nigel" and something starting with an *E*. I couldn't make out the last name.

At the foot of the gangway, the ship's photographer, a cheery olive-skinned man, was energetically recruiting folks to pose for a disembarking shot against a canvas backdrop of Mykonos, which seemed kind of silly to me because, by simply turning his camera the other way, he could have used the real Mykonos as his background. I pointed this out to Lettie.

Three buses waited in a line, each driver herding people aboard then taking off up the hill as soon as his bus filled. A fourth bus appeared from over the hill, punching through a cloud of the departing bus's dust, and took its place at the back of the line.

"They really should have put the town closer to the dock," Lettie said.

Ollie and Marco glanced at each other and grinned.

"Wait up," Ollie called to two men I didn't know. The men turned and came toward us. "I want you to meet Mr. Leclercq and Mr. Stone," he said to us. "These are the guys we played poker with last night. They were kind enough to let us use their suite." This was the most formal introduction I'd ever heard from Ollie Osgood, and a chill went through me when I realized these three men had been George Gaskill's sole companions in the two or three hours before his death.

The older man extended his hand to me first, then to the others. "Malcolm Stone," he said, and Willem Leclercq followed suit. Leclercq slipped off his sunglasses and looked at me with his very blue eyes. He wore a tropical flowered shirt that looked expensive and olive-drab cargo pants. *Bon vivant,* I thought.

As Leclercq shook hands with Marco, he said in a French-sounding accent, "I understand you've been helping security to find George Gaskill. Is there any further word? Have they found him yet?"

"No, and at this point, I think they are not going to find him at all. I think Mr. Gaskill is gone…" Marco stopped abruptly and squinted into the morning sun.

"Rum business, that," Malcolm Stone said, shaking his head. No one seemed to have anything else to add.

The four of us started up the hill toward the buses, and right away I realized I'd worn the wrong shoes. My sandals collected gravel, requiring me to stop and shake one foot or the other every few feet. I hoped the whole island wasn't gravel.

"What did he mean, 'rum business'?" Lettie scrambled to catch up with Marco and me. "Is he suggesting George was drunk?"

"No, Lettie, it's a British expression. It means something like 'bad business,' I think."

On the other side of the hill, a beautiful little Greek town, white-washed to a dazzling brightness, hugged a crescent-shaped bay. Colorful boats bobbed at anchor in the sea and dotted the sandy beach. A red-domed church on the opposite hill seemed to be where our bus driver was pointing when he told Marco, "Little Venice, over there."

MARCO AND I STOPPED BY the local Hard Rock Café and bought T-shirts for my grandchildren while Ollie and Lettie forged ahead up a narrow, winding street toward Little Venice.

Exiting the Hard Rock, I looked up the hill and spotted Brittany Benson, the dancer, emerging from a shop along a row of white cubes with brightly painted doors. Close behind her, Leclercq and Stone dashed out the same door, obviously calling to her as they went because she turned and stopped. They gestured toward the package Brittany was carrying, a bag roughly the size of a toaster. Brittany shook her head and seemed to clutch the bundle more tightly. I tugged at Marco's shirt sleeve and pointed.

Leclercq pulled out a wallet and extracted what looked like paper currency, extending it to Brittany. She shook her head. Stone reached toward her package but Brittany backed away, stumbling and righting herself quickly. She walked away, then turned and said something to them. Leclercq, his wallet still in his hand, withdrew another item that looked to me as if it was probably a business card. Brittany shifted her load to one arm and shoved whatever Leclercq had handed her into her shorts pocket.

Bag of T-shirts in hand, we followed Ollie and Lettie's route up the narrow street but I had to stop near the top because my sandals were full of rocks again. Ahead of us I spotted the photo opportunity of a lifetime. Ollie and Lettie, standing in a gap between two rough whitewashed walls with a swath of blue sky and a strip of bluer water behind them, had just turned to face each other when Ollie put his hands around Lettie's waist and looked down at her.

I grabbed my camera out of my purse, fumbled for the "on" button, and located them in the little view window in time to catch the look of love on both faces just before their lips touched.

"Christmas gift!" I said to Marco. "If this turns out well, I think a framed eight-by-ten would be about right." I flipped the camera mode to "playback" and saw the moment again, frozen in time. "Perfect."

We explored alleys and shops for an hour before my stomach told me it needed lunch. Marco confessed he hadn't eaten all day and steered me into a small coffeehouse overlooking a bay. The windows on one side of the room stood directly over a wave-lapped cliff that rose straight from the water about a hundred feet below the base of the building. I had a moment of vertigo looking down from one of the windows and suggested we sit at a table a little farther back. If one accidentally fell into the glass and it broke, one's next stop would be the Aegean Sea. Or the rocks, which would probably hurt even more.

Our waiter spoke no English at all so I left the ordering to Marco, who, as a native to the Mediterranean area, was accustomed to dealing with language problems. Strange instrumental music played softly in the background and, through the windows, a row of five windmills with bare blades and grass roofs lined the crest of a promontory across the bay. What a wonderful place.

About then I noticed Marco and I were the only mixed-gender couple in the room. Mostly in pairs and mostly men except for two women sitting with their backs to a window, they lounged with their coffee and cigarettes, arms slung casually across seat backs.

"This is a gay bar, Marco."

"On Mykonos, gay bars are the rule and not the exception, Dotsy, and do not stare. It is bad manners." He conferred with the waiter about our order while I studied the artwork on the walls, recovering from that rebuke.

Our food arrived. Marco had ordered me a sort of fish-kebab with vegetables and rice. One of the skewers held nothing but a longitudinally impaled octopus tentacle, its suction cups lined up in a double row down one side. Sliced up, it tasted okay. While I ate, I considered how to respond to his "bad manners" crack. I wanted him to know I am not a homophobe and I have not recently fallen off the turnip truck. I considered it, but decided to say nothing. Much better to let my wound fester until it erupted in a torrent of green bile.

"I've been thinking about what you told me yesterday," I said, taking a totally different tack, "about antiquities in warehouses and such. What do you know about the illegal market? The smuggling and all?"

Marco lowered his forkful of rice back to his plate. "Quite a lot, actually. The Carabinieri are working with Interpol and with Scotland Yard in England. We have been for several years. The smugglers bring their goods from Turkey, from Crete, from all around the Mediterranean, through Italy on their way to Germany, England, and to America. Through Greece, too, of course, but there are a couple of families in Italy who have a well-organized smuggling syndicate. The looting of Etruscan artifacts in Italy has been big business for a long time, you know."

"I know," I said. Marco knew of my interest in Etruscan civilization.

"UNESCO has passed some laws that are making it more difficult for them to get away with it. For a long time, Switzerland allowed no-questions-asked importing and exporting so Geneva was a haven for the international black market. They are cracking down now, but the smugglers are also getting smarter."

"Are these things that have been actually stolen or are they items that local people have just happened to dig up?"

"Both." Marco leaned over his plate and tapped his forefinger firmly on the table. "But whether they break into the museum, knock out the guard, and smash open the glass cases or whether they pay a poor farmer in Crete more money than he can make in a month for a vase he has found, it makes no difference. It is stealing our heritage. Our history. And not just from the Italians and the Greeks, no! It is stealing from the world!"

"Hey, you're preaching to the choir here." I sat back, ducking his sweeping hand gesture.

"What do you mean?" he asked.

When will I learn to speak in plain English when I'm talking to Marco?

THE DOOR TO THE STREET opened and Lettie walked in, accompanied by the two strangest pelicans I had ever seen. Waddling nonchalantly, as if they were coming to tea, they elicited barely a ripple of laughter from the other patrons. I supposed this was the done thing on Mykonos. These pelicans, the official mascots of Mykonos, were snow-white except for their heads and pouched bills. The area around their eyes was pink, the top of their bills, a long streak of blue, and the pouch part underneath was lemon yellow. They must have weighed thirty pounds apiece because their heads were higher than Lettie's waist.

Lettie carried a huge mesh bag full of sponges.

She calmly took an empty chair at our table and squished the bag of sponges between the chair's legs. A waiter tried to shoo the pelicans out, but they were in no hurry to leave until he tossed something, probably fish, out the door and into the street. The birds waddled out the door.

"I thought you might like to walk down to the harbor with me," Lettie said. "Ollie's there now, gabbing with the fishermen, although I don't know how either they or he knows what they're saying. He's speaking English and they're speaking Greek."

"Did he buy the sponges, or did you?" Marco asked.

"Oh, aren't they ridiculous?" She pulled the huge bag out from under her chair and plopped it on her lap. "These are real natural sponges. Sponge divers bring them up. Ollie says he's going to give them as Christmas presents to his crew." She turned to Marco and explained, "Ollie is a building contractor. He usually has fifty to a hundred men working for him."

"I bet a sponge is just what they've always wanted," I said.

"Well, maybe not. But Ollie said, 'How many of these guys are ever going to go to Greece themselves? Most of them have never seen a real sponge.'"

"You can buy them at home, you know."

"Don't tell Ollie. Just tell me how I'm going to pack these things up."

Lettie and I headed for the door while Marco paid the bill. I glanced over my shoulder in time to catch the grins on the faces of the other patrons and resisted the temptation to say, where Marco could hear me, "Don't stare. It's bad manners." We wound our way through several narrow streets and alleys in a roughly downhill manner. The aromas and sounds coming from the open shop doors we passed were a sensual smorgasbord. I tried to make mental notes to write in my trip journal later.

"The harbor is at the end of this next street, I think."

"Wait a minute. I have to dump the rocks out of my sandals," I said, vowing to wear closed-toed shoes at our next island. As I held onto Marco's arm and lifted my left foot to shake it, I heard noises. A scream. Shuffling. A loudly barked order. Someone yelled, in English, "Get back! Get back!"

Marco left me leaning on thin air and ran to the nearest alley, one that ran downhill and to the right. He stopped.

"Oh, Dio!"

Lettie and I hurried along to join him. The alley opened out to bright sky at the other end, but I could go no farther than the entrance because Marco stopped me with his outstretched arm. He didn't stop Lettie, who, being a bit shy of five foot one, ducked under his arm.

Afternoon sun poured into the far end of the alley, highlighting red-streaked walls, red puddles on the cobblestones. It must have been a horrible battle. From a dark mound at the base of one wall, a bare arm stretched out and up at an awkward angle.

Beyond the mound, one face, then two, then another, peeped around the corner and vanished when a voice warned, "Get back!" or something like it in Greek.

Lettie, standing between us and the dark mound, hunched over suddenly, her shoulders tight. I thought she was going to throw up. Instead, she turned and called back, "Marco! Come here!"

"No! This does not concern us. You come here!"

Lettie didn't budge.

"This is an island problem. A Mykonos problem. We will stay out of it!"

She turned back to the dark mound, inching closer, bending forward. I wanted to run to her, to stop her before she touched the body. You can never tell what Lettie is going to do. But she raised one hand to her mouth, studied the lump for a second, then said, "Yes, it does concern us, Marco. It's our photographer!"

"I have to go and get her, Dotsy," Marco said, folding both my hands in his and pushing me firmly back and out of the alley. He slipped up behind Lettie, put an arm around her shoulders, and led her back to me. Her face was pale.

She walked unsteadily, leaning on Marco, staring blankly toward her own feet.

Marco handed her off to me. "Take her away and get her some fresh air. I will stay here and try to help. And will you make certain someone has told the police?"

That last order was unnecessary because, as he said it, three policemen in summer shirts with emblems on their sleeves appeared at the far end of the alley. I walked Lettie down the street listening to her halting description of the photographer's bloody remains. I looked for familiar faces. Anyone I recognized from the ship. It seemed to me, if I found myself in a police interview later, they might want to know who else was in the vicinity.

Luc Girard, the archaeologist, was at the bottom of the steep slope, walking toward us, and Sophie Antonakos was a few yards ahead of us, going down. She slipped on a cobble and a brush flipped out of her open purse as she twisted to right herself. Girard picked it up for her, but Sophie, stooping at the same time, cracked heads with him. He smiled sheepishly, handed her the brush, and rubbed his forehead as he passed us.

Where our street opened out onto a plaza fronting the harbor, Brittany Benson sat on a block of stone, surrounded by several packages. Sophie ran up to her, twittering, "Oh, no! I ran into Dr. Girard. I really ran into him! I was so embarrassed."

Ollie rounded the corner of the next street over—logically the one that would intersect the alley we'd just left but who could tell in this rabbit warren—and headed toward the water. I called out to him. He turned, waved, and then ran toward us.

"What's wrong with Lettie?" he asked, gathering her into his arms.

As I explained, Ollie held Lettie at arm's length, studied

her face, pulled her close, and kissed the top of her head. I noticed Ollie was toting another mesh bag of sponges, as large as the one Lettie had. Snuggled together with both bags, they looked more like a foursome. Ollie suggested we'd better head back to the ship right away.

We had to pass the other end of the alley as we climbed back over the hill and as we did so I paused, standing on tiptoes to see over the heads of what was now a crowd. A police officer stood, feet wide apart, barring rubber-neckers from the alley. I heard Marco's voice, somewhat damped by the alley walls, shouting, "Stay back!"

SEVEN

BACK ON THE SHIP, I knocked on Kathryn Gaskill's door but got no response. Thinking she might not be dressed or might not feel like opening the door, I retraced my steps three doors down, slipped into my own room, and dialed her number. No answer. Maybe she's talking with the investigators, I thought. I didn't even consider the possibility that there was good news. That they'd found George. Stepping back out, I felt the hallway near their door had taken on a sort of pall, which, it seemed, would neutralize laughter and suck it into the walls. *Maybe she's getting a bit of fresh air,* I thought. I walked back to my room and checked the floor inside my door for a note slipped under. It occurred to me that I didn't know Kathryn well enough to know if she was the note-leaving sort or not.

I renewed my lipstick, brushed my hair, and scanned the deck plans in my brochure to locate the library. Luc Girard's lecture was to be held there at five o'clock and it was already four-fifty. The library, according to the brochure, was on the starboard side of the Ares deck, one deck up, so I took the stairs. The library's entrance was by way of an exterior door off the promenade. Through a round porthole window in the varnished teak door, I saw no lights inside, but there was a note taped to the brass porthole fittings: *La conférence de Dr Girard sera tenue à 18h00, pas 17h00.*

And below this: "Dr. Girard's lecture will be at 6:00 p.m., not 5:00."

I ran into Ollie and Lettie on my way back to the stairs and they suggested a drink in the lounge on the Poseidon Deck. Up two more levels. It was a large, well-upholstered room with U-shaped sofas and lots of throw pillows. Lettie and I sat facing the windows on one arm of a U and Ollie, opposite us, occupied a section of sofa normally sufficient for two people.

"You've changed clothes, Ollie," I said.

"I've been handling fish all afternoon. Lettie made me take a shower."

"I asked him if he needed a sponge for his bath. We have plenty." Lettie stuck her foot around the coffee table and gave Ollie's tent-pole leg a light kick.

Ollie cleared his throat and paused a moment. "Lettie tells me the man you found in the alley was our ship's photographer."

"It was," Lettie said.

"I don't think I'd have recognized him," he said. "Who looks at a photographer when he's taking your picture? He's always got that light shining straight in your eyes."

"But you can count on Lettie to recognize anyone she's ever seen before."

"Of course I recognized him. We'd just passed him on the dock. He had a cute sort of round face and he was wearing a blue-and-white striped shirt." Lettie paused and studied her hands for a moment. "The shirt wasn't blue and white when I saw him later. It was red." Her voice faltered. "So much blood. You wouldn't think a person could have so much blood in him."

"Did you see a knife?" I asked. We hadn't discussed this at all on our walk back to the ship. We hadn't waited for a bus to tote us across the hill, and the three of us had made the whole trek in silence.

"No."

"Did you see any cuts on his arms? I mean, if there were cuts, it would indicate he'd fought his attacker."

"Oh yes. His arms were all cut up. His chest, his arms, his neck. All cut up."

"It must have been a battle."

"A lop-sided battle," said Ollie. "Apparently only one of them had a weapon."

"I sure hope they find the weapon. The knife or whatever it was."

We talked about it at length, but all we knew was based on the one brief look Lettie had, and that wasn't nearly enough. The waiter brought our drinks. The lounge was starting to fill up as people returned to the ship. We were already a half-hour past the time we were supposed to have left the dock. A man came over and asked us if he could take the empty chair at the open end of our seating nook, but before he could take it, a hand grabbed his shoulder.

Marco stood behind him. "Sorry, but I need this chair," he said. The man bowed politely and left.

"What a day, eh?" Marco pushed the chair close to my end of the sofa and sat. He smelled of sweat. *"Li mortacci..."* He squinted, pinching the bridge of his nose between his thumb and forefinger.

"Tell us," I said, and the three of us stared at him.

"His name was Nikos Papadakos and he was from Crete. His family, his wife and children, still live in Crete. He had worked on this ship for two seasons. Everyone liked him."

"Not everyone," Lettie muttered.

Marco gave Lettie a sidelong glance. "Everyone they've talked to so far. A lot of people from the ship were down in the area near the waterfront when it happened. The police grabbed everyone they could find and talked to them. At first, their chief wanted to hold up the ship's leaving until they could sort everything out, but the ship security and the FBI men came down and talked to him. They pointed out that the people on the ship are as good as in jail when it comes to escaping."

"Absolutely," Ollie said. "Much easier to escape from an island with a dozen marinas than from a ship."

"Have they found a weapon? What was it? A knife?" I asked.

"Almost certainly a knife, and no, they have not found it."

"Do you think our photographer had a weapon, too? Lettie says he was all cut up."

"It is hard to say. He has lots of defensive wounds all over, but if Papadakos had a weapon, the killer must have taken it with him."

Ollie leaned back and threw one arm across a cushion. "Are they letting you work the investigation with them?"

"No, no, no. I am just a passenger. I am not part of the investigation. They let me help them in the alley because I made myself useful. I am good at crowd control." Marco grinned a little. "All I have told you, I learned by listening to them. When they were talking to people from the ship, they were mostly using English. When they talked to each other in Greek, I did not understand everything they said."

"And nobody heard anything?" I said. "I find it hard to believe a vicious attack like that could take place in a little alley, so many people within earshot, and nobody heard a thing!"

"I agree. I think when they have a chance to talk to everyone, they will find someone who does remember something."

I looked at my watch. "Will you excuse me? I want to catch Luc Girard's talk in the library and it's almost time.

Will I see you at dinner?" I touched Marco's shoulder as I stood to leave.

He jumped up, knocking his own chair over, and bowed slightly. "I will take a shower and change clothes. Shall we meet here and go down to dinner together?"

Yes. Please take a shower, Marco, is what I thought. "About eight," is what I said.

EIGHT

LUC GIRARD SHIFTED A TALL, white-ground jug from the corner of the reading table to a safer spot near the center. The first to arrive for the lecture, I screwed up my courage and introduced myself to the man I had admired on video. He stepped around the table and shook my hand.

"I'm thrilled to meet you in person, Dr. Girard," I said, hating the cloying formality in my voice. I told myself to lighten up. "I teach ancient history at a junior college in America and I have discussed your work with my students. You were working, I believe, on an excavation in Crete?"

"Yes. With Dieter Matt. But no more." He said it with a finality that told me Dr. Matt and he had had a falling-out. Luc Girard's face puzzled me. Caramel-colored eyes behind horn-rimmed glasses, a delicate mouth, shaggy hair, and a sparse goatee. He seemed, at once, both formidable and vulnerable.

I turned my attention to the items on the table. "I see you have both red-figure and black-figure pottery. Which is older?"

Girard walked back around the table and picked up a brick-red vase with black figures around its middle. "This is older. About 450 B.C." He pointed to a black vase with red figures. "The idea for reversing the process came later, and the white-ground came still later. He picked up the jug—he called it a lekythos—and showed me the museum identity marks on its base. The red-figure and black-figure vases were reproductions, he told me. He disappeared under the table and popped back up holding my favorite of all prehistoric works, the marble Cycladic figure known as the harp player. A work of art that would hold a place of honor in any exhibition of modern sculpture, but carved more than 4,000 years ago. Clean lines, graceful curves, a mastery of space.

I gasped. "The Harp Player! Surely you're not…" Then I realized how silly that was. "It's not the original, is it?"

"Of course not. The original is in Athens. I like to show people reproductions of the things I talk about, when the genuine article isn't available. You dig?" He had a French accent but he seemed at ease with English.

"What about the Cycladic fertility figure in the display case by the stairs?"

"It is genuine."

"How can the ship risk putting such a valuable item on display? In fact, how does the cruise line acquire these things to begin with?"

Girard gave me a penetrating look and paused a second longer than necessary before answering. "It is curious, isn't it?" He lowered his head and continued staring at me over the tops of his glasses. "You dig?"

People were filing in now and rearranging chairs to suit themselves. I gave Dr. Girard one more look, aching to know what he was trying to tell me with his eyes. He turned back to his artifacts and I slipped outside, assuming it would be a few minutes before the lecture started. Did Girard realize how funny that little expression of his, "you dig?" sounded coming from an archaeologist?

On the promenade outside the library door, I found Sophie Antonakos gazing out to sea with one espadrilled foot on the bottom rail. *Déjà vu.* Hadn't I seen her at this same spot about three o'clock this morning? She held her chestnut hair back with one hand. A mass of corkscrew curls blew in the wind. I slipped up beside her.

"Are you waiting for the lecture, too?" I asked.

She jumped as if I had surprised her. "Oh! No, I was trying to get up the nerve to apologize. I bumped into Dr. Girard a while ago. It was an accident, but he was so nicely picking up my brush for me when I ruined it all by cracking my head against his."

"I'm sure he knew it was an accident." I saw no need to tell her I'd witnessed the event.

"You don't think I should apologize?" Sophie glanced anxiously toward the library door, and I got the feeling she was looking for an excuse to talk to Luc Girard.

"Are you free for a few minutes? Why don't we go to the lecture together? If you can't stay for the whole thing, you can duck out anytime you want."

"Oh." Sophie bit her lower lip. "I am interested in archaeology, actually. Not that I know very much, but I've done a lot of reading. I haven't been to college," she said.

Before Sophie could talk herself into more abject unworthiness, I took her by the elbow and ushered her through the library door. By this time, most of the seats were taken, but I spotted a step stool near the wall-mounted atlas stand and led Sophie to it. We managed to rest one-and-a-half butt cheeks each on the stool.

Luc Girard began. "The islands we are now in are called the Cyclades, and it is here, in prehistoric times, that some of the finest art the world has yet seen was born." His lecture had been billed as a comparison of Cycladic and Minoan civilizations, but after a few minutes in which he told us, rather than two separate civilizations, we should think of them as one civilization that evolved into the other, he detoured into a discussion of how to tell genuine antiquities from reproductions.

I glanced at Sophie several times and what I saw on her face was pure adoration. Almost rapture. Was she that keen on archaeology or did she have a crush on the man? Or both? Luc Girard was a fine-looking man and, although I'm bad at estimating people's ages, I'd have guessed he was a few years older than Sophie. Late thirties, probably.

"Now that I've shown you how to tell the real from the fake, make certain, when you buy, you always buy the fake."

The audience tittered.

"Because it's illegal to take real antiquities out of the country," he added. He picked up a reproduction red-figure vase, handed it to the woman nearest him, and told her to pass it around. He started a couple of other items around the room, then the white-ground lekythos. This made me nervous because it was the real McCoy. As they passed it along, everyone turned it upside down and looked at the black numbers, which pegged it as an authentic museum piece. The lekythos made the round of the room to the last man who sat near the door and about eight feet away from Sophie and me. He held it out toward Sophie, but the gap made it necessary for her to get up and lean over toward him. He passed it to her.

She dropped it.

If it had fallen straight to the carpet it might not have broken, but it fell onto a brass doorstop that had been pushed aside when they closed the door. Sophie cried out like a wounded kitten and ran from the room. By the time I got out to the deck, she was nowhere to be found. I returned to the library, not knowing what to say but knowing I had to say something. Girard was on his knees, slowly placing each piece of the broken lekythos on the seat of a nearby chair.

"Is there anything we can do to help, Dr. Girard?" an elderly man asked.

"There's a tray behind the table," he said softly. "Bring it to me."

Someone handed him the tray and the rest filed quietly out. It was just him and me now. He moved the broken shards reverently from the chair seat to the tray. He lowered his head to the carpet and looked sideways, licked one finger to pick up a tiny sliver.

"I'm so very sorry this has happened, Dr. Girard. Sophie, the poor girl, I know she's devastated. She admires you and your work so much."

"Ask Sophie to see me at her earliest convenience."

I promised I would.

KATHRYN GASKILL OPENED her door, took my arm with her small, cold hand, and pulled me into her room. She obviously hadn't allowed the staff in to clean because her bed was still unmade and a couple of bathroom towels lay on the floor. I stepped over them and seated myself at her dressing table. Now wearing a green wrap-around skirt and yellow blouse, she stood in the center of the room, her hands over her mouth, staring at the wall as if she had forgotten where she was and what she was doing.

I waited a full minute in silence before she turned and acknowledged my presence. "I came down about an hour ago, Kathryn, but you weren't here."

She said nothing.

"Any news?" I asked.

"I was up on the…other floor. In the security office. I was talking to the FBI men and those other men." Kathryn was one question behind me.

"Any news?"

"No sign of George. They searched every inch of the

ship while you were ashore and they've still got two helicopters and some little boats out looking for him. They said they'll keep it up until dark, but it's useless. I told them George is a poor swimmer. He can't tread water for more than a few minutes, so even if he was conscious when he hit the water he wouldn't have lasted long."

"Have you eaten anything today?"

"No."

"Would you like to go to dinner with us? Or I could have them bring dinner to you." I flashed on a picture of the five of us and one empty chair at the table, like last night but minus George. Not such a good idea, perhaps.

"I can have them bring meals to me anytime I want." Kathryn glanced at the phone. "But I think I would like to go with you. I can't stay in here forever." She walked past me and into the bathroom. I heard water running. When she came out, holding a wet cloth to her face, she said, "They think Ollie Osgood did it. They think he killed George for the poker winnings he left the casino with."

"That's ridiculous."

"He and Lettie are good friends of yours. Of course, you never want to think that someone you know…"

"Don't even try that, Kathryn." I felt my hackles rising. "Ollie Osgood is a successful building contractor. He makes more than five thousand dollars in a week." As I said it, I realized my numbers were probably way off on the high side. I had no idea how much Ollie made, but I felt no inclination to soften the impact by making a correction. "You don't kill somebody for less than two weeks' pay!"

"He was the last person to see George alive."

"There's no way to know who was last. What about the others who were in the casino when George picked up his winnings? Who's to say they didn't follow him out and wait until Ollie went to his own room?"

"Everyone who was in the casino at the time has been questioned." Kathryn gave me a steady stare. "They gave each other alibis. They swore nobody left for at least an hour after George and Ollie left."

I counted to ten and changed the subject. "Is this the first cruise for you and George? I mean, why did you choose the Greek Isles? There are lots of cruises closer to home."

"That's exactly why we chose the Greek Isles. We wanted to go as far from home as possible." She folded her arms across her stomach and sat on the edge of the bed that would have been George's, the one that hadn't been slept in. "Poor George has had such a rough time since he lost his principalship. I told you about his troubles, didn't I?"

"You mentioned it. Tell me." I kicked off my sandals and moved to the sofa, tucking my feet behind one cushion.

"George was a great history teacher. Students, faculty, administrators, everybody, respected and admired him. Kids used to come to him with their problems. Other faculty members asked his advice. They talked him into taking over as principal when the former one died and that's when he found out about all the dirt, the petty squabbles, the politics, which had been under the surface all along, but which he'd never been aware of before. Certain factions on the faculty were trying to get him fired and others would come to him with all sorts of rumors and demand he take action. Well, you can't fire somebody because somebody else says she's getting too friendly with her students, can you?"

"Of course not. And I know what you're talking about, Kathryn. My own college has those factions, those cliques, but I've learned to stay out of school politics."

Kathryn gave me an impatient look and went on. "There

was a certain young lady a teacher sent to George with a note charging her with cheating. The teacher had solid proof, so George suspended the girl. Her parents protested, because she was a graduating senior and a suspension would, they claimed, jeopardize her chances of getting into the college of her choice. I say 'they claimed' because her whole high school record made it unlikely she'd get into any decent school.

"She told her parents George had come on to her. Kissed her. Fondled her. Told her he knew she wasn't really cheating but if she ratted on him, he'd suspend her. Totally ridiculous, of course, but parents will believe anything their little darlings tell them." Kathryn's upper lip curled on the word darlings. "She said she told George she would indeed tell all, and that's why he suspended her.

"Somehow, the thing snowballed. George refused to back down on the suspension, and the girl embellished her story until it was, 'He raped me.' She got some of her friends to say George was always leering at them during cheerleading practice, that he gave unlimited hall passes to girls who 'cooperated' with him. And, of course, there were certain faculty members who were delighted to add fuel to the flames, any way they could. Oh, it was just awful!" Kathryn paused and turned her splotchy-red face toward the wall. When she went on, her voice was softer.

"It went to court. George was charged with taking indecent liberties with a minor, because the rape charge, they knew, would never stick. All the girl's friends testified that…well, it seemed as if they were competing to see who could make up the most outlandish story! It got worse and worse. George resigned because he knew he couldn't be an effective principal after all that, but it wasn't good enough for them. They wanted blood."

"And the verdict?"

"George was convicted but he was spared a prison term. He's required to register as a sex offender everywhere he goes. Wherever we live, our neighbors always find out he's a sex offender because all they have to do is go on the internet." Kathryn had been fiddling with a hairbrush as she talked, but now she wrung it in both hands, banged it on the edge of the bed, and flung it against the far wall. The brush ricocheted, landing back at her feet. "He can't get a decent job. We have no friends. Even me, I know my co-workers talk about me behind my back. You know, 'Kathryn's husband is a sex offender!'"

The phone rang. Kathryn, still shaking, asked me to answer it for her. It was Marco and he was looking for me. I told him I'd meet him in the lounge as agreed, but I might be a few minutes late. I went to my own room and called the main number, asking them how I might get a message to a member of the staff. "For Sophie Antonakos. I don't know her room, but she's a dancer."

"I'll give her a message for you, Mrs. Lamb."

"Tell her to call or come see me as soon as possible."

NINE

THE LOUNGE WAS JAMMED. As I edged my way around the room in search of Marco, bits of conversation flew past me and they all seemed to be about the twin tragedies. The disappearance of a guest from America and the chilling murder of the photographer. Of the two, it seemed the latter concerned them more. Quite natural, since the photographer was the one who had greeted and photographed every one of them. They had all heard his cheery "Say tsatziki!" at least once.

"He was stabbed! In the alley!"

"I can't believe no one noticed a man running around with a bloody knife."

"They said there was blood all over the deck back there."

"I, for one, am about ready to ask for my money back."

Marco, I saw, had been buttonholed by a dough-faced woman shaped like a butternut squash. She had him by the arm and was blinking something like Morse code at him with her eyelashes. Beside her was a younger woman, rather plain and wispy-looking. I got close enough to hear the older one twitter, "You simply must help them solve these cases. A Carabinieri captain! You simply must!"

Oh, barf.

At the far end of the lounge, Luc Girard and a man in a white dinner jacket held a large book between them while Girard ran his finger across the page. I turned sideways and ran a gauntlet of arms holding cocktails. Girard closed the book and handed it to the other man when he saw me coming his way.

"I left a message for Sophie to call me," I said. "Remember? The girl who dropped the lekythos?"

"Of course, I remember." He introduced me to the man holding the book. "We've been discussing the return of the Euphronios vase to Italy."

"A Greek vase? To Italy?"

"It was dug up from an Etruscan tomb somewhere north of Rome so it belongs to Italy."

"Of course." Being something of an Etruscan enthusiast myself I was surprised I didn't already know about it. "The Etruscans seem to have been enamored of Greek art and philosophy," I said.

The dinner jacket man raised one eyebrow as if he was surprised to hear such a comment from a woman with an American accent.

"Quite right." Luc Girard went on. "It was traded under false pretenses and purchased by the Metropolitan Museum in New York where it has remained for some years. Its return to Italy is the result of an agreement between Italy and the Metropolitan Museum."

"Perhaps this will set a pattern for the return of other antiquities," the dinner jacket man said, nodding to me. Taking the book with him, he turned and left.

Girard told me the Greek red-figure vase—signed by the painter, Euphronios, and unearthed 2,500 years later—was a masterpiece and in pristine condition.

"I don't understand," I said. "How is this buying and selling done? Surely the Metropolitan Museum wouldn't have bought the vase with no provenance, no paper to prove where it came from."

"These antiquities dealers have a hundred ways to falsify provenance. In this particular case, the vase came with papers that actually described a similar but much less valuable piece. This other piece has miraculously disappeared." His mouth turned up a little on one side. "You dig?"

Sophie Antonakos appeared at the door to the lounge and waved at me. I made come-here motions with my own hand, but she shook her head.

"I see our little fumble-fingers now," I told Girard. "Shall I try to get her to come in?"

Girard shook his head. "Could we both meet with her in the library? It's too noisy in here. How about after dinner? Are you free?"

I made my way to the door, glancing toward Marco as I went. He caught my eye and made a desperate sort of throat-cutting motion with his hand, a gesture I interpreted as meaning, "Please rescue me from this woman before I cut my own throat." I pointed toward the door and kept walking.

Sophie had tucked herself discreetly behind the open door to the hall, pulling me aside as I stepped out. "I can't come in, Mrs. Lamb. I'm not dressed properly."

"You're dressed fine, but Dr. Girard suggests we three meet in the library after dinner. Say about nine? Better make it nine-thirty," I added, remembering that dinner last night had been a rather lengthy affair.

"What is he going to do to me?"

"Do to you?" I laughed. "He's not going to do anything to you, Sophie. He's quite harmless, I think. And by the way, call me Dotsy."

I joined Marco, who by this time had shaken off the squash-shaped woman, and together we located Ollie and Lettie. Willem Leclercq and Malcolm Stone were talking to them.

Ollie took my elbow and turned me away from the

conversation group. "I've asked Leclercq and Stone to join us for dinner. Is that okay?"

"Why ask me? I'm not the social director," I said. "But Kathryn Gaskill says she might join us, too. Do you think it will be awkward?"

Ollie reddened. He paused for a minute. "She has as much right to that table as we do. We can't ban her because her husband's dead and she thinks I killed him. Either me or Leclercq or Stone. Wow. The victim's widow and the three top suspects at the same table." He paused and ran a hand over his bald head. "Maybe me and those two guys could take a different table. Make it seem like they invited me to their table."

"That's not necessary." I felt as if I should give Kathryn and the men credit for having some couth. "We'll simply stay off the subject of what's happened to George."

WHEN WE ENTERED the dining room, I saw Kathryn was already sitting at the table we'd had the previous night. She was decked out in widow's weeds: black dress, black shoes, black necklace, and a little black bow in her black hair. Our waiter quickly grabbed two more place settings from his little service bay, but I whispered to him that only one more setting was needed since Mrs. Gaskill's husband would not be with us. The poor waiter, just grasping the situation, backed away so quickly he sent a tray on the portable stand behind him skittering across the carpet. I managed to get Marco and myself seated on either side of Kathryn. Sort of like insulation.

Since "How has your trip been so far?" and "What did you do today?" were forbidden topics, Lettie started us off with, "This is such a beautiful time of year to be in Greece. I've heard it's horribly hot in mid-summer. I told Ollie, I said, 'I'm glad you were able to take time off now,' because he can't leave town when he's in the middle of a construction project."

Kathryn said, "For us it was a matter of finding time between surgeries. George has been having dental work done—caps and things—and he's scheduled for bypass surgery soon after we go home." Kathryn was still referring to her husband in the present tense. "You never know, do you? George told me he wanted to take this trip before his surgery because he'd always wanted to see the Greek islands and with heart surgery, you never know." Kathryn's napkin flew to her face as if she had just realized George wouldn't be needing that operation after all.

Marco changed the subject and directed a question to Leclercq and Stone about their search for antiques. Leclercq reminded us this was a buying trip for him because he was looking for furnishings for a wealthy client's new home, and Stone's job was to advise him about the purchases he hoped to make. A nice, safe topic. Good job, Marco.

Lettie told us about Ollie's buying every sponge on the island and Marco got us all laughing at his description of Lettie entering the urbane coffee house with a bag of sponges and two pelicans. The laughter sort of morphed into coughs and throat-clearings as everyone decided they should act, if not somber, at least sober.

"That reminds me," I said, looking at Leclercq and Stone, "Marco and I saw you two today on Mykonos. You were talking to one of the dancers from the ship. She had a package, I remember."

"Ah, yes!" Stone came to life. "We were browsing through one of the little shops when Miss Benson came out of a back room with the absolutely most wonderful geometric-style krater. A krater to die for. Probably eighth century B.C." Stone's way of speaking was effete, I thought. I could definitely see him in an antique shop. "She let us look at it for a moment and then she left so I said to Willem, 'We must get that krater. If you and your client don't want it, I certainly do.'" He waved a hand toward Leclercq and looked around the table, making eye contact with each of us, as if to assure himself we agreed with him that some things were too wonderful to be passed up. "So we followed her outside and offered her nine hundred Euros for it, but she said, 'No.' Then Willem said, 'Tell us what you paid for it and we'll double it.'"

"She still said, 'No.' She simply would not negotiate. Then she explained she was picking up the krater for a friend and she had no idea what he'd paid for it. We asked her if she would talk to her friend for us or give us his name so we could deal with him directly. But she wouldn't tell us his name."

"So what could we do?" Leclercq said. "Malcolm told me we'd be crazy to let this thing slip through our fingers, so I gave her my card and asked her to please pass it along to her friend. I hope she will. Malcolm, what did you say her name was? I've forgotten it already."

"We met her this morning when we were waiting in line to get off the ship," I said. "Her name is Brittany Benson."

All eyes at the table shifted from me to the woman next to me. Kathryn Gaskill's head jerked forward and horror spread across her face. I glanced across and beyond our table, trying to follow her eyes, to see what she saw, or hear what she heard, that had petrified her. She jumped up from the table, toppling her chair backward, and ran from the room.

"EXCUSE ME." I started to dash off after Kathryn and then turned, shaking my head at Lettie who, I knew, would follow me if I didn't stop her. Five dumbfounded faces stared back at me, but no one followed me out.

I ran up and down the hall outside the dining room noting from the lights above the elevators that none of them were descending, so it was unlikely Kathryn was heading to her room. In an L off the main hall, I found a ladies' bathroom and pulled the door open. Kathryn stood in the middle of the room, her back to a wall of mirrors and sinks, trembling.

"What is it, Kathryn?"

"That name. Didn't you say…Brittany Benson?"

"Yes. I'm sure that's the name she gave me when I met her this morning."

"That's the name of the girl I told you about! The girl who accused George of rape!"

I tried to think fast, but trying to think fast always seems, to me, to make the process actually slow down. "There must be a lot of girls by that name. I'm sure it's not the same one." I led her to a chair in the corner and babbled on. "Benson's a very common last name, and Brittany, why, it's one of the most popular girls' names in the U.S."

Kathryn looked at me as if I had lapsed into another language.

"And besides, you saw her last night, Kathryn. The tall, pretty girl in the center of the dance line? You remember? You commented that she was the best dancer on stage."

"Did I? I wouldn't recognize her now anyway. She was in high school the last time I saw her, and even then, I only saw her a few times from a distance. On the other side of the courtroom."

I continued trying to soothe Kathryn, and eventually she let me walk her back to her room, but all the while I was thinking about the one thing Brittany had told me about herself—that she was from Pennsylvania. Hadn't the Gaskills mentioned living in Pennsylvania before they moved to Indiana?

SOPHIE ANTONAKOS WAS waiting in the library when I got there. Marco had tootled off to see what he could find out about how the investigations were proceeding, and—at my suggestion—to ask around about Brittany Benson. We agreed to meet later in the bar on the top deck. Ollie and Lettie went to the pool area of the Poseidon deck for a little dancing.

"I had to come dressed for my performance, because I didn't know how long this would take," Sophie said, spreading her peasant skirt across the arms of her chair. She wore a heavily embroidered vest and skirt with a white apron. "We go on stage at ten." Her back rigid, she stared at the library door as if she expected the grim reaper to enter at any moment.

"Relax, Sophie," I said, seating myself in a chair beside a large, ancient-looking globe. "The girl you were with this morning. Didn't she say her name was Brittany Benson?"

"Yes."

"How well do you know her?"

"We're roommates. We have…"

Sophie didn't finish her sentence because Luc Girard came in, introduced himself formally to her, and handed her a small box. "Open it," he said.

I got up and leaned over Sophie's shoulder to see. Inside the box was an ornate gold item, probably a piece of jewelry, I thought. It was about four inches long and it lay on a bed of cotton.

"I heard you were from northern Greece, Miss Antonakos. This was recently found by a colleague of mine. Near Pella, I believe. What can you tell me about it?"

"Me? But I am not an…"

"I know you aren't but never mind. Tell me anything and everything that comes to your mind when you look at this thing."

Sophie's hand shook as she lifted the little item and turned it over. I was ever so glad it was unbreakable.

"It is a diadem," she began. "It appears to be gold but one would have to weigh it to be sure. It's made of twisted wire and hammered metal, many spirals, and in the center there is a Heracles knot." She turned the item toward Girard, her pinkie finger pointing to the design in the center. "If it's a genuine antiquity, it would date from the time of Philip the second or later. It may have been a wedding gift. It originally had five gemstones soldered across the middle but they are all missing."

Girard tilted his head, twiddled his mustache. "You have studied archaeology, Miss Antonakos."

"No, sir. I like to go to museums, though, and I read books. I have been many times to all the museums. But I have never been to college."

This was the second time I'd heard Sophie mention her lack of a college education. I had a sneaking suspicion I knew where this was heading.

"About that white-ground lekythos, Miss Antonakos. The accident this afternoon." Girard sat back and laced his hands across his chest, resting his elbows on the arms of his chair. A stray strand of hair fell between his right eye and his glasses. "Accidents happen."

"Oh, but I should have been more careful! I've been thinking, Dr. Girard. I don't know how much it was worth, but I could have the purser make over my paychecks to you until you say it is paid for."

"No, no, no. Let me tell you something. Last year I was working with Dr. Dieter Matt, the German archaeologist, at an excavation in Crete. Have you heard of Dieter Matt?"

Sophie nodded. "And I've also heard of you as well."

"We found several nice amphorae and I was working to clean them up. These were huge things, more than a meter tall. I let one slip off a bench while I was working on it and, of course, it broke. Dr. Matt flew into a rage. He called me every humiliating name he could think of and he did it in front of the entire crew. I couldn't work there anymore. I was supposed to be in a position of authority, and I had been made to look like a fool. So I left."

Girard's voice was soft but it held no hint of tenderness. "I made up my mind, then, I would never do that to anyone who had simply made an honest mistake." He looked at me and added, "Stuff happens. You dig?"

I grinned.

"I have a suggestion, Miss Antonakos. There is a way you could repay me. I need an assistant, and if you could find the time between your other duties," Luc said, gesturing toward her costume with the forefingers of his laced hands, "you could help me catalogue and describe the artifacts I have on the ship. You could organize them for me before each of my lectures. Do you speak Greek?"

Sophie didn't seem to realize what a silly question that was. She nodded.

"I have to make speeches in Rhodes, in Crete, and in Athens from time to time. When the ship is docked in those places. If my audience is mainly Greek, I try to deliver my lecture in Greek. But my Greek isn't very good. I'd like for you to read my notes and put them into good, modern Greek for me."

Sophie nodded vigorously.

I looked at my watch. "I think this sounds great but, Sophie, don't you need to scoot? You're supposed to be on stage in three minutes."

"Oh!" She jumped up, toppling the brass compass on a stand beside her chair and launching it on a new search for north. She lunged forward and caught it before it hit the floor.

Girard watched as she righted the compass, patted it affectionately, and backed through the door to the deck, apologizing under her breath all the way.

"She'll be all right," he said. "I think."

"You're quite a detective, Dr. Girard. You already knew Sophie was an archaeology enthusiast."

"I also know she comes from a very poor family and she has a lot of potential. As a scholar."

Why, I wondered, did he find it necessary to add those last three words? I picked up the box with the diadem and looked at it more closely. The craftsmanship was superb. I hefted it in my hand and felt its weight. "And speaking of detectives, do you remember our conversation before dinner about the vase? The Greek vase that's to be returned to Italy?"

"The Euphronios vase. Yes."

"Did the Italian Carabinieri have anything to do with it? I ask that because I have a friend on the ship who is a detective with the Carabinieri in Florence and he has a keen interest in stolen antiquities."

"I'd like to meet him. But to answer your question, no. This wasn't a case of anything having been actually stolen, except in the sense that it was excavated illegally to begin with. It was a case of altered identity papers and misrepresentation. But the Metropolitan Museum in New York knew what they had. The question was whether or not they had to return it to Italy."

"I see."

"The Italian Carabinieri are doing great work, though. They work with Interpol very effectively."

"And with Scotland Yard?" I asked because Marco had mentioned working with that London-based agency.

"Sometimes," Girard said, and his tone of voice may have betrayed a tiny bit of Anglo-French rivalry. "This business of theft, though. There's hardly a museum in the entire Mediterranean area that hasn't been hit. Broken into. Looted. The Corinth Museum. Did you hear about that? Thieves broke in, beat up the night watchman, and stole hundreds and hundreds of priceless works. Look!" He jumped up and flew to the book shelves behind me. "I want to show you."

Girard ran his fingers along one row of books, then along the next row down. He pulled out a thin, soft-cover book and opened it. "In here they have pictures of all the items stolen from the Corinth Museum. See?" He flipped through the pages and handed me the book. In it were photos and descriptions of hundreds of vases, busts, kraters, and sculptures. "Most of these things have been found and returned, thank God."

"Where did they find them?"

"Believe it or not, they were in a warehouse in Miami, Florida." He showed me another, somewhat thicker, volume. "And this one has photos of some of the artifacts currently missing from other museums. Only museums in Greece."

"Incredible."

"They could do another one as large as this for items missing from Italy, or from Turkey, or from Egypt."

I thumbed quickly through the thicker book, entitled LAMBDA. I imagined LAMBDA was an acronym for something and certainly an apt title. Lambda, the Greek letter L. L for lost. I wished I had more time to study this book.

Girard read my mind. "You may take it with you if you like. Bring it back here when you're finished."

TEN

MARCO MANAGED TO WEASEL his way into the meeting in spite of Chief Letsos. In the small room that served as an office for shipboard security, the men directly involved in the investigations of the disappearance of George Gaskill and the murder of Nikos Papadakos were gathered. Chief of Security Letsos sat behind the desk, twisting a rubber band around his fingers, glumly chewing on a toothpick. His baby-faced assistant, Demopoulos, stood in one corner, his hands clasped behind his back. United States FBI Special Agent David Bondurant had taken one of the two chairs on the opposite side of the desk from Chief Letsos.

Perched stiffly on the other chair was the sole policeman from Mykonos who had stayed aboard after the others had been called ashore to help with the murder probe. Murder was not an everyday occurrence on Mykonos and this particular policeman looked overwhelmed by recent events. Letsos introduced him to the others as Lieutenant Villas.

The question was: Who's in charge? The other question was: Of what? Special Agent Bondurant had already made it clear he considered himself in charge of the George Gaskill affair. George had been an American citizen, Bondurant had fifteen years' experience in criminal investigation, and he had access to all the investigative tools of the FBI. Shipboard security, as Bondurant had forcefully pointed out to Letsos, had access to a pair of handcuffs and experience with scanning boarding cards.

Technically, the photographer's murder was the bailiwick of the Mykonos police, but Lieutenant Villas, sitting beside Bondurant, his left leg nervously bouncing, would obviously have been delighted to hand it over for any reason or none at all. His own chief, back on the island, had charged him with the task of finding out who on the ship knew what about the murder of the photographer.

Marco had told Letsos about Kathryn Gaskill's reaction at dinner to the name Brittany Benson. He repeated what Dotsy had told him about the Brittany vs. George court case and George's subsequent status as a sex offender. When he suggested they look at the ship's personnel records on Miss Benson, Letsos pawned him off on his junior officer, Demopoulos. It was while that young man was calling around to find out where personnel records were kept that Special Agent Bondurant walked in. Marco identified himself as a fellow crime-fighter, and name-dropped a couple of mutual acquaintances, other FBI attachés in Europe with whom Marco had worked.

Meanwhile, Letsos had walked in with Villas, and it would have been rude for him to have told Marco to leave. He said it with his eyes, with a glowering glance toward the door, but Marco refused to take the hint. So there they were. The five of them.

"They have found the knife," Villas announced. "At least they think it's the knife used to kill your photographer. Someone found it in the shallow water of the rocks along the bay in Little Venice."

"We can forget about fingerprints, then."

"The knife looks similar to those sold in one of the shops in Mykonos Town. When they talk to the owner of the store, they will probably know for sure."

"With luck, the owner will also remember who bought the knife," Bondurant said, "or at least be able to describe the buyer."

Marco said, "It seems to me, as vicious as the attack was, there should have been a very bloody person running down the streets of Little Venice. Strange, no one saw him."

"They think the attacker may have come prepared with protective clothing. He could have taken it off and stuffed it in a bag, after he finished." Villas looked around the room, as if for confirmation that this was a reasonable idea.

"Did you see the body?" Marco asked. "It was a mess. Such a mess that it was either done by a person who was angry, out of control, or by a person who did not know what he was doing."

"Stabbing blindly?"

"Exactly."

Security Chief Letsos flipped his toothpick with his tongue. "Let's let the Mykonos police worry about that one. We have enough to worry about already. We've interviewed Oliver Osgood, Willem Leclercq, and Malcolm Stone. They are the three men who were playing cards with Gaskill last night. Osgood is still our best suspect, because he was with Gaskill until they parted to go to their rooms. As far as we know, he was the last person to see Gaskill alive. Those three men lost almost two thousand Euros each, but Stone and Leclercq alibi each other. They both say they didn't leave their suite after Osgood and Gaskill left. They went to bed."

"But they have separate bedrooms in their suite," Bondurant said. "Either of them could have left after the other went to bed."

"Possible, but unlikely."

"Or they could be alibiing each other. One of them could be protecting the other."

"Possible," Letsos repeated. "We've collected blood samples from the deck and we should be able to get a sample of Gaskill's DNA from at least one of the personal items we've taken from his room. Drinking glass, hairbrush, razor, and such."

Demopoulos, still standing in the corner, cleared his throat and held up one finger. "Excuse me, sir. The hair?"

"Oh, yes. Where is it?"

Demopoulos drew a plastic bag off the top of the filing cabinet beside him and handed it to Letsos. Inside the transparent bag was a stringy black mass large enough to clog a sink drain.

Letsos grimaced as he took the bag from Demopoulos and held it up. "This was pulled out of the water this morning by one of the Mykonos police boats. They began at the stern of our ship and continued on a course one hundred eighty degrees from the course we were steering last night. In other words, they were trying, as nearly as possible, to retrace our path. When they got to a spot that was approximately where we would have been at one o'clock this morning, they stopped and looked around for a while. This is all they found." Letsos looked embarrassed, as if he expected the others to laugh.

"What is it?" Bondurant asked.

"It seems to be a part of a wig. Like a man's hairpiece," Villas said. "I was on the boat when we found it."

"Did Gaskill wear a hairpiece?"

"Why was it floating? If it's hair, shouldn't it have sunk?"

Letsos squeezed the bag, rose, and passed it across the desk to Bondurant. Bondurant held it up to the overhead light. He mashed it and said, "It's greasy. It's got so much hair oil on it, it must've been like a duck. Couldn't sink! Too much oil on its feathers."

Marco and Bondurant laughed.

"Our friend from the Carabinieri, here," Letsos said, jerking his head in Marco's general direction, "sat with Kathryn Gaskill at dinner this evening. He tells me she had a rather violent reaction when the name of one of our ship's dancers was mentioned." He paused, and then said. "Would you tell them, Captain Quattrocchi?"

Marco described the dinner table scene and filled them in on the story Dotsy had told him.

"We'd better talk to this Brittany Benson," Bondurant said.

"I intend to," Letsos said as if he resented the implication he wouldn't have thought of that himself. "She's on stage at the moment."

"Could a woman have done this?"

"Sure. A young, physically fit woman? A dancer? Versus an over-the-hill car salesman who'd had at least five drinks?"

"It would be quite a coincidence, wouldn't it? Rapist and victim meet on a ship halfway around the world from the crime?"

"The charge may have been false," Marco said.

"In which case, the young woman would have no reason for revenge. It would be Mr. Gaskill who would harbor a grudge." Bondurant glanced around at the other four, a deep furrow between his eyes. "Could either of them have known the other was on the ship?"

"You mean before the cruise started? Not likely. But they could have bumped into each other at any time after that," Letsos said, taking the plastic bag containing the hairpiece back from Bondurant. He held it up and, by way of dismissal, said, "We'll see if Mrs. Gaskill can identify this tomorrow morning. She's probably asleep by now. And we'll try to catch Miss Benson when she leaves the stage."

ELEVEN

A NOTE FROM MARCO lay on the floor inside my door. I'd forgotten he said he would wait for me in the Zeus Deck bar. I was so absorbed in the book Dr. Girard had given me, I'd found a seat between the outside doors and the stairway and sat there looking through it for some unknown period of time, unaware I hadn't actually gone to my room. When I finally did make it back to my room, it was well after eleven, and I was dead tired. Of course I was tired! I'd been up since 3:00 a.m., with less than two hours' sleep.

I recognized Marco's squared-off style of printing. I opened the note and read: "Dear Dotsy, Where are you? I am tired of drinking by myself. I am going back to the bar for a few more minutes, but I am going to leave at midnight. Marco."

I looked up the number for the Zeus Deck bar on the telephone info card, dialed it, and left a message for Marco saying I was crashing and I'd see him in the morning.

I SLEPT THE SLEEP of the righteous until seven the next morning, dressed, and scanned the day's activities in the "Oracle," the flyer the cabin steward shoved under my door each night. We were to visit the island of Patmos today. Patmos is the traditional site where St. John the Evangelist wrote the book of Revelation. Apparently, our ship would have to anchor outside the harbor and we would need to take a small launch to shore. It was too early to wake anyone else up, so I breakfasted alone and rode the elevator up to the Zeus Deck, the top level and one I hadn't seen yet. Except for the bar/lounge on the bow, now closed, the Zeus Deck was dominated by a large gymnasium covered with bubble-shaped skylights. The ship's smokestack rose above the forward end of the gym. I felt a twinge of guilt when I looked at the doors to the bar. That was where I'd have met Marco last night.

Aft of the gym, I found a small sun deck with chairs and tables scattered around. Two people sat at one table drinking coffee. With a small shock, I saw one of those people was Kathryn Gaskill and the other was the man I'd noticed in the debarkation line yesterday and pegged as "trying too hard to look casual." I paused, turned to the rail and gazed across the water. It was blinding in the morning sun. *Don't be silly, Dotsy. Go over and talk to them,* I told myself. I walked over.

"Dotsy, this is Nigel Endicott. He's from Vermont."

Nigel Endicott rose and shook my hand. A man of indeterminate age, his skin said "fifty-something," but his hair, the gold ring in one ear, and the tattoo on one arm said "thirty-something." He wore black-rimmed glasses and his hair, scrunched up with gel into the tousled style the young men all wore, had a sprinkling of gray mixed in with the dark.

"Are you traveling alone, Nigel?"

"Yes. I was just telling…"

"Kathryn," Kathryn prompted.

"Kathryn, that since my retirement I've been renovating the farmhouse I bought a couple of years ago and I needed a break. I plan to spend my retirement there, 'far from the madding crowd,' as they say."

"Oh, but surely you're too young to retire."

"Not really retire. I'm just retiring from the rat race. I want to do organic farming and sell the results of my labor.

My farmhouse is on ten acres of land." Nigel had a trace of an English accent.

I felt as though I shouldn't bring up anything to do with George because I had no way of knowing whether Kathryn had told Nigel Endicott about it. It seemed logical that, unless she was deliberately avoiding the subject, she would have mentioned it the very first thing. "My husband was murdered on this ship yesterday." Hardly the sort of thing that would slip your mind, but it occurred to me Kathryn might be in need of a break because the tension for her must be unbearable. I could see myself, in her place, heading for a deserted deck with my morning coffee. If someone did join me and want to talk, I'd stick strictly to small talk. Quite natural, I thought.

I left them and took the stairs down three levels to the stern of the Poseidon Deck. This was where Lettie and Ollie had been heading last night for music and dancing in the area around the pool. The deck was abandoned now, so I grabbed a chair and, looking up, saw Kathryn and Nigel still sitting where I had left them. The pool area was open to the sky because the top three decks only went back part way. I moved to a chair that was closer to the bulkhead until I could see none of the upper deck, so Kathryn and Nigel wouldn't think I was watching them.

I hoped Ollie and Lettie had had a fun evening. Poor Ollie. This was the first vacation he'd had in ages, the first time he'd ever been out of the States, and here he was, a murder suspect. I didn't need to waste a single minute wondering if he was guilty. The very idea was ludicrous.

I wanted to know more about Leclercq and Stone, the other suspects. Why were they so anxious to get their hands on that krater of Brittany Benson's? Why had they been so hospitable in offering their suite for a poker game with two total strangers? Ollie said they had been generous with the drinks and they had the poker table all set up when they got there.

Antiquities. That's what Leclercq was shopping for, wasn't it? Funny how this was becoming a recurring theme. Leclercq, looking for ancient Greek relics to furnish a client's new home. Stone, an antiques expert. Luc Girard, world-renowned archaeologist and authority on antiquities. Sophie Antonakos, poor girl from central Greece who, nevertheless, can pick up an antique diadem and immediately spout a scholarly discourse on it. Brittany Benson, showgirl from America, who runs around Mykonos hugging a prize antique krater.

And the *Aegean Queen,* cruise ship with a theme. It flaunted genuine antiquities in showcases all over the ship.

Okay, but was any of that connected to the murders of George Gaskill and Nikos Papadakos, our late photographer? Were the two murders connected to each other? I thought about it for a while and decided I needed to talk to my son, Charlie.

CHARLIE, MY NEXT-TO-ELDEST, was principal of a high school in northern Virginia, a most trustworthy boy and an absolute straight arrow. I knew I'd have to word my request carefully because Charlie wouldn't violate the law or even bend the rules, and I wasn't a hundred percent sure what I wanted him to do was ethical. Or legal.

I couldn't call him now because back home it was three A.M. but I recalled passing a sort of computer room on my way out. An internet café. It had been closed when I walked past, but now my watch said 9:05 so I decided to check again and, lucky me, it was just opening. A woman behind a desk surrounded by computer stations explained the rates to me but they all sounded expensive. You paid by the minute to access the internet from one of their computers, and she warned me that pages took some time to download. Assuming I'd have to mess around a good bit before I managed to even get into my own email, I could see this costing a bundle.

Then she made me a more reasonable offer. For a few dollars (added to my bill) I could send one email to one address. If I got a reply, it would cost me a few dollars more. I sat down with pencil and paper to compose my message to Charlie.

Meanwhile a large woman with an American accent barged in and asked about using a computer. She looked like the woman who'd been batting her eyelashes at Marco last evening in the lounge. The attendant explained things to her, reciting the same spiel she'd given me.

"Why is it so slow?" the American woman groused. "Don't you have cable?"

"Oh yes, madam," the attendant answered with a straight face. "But it's a very long cable. Goes all the way back to Athens. It's elastic."

The woman stomped out, and I sent my message to Charlie's email box at work:

Hi Charlie,
We're having a great time, but I have something I want you to do for me. Find out all you can about a man named George Gaskill. He was principal of a school in Pennsylvania about ten years ago. I know it's not much to go on, but you could maybe pretend you're thinking about hiring him. If you find the right George Gaskill, they'll tell you not to hire him because he's a registered sex offender, but go on anyway and find out all you can.

Also, find out about a former student, Brittany Benson, who attended the school at which Gaskill was principal and who was complainant in a court case charging him with sexual abuse. I'm not making this up! I know students' records are sealed and employees' records are confidential, but I'll bet you can find a way. You could check court records, news coverage, and stuff like that.

Also, Brittany Benson was a cheerleader and George Gaskill now lives in Elkhart, Indiana, and he works at a used-car place. This is important, Charlie, otherwise I wouldn't ask.

Love, Mom

I left the internet café and took the stairs down to the Osgoods' room. Lettie was there but Ollie, she told me, had been called to the security office by Special Agent Bondurant.

"Marco called a while ago," Lettie added, "looking for you. He said to tell you to come to his room."

I noticed Lettie had pulled out one of the dresser drawers and one of the sofa cushions. Both were on the bed now, the squarish cushion crammed inside the drawer. As she was talking, she yanked two huge mesh bags full of sponges out of the closet, an avalanche of shoes following in their wake.

"I'm afraid to ask," I said.

"I've figured out how to get these silly things back home without going over on the number of bags they allow you to take on the plane. Watch." Lettie held up a couple of large space-saver bags. "I brought these in case we needed more room in our luggage, and guess what? We do."

She stuffed one bag with sponges and ran her fingers across the open end. "These have a special seal so you can squeeze air out but it can't go back in. Sponges are mostly air, so…" She put the full bag on the bed, put the drawer with the cushion inside on top of it, and sat on the cushion. Sat hard and bounced a few times. Air hissed out from under the drawer. When she stood up and lifted the drawer, I saw the vacuum bag was flatter, but not by much.

"They're too stiff, Lettie. A sponge has to be wet to be squishable."

"But I can't take wet sponges on the plane. Oh, hell." She stood, staring at the problem with her left fist poised thoughtfully under her chin, then snapped her fingers and took one sponge into the bathroom.

I heard water running.

"Ta da! Look." Lettie returned, holding out two fists. "Pick a hand."

They looked the same. I felt ridiculous but I pointed to a random hand.

She opened both of them anyway, and a sponge ballooned out of her right hand. The left one, of course, was empty. "They don't have to be really wet. Just damp. See?" She snapped the sponge downward so if there had been any extra water in it a spray would've streaked across the carpet. "I wet it and wrung it out in a towel. When they're damp, you can squeeze them down to nothing."

"So what are you going to do? Wet all of them?"

"Yep. And wrap them all in big towels and get as much water out as possible, then I can squash them really flat!"

"I'd better go see Marco," I said.

MARCO OPENED THE DOOR and, without a word, turned and walked back into his bathroom. I closed the door and stood awkwardly in the middle of his bedroom, enjoying the man-smell of aftershave and soap. Except for the brush and towel on his bed, his room was neat. I'd wondered if Marco was a neat freak or a slob, and here was my answer. Neat. On his desk lay a small, clear tube with cotton stuffed into the open end. Without touching it, I bent over and looked closely. The cotton swab I'd given him yesterday lay inside the tube, the cotton on one end stained a dark red-brown.

"Is this a sample of the blood from that pool on the deck?" I called out, loudly enough that he could hear me over the noise of water running in the sink.

"Yes. Do not touch it."

"Why did you put cotton in one end?"

No answer. I was getting the silent treatment. I looked at the tube again and recognized it as a complimentary shampoo vial. I had two in my room, one with shampoo, one with conditioner. Police, I knew, had special containers for storing collected samples but obviously Marco hadn't brought any with him so he'd improvised.

He emerged from the bathroom swiping his face with a hand towel and shot me a cold look. "I put the cotton in to keep dust out. I did not want to put the cap back on because the tube is not sterile and sealing it with moisture inside would make the bacteria grow."

"Marco, I'm sorry I didn't go to the bar last night. Did you get my message?"

"Yes. It is okay." But his voice was still cold. "Have you had breakfast yet?"

I said I had, but I'd sit with him and have a second cup of coffee while he ate. I stopped off at my room on our way to the stairs and picked up the LAMBDA book Dr. Girard had let me borrow. At the showcase on the stairway landing, we paused to look at the Cycladic fertility figure and I flipped through the book. "They're all so similar, these little marble women," I said. "But I don't see anything in the book that looks exactly like this one."

"That is good."

While Marco waited for his breakfast to be brought to the table, he studied the LAMBDA book. Whether because he was interested in the stolen Greek antiquities or because he didn't want to talk to me, I couldn't say. His croissant and fruit arrived and he finally looked at me and smiled. My heart did a little bounce.

"Special Agent Bondurant, the man from the FBI grabbed Brittany Benson as soon as she finished her performance last night," he said.

"Were you with him when he did?"

"No, I was in the bar. Waiting for you."

Oops. I asked for that.

"Brittany says she went straight to her room after their show the night Gaskill was killed. Sophie, her roommate, was with her the whole time. They talked for a while and went to sleep. Sophie backs her up on this."

"I guess that's that." I tasted my coffee and added a blip of cream. "Wait a minute. I saw Brittany at three A.M! On the promenade deck, you know, the one running all the way around."

"You need to tell this to Bondurant. Was she alone?"

"No, she was with Sophie. I know it was Sophie, because I recognized her as the girl who had fallen on her face when she ran on stage."

"Did you talk to them?"

"No. I should've asked them if they'd seen anyone, but I suppose I was too preoccupied with finding George myself."

Marco and I decided to meet again when the boat dropped anchor in Patmos harbor, and then we left the restaurant in search of Bondurant. We found him in Security Chief Letsos's office, poring over the contents of a three-ring notebook.

Marco introduced me to the FBI special agent and I told him my story. He dropped his notebook on the floor and listened, his legs stretched out casually and crossed at the ankles.

Bondurant heard me out, then asked, "What were they wearing? Were they still in costume?"

I had to really think about it. I wished Lettie had been with me because, with her near-photographic memory, she could have described everything they had on, right down to their shoes. "No, they weren't. They were wearing bathrobes."

"Bathrobes?"

"Yes. It didn't strike me as odd at the time. All I was thinking about was finding George Gaskill."

"Were they wearing shoes?"

"I don't remember."

"Did they see you?"

"I don't know."

Bondurant turned to Marco and said, "We took that sample of hair to Kathryn Gaskill a few minutes ago. She positively identified it as her husband's hairpiece."

"Dio! Per carita."

"Mrs. Gaskill went berserk when we showed it to her."

"What are you talking about?" I asked.

"On his way down to Davy Jones' locker, George Gaskill left something behind. His hairpiece was waterproof because it had so much oil in it. It floated." The FBI man grinned the tiniest bit.

BONDURANT WALKED ME to the door but indicated he wanted Marco to stay, so I took the LAMBDA book and went back to Lettie's room. She proudly showed me two thin, bumpy boards, each about a half-inch thick, which I soon recognized as vacuum bags containing hundreds of squashed sponges. She had managed to convert them from the approximate volume of a steamer trunk, to the size and shape of two cafeteria trays.

"Ollie is really upset, Dotsy. Bondurant called him back to the office this morning and he's been gone for more than an hour. He wants to go home, but they won't let him go!"

"I was in the office with Bondurant myself a few minutes ago. They found George Gaskill's toupee floating on the sea."

"Was Ollie there?"

"No."

Lettie's face went blank. "How long were you in there?"

"Fifteen minutes?"

"So where's Ollie? He's had time to get back." Lettie bit her lower lip and glanced out their porthole window. "I have to go look for him. When he left the room, Dotsy, the last thing he said was, 'If it's more of the same, like yesterday, don't wait for me to come back. I'm gonna jump ship and join George Gaskill.'"

"You know Ollie wouldn't kill himself. Really!"

"Are you sure? Or are you going to help me find him?"

TWELVE

LETTIE AND I CHECKED the Ares deck, the one I called the promenade deck, first. Ollie and Lettie's room was on this deck and, like all the other outside rooms, had a small, round porthole window instead of a large rectangular one like mine. I imagined this was to afford the rooms' occupants more privacy because a steady stream of walkers and joggers flowed past these windows. My window, on the other hand, was flush with the outside of the ship and looked out onto nothing but blue sea and sky.

"If Ollie is walking around on this deck, I think I'd have spotted him walking past," Lettie said. "Our curtain is open."

"Since we're already here, let's check it."

We made the circuit going in opposite directions, as Kathryn and I had done at three A.M. yesterday morning. No Ollie. We descended one floor and checked the little stern deck from which George Gaskill had disappeared. At the bank of elevators, I studied the deck diagrams posted on the wall.

"There are two levels below this one, but they have no outdoor decks. Just rooms, engines, and stuff. The next deck above yours, Lettie, is the Dionysus Deck where the whole thing is open to everybody. Dining room, main desk, show lounge. Above that is the Poseidon deck with the pool, casino, bar, etcetera. The Ares deck is nothing but rooms, and the Zeus deck is on top. I was up there earlier."

"Let's go up one floor."

On the Dionysus and Poseidon decks, Lettie and I split up again, Lettie taking the stern, me, the bow. On the Zeus deck, Lettie headed for the stern, and soon shouted back to me, "I found him!"

Ollie was standing at the rail near the table where Kathryn Gaskill and Nigel Endicott had been sitting earlier. He barely turned his head when Lettie came up beside him. I was debating whether I should join them or not, when Lettie turned to me, shook her head, and I beat a retreat around the bubble-top gymnasium.

Standing now in the middle of the top deck, I had the gym on my left, the observation bar on my right, the sea beyond the rails behind and in front of me. In the distance an island I assumed was Patmos peaked over the horizon.

A young couple emerged from the gym and walked across to the bar, tried the door, opened it, and walked in. The bar was now open. It was too early for a drink, I thought, but while Lettie and Ollie talked I could get a Coke and check out the view from the bar's big windows. I went in.

Inside the door I found a Plexiglas case containing a large black-figure amphora, or jug. The amphora had two vertical handles attached to opposite sides near the neck, a base so small it made the vessel look quite unstable, and a red-orange panel on the front that framed the helmeted figure of the goddess Athena standing between two columns. Beneath Athena's feet was an inscription in ancient Greek.

An engraved plaque near the foot of the amphora identified it as a "Panathenaic amphora. Early sixth century B.C. The inscription reads, 'I am one of the prizes from Athens.'" This information was repeated on the plaque in four other languages. The games in Athens, I knew, were similar to those in Olympia, Greece, but started a century or two later than the Olympics. This would have been one of the jugs, filled with olive oil from the sacred grove of Athena, that were awarded to winning athletes.

I thumbed through the LAMBDA book until I found the photo of the Panathenaic amphora I had noticed earlier. It was identified by a number assigned to it by the museum from which it had been stolen. It was 265 centimeters tall and it showed five black-figure sprinters in the area where, on the amphora in front of me, I saw a figure of Athena. All the sprinters, painted in silhouette, had one leg and the opposite arm raised, like a chorus line of Rockettes.

Two hundred and sixty-five centimeters. That would be about three feet. The amphora in the case was about three feet tall as well. I wondered why this one depicted Athena rather than athletes.

"There you are," Lettie said. She and Ollie had sneaked up behind me.

"Check this out, Ollie," I said. "This is a prize for an athlete from the sixth century B.C."

Ollie laid a meaty hand on my shoulder. "I'm going to get myself a very large drink. If you want me, I'll be in the bar."

"I hope he doesn't drink too much. He's depressed enough to drink himself blotto." Lettie peeked around the corner at Ollie's retreating figure.

"I thought Ollie loved anything to do with Olympics." I remembered the time I called Lettie and she'd whispered to me she had to switch phones because Ollie demanded absolute quiet when he was watching the Olympics on TV.

"That shows you how stressed he is. He'd rather have a drink than see an Olympic prize."

I gave Lettie a short lecture about the amphora, on which I had been an authority for about four minutes. She took the LAMBDA book from me and turned the photo toward the light.

"Everything in this book has been stolen? Golly."

I peeked around the back side of the amphora and saw the sprinters. Just like the ones in the photo, each had one leg and one arm up, the other leg straight and extended back. I couldn't tell how many figures there were because the piece was too close to the back wall of the display case.

"Lettie, look. This jug has sprinters on it like the one in the book. Why didn't they turn this side to the front? It's more interesting than the other side."

Lettie stepped around beside me, looking at the amphora, then the photo, then the amphora again. "This is the same one."

"Very similar, yes. But they must have made one of these for every contest."

"No. It's the same one, Dotsy. Look. Look right above the second runner from this end. In the black part. Do you see where the black has flaked off in the shape of a V? And about a half-inch down, there are three sort of pock-marks going downhill."

"Okay." I looked and saw the blemishes she was talking about.

"Now look at the picture."

The amphora in the photo had identical damage. In the black area above the second sprinter from the left there was a V-shaped spot of exposed clay with three dots below it. Going downhill.

"It's stolen! I have to tell Dr. Girard."

I FOUND LUC GIRARD in the library with Sophie Antonakos. He'd already put her to work. Surrounded by a dozen or more relics and a ruler, she seemed to be measuring and recording data in a notebook while Dr. Girard sat hunched over a box full of sand. A glue pot stood beside the box and shards of pottery poked up, willy-nilly, out of the sand. He was gluing the broken lekythos back together and I didn't wonder that he hadn't entrusted that job to Sophie Stumblebunny.

"What would you say if I told you item number two-nine-four-three is upstairs in the observation bar?"

Sophie dropped her pencil and Girard's head popped up from his work. His mouth opened but nothing came out. I handed him the LAMBDA book and pointed to the photo of the Panathenaic amphora. He dashed out the library door, taking the book with him.

Sophie looked at me. "What do you mean? How did you find it?"

"It wasn't hard. It's on display in the big showcase right inside the door of the Zeus deck bar. Haven't you ever been up there?"

"A few times, yes. Do you mean the big amphora from the Athens games?"

"Exactly."

"I don't know where the people who furnished the ship got the things they have on display, but I have wondered where they came from. They all appear to be real. Not—how do you say—reproductions."

"Who would know where they got them?"

"I don't know." Sophie studied her feet for a few seconds. "Maybe the purser? He might have a record of the purchases."

"Good idea. What about the captain?"

"Captain Tzedakis? He might. He probably knows the owners of the cruise line." Sophie agreed to ask around about who was in charge of purchasing what.

"Another thing, Sophie. About your roommate, Brittany."

Sophie's eyes widened as if she was surprised I remembered her roommate's name.

"A man I met yesterday saw Brittany with what he said was a 'to-die-for' antique krater. She had picked it up at a shop in Mykonos Town but when he tried to buy it from her, she wouldn't even talk about making a deal. Not that she should, of course, but I wonder. She said it was for a friend of hers. Do you know anything about it? She turned down an offer of nine hundred Euros."

"I think it was probably for her boyfriend, Rob. She talks about him all the time. He's rich, I think."

"Where does this Rob live?"

"In Switzerland. Geneva."

"Did you see the krater yourself? She must have brought it back with her yesterday unless she had it shipped."

"It would make no sense to pick it up and then ship it," Sophie said. "If he wanted it shipped, why not have the shop do it?"

Sophie, I decided, was a sharp cookie.

She stared at her feet for another moment, then said, "Brittany and I each have our own closet and we both stow things under our beds. She could have brought it back to our room."

"Could you look?"

"Go through her belongings? No!" Her back went rigid. "I'd be very angry if she went through my things!"

I sat quietly, letting the importance of what we might be talking about—the theft of priceless antiquities—sink in. "Well then, could I come to your room sometime and visit you?"

"Certainly. Any time." Sophie, I thought, understood.

A perspiring and disheveled Luc Girard burst through the library door. "*Merde!* I don't believe it!"

"Whom should we tell? The captain?"

Girard ran a hand through his hair. His eyes darted left, right, left, and he covered his mouth with both hands. "Didn't you tell me you know of a Carabinieri captain on the ship? I think I should talk to him before we tell anyone else."

THIRTEEN

MARCO AND I CLIMBED aboard the launch and found a spot on the bow so we could see Patmos as we approached it. I turned and shot a photo of our ship after we had put a bit of distance between it and ourselves. The launch, zipping across the water, blew a warm, sensuous breeze through my hair.

Marco slipped an arm around my waist. He lightly kissed my temple and I turned to receive the kiss on the lips I knew waited for me. I felt a knot form in my stomach as he kissed me again.

"At last," he said. "I've been waiting for that kiss for two years."

The demons within me banged against my ribcage and I turned my face toward Patmos. Marco was threatening to make me deal with how screwed up I was. My divorce from the swamp rat some five years ago had left me with a bucket-load of problems and it didn't take a psychiatrist to tell me what they were. Teaching ancient and medieval history at a local community college had helped mend parts of my shattered self-image, but to trust again? To let myself be vulnerable? I couldn't do it yet.

I felt Marco's arm stiffen and drop away.

"Did Luc Girard find you?" I asked.

"Luc? You are on a first-name basis with him already, eh? Yes, he found me. We went up to the top deck together. It is the stolen amphora, all right. We think they may have been aware of the photograph being circulated. The one in the LAMBDA book. So they deliberately put the display case close to the wall and turned the amphora so the side shown in the photographs would be hidden."

"What are you going to do about it?"

"Me? Nothing, for now. We are going to talk about it later."

I turned and looked at him.

"Girard needs to proceed carefully," Marco said, staring across the water toward the approaching island. "The cruise line is his employer, after all."

"You mean he wants you to do nothing so he won't risk losing his job?"

"I mean we must proceed carefully."

"I think we should check up on every item in the display cases all over the ship. They may all be stolen!" I may have said this a little too loudly, because I sensed heads had turned toward us. I looked to my left and saw Brittany Benson and Willem Leclercq standing together and no more than ten feet from Marco and me.

Ollie and Lettie were the first people off the boat when we docked. Ollie was drunk. Marco and I watched as Lettie guided her voluminous husband around vendors' stalls and darting children to an olive tree. She propped him up against the tree and glanced around, an anguished expression on her face.

"Should we go and help her?" Marco asked.

"She can handle it. Let's not embarrass her."

Marco and I went first to the Holy Cave of the Apocalypse where St. John saw the vision that inspired the Book of Revelation, then back down a cobblestone path to the harbor town where Marco spotted Ollie careening dangerously along a seawall. He left me to go and help poor Lettie out.

I found a bench under a tree and sat. I kicked off my

shoes and then noticed the man on the other end of the bench was Malcolm Stone, the antiques expert from England. He had a brown paper package about the size of a hardcover book.

"Did you find a bargain?" I asked.

"No, I paid dearly." Malcolm paused, then added, "Dotsy, isn't it?"

"Right. Friend of Ollie Osgood. We had dinner together last night."

"Of course. Have you seen Osgood? He's drunk as a skunk."

"It's because the FBI and ship security are leaning hard on him about the murder of George Gaskill. He's about had it."

"Is there anything I can do? They've given me and Willem the third degree, as well."

I couldn't think of anything he or I could do, other than figure out who had killed George.

He turned his package over and began loosening the tape. "This is something I ordered a year ago. It was made for me by a monk in the monastery up there." He jerked his head toward the eleventh-century Monastery of St. John at the top of the hill behind us. Unwrapped, it proved to be an icon of St. George running his lance through the legendary dragon. It looked old, but I knew they had ways of antiquing newly painted icons.

"It's lovely."

Stone looked at it in silence for a minute, and then said, "My wife's father's name was George and she always kept an icon similar to this one in the office at the back of our shop. It's an antique shop I still own and operate in Brighton. Her father's family was Greek. He, my father-in-law, had given it to her when she was young."

"What happened to it?"

"I took an axe to it. I chopped it into a hundred pieces."
Stone began rewrapping the icon, found the end of the
tape, and pressed it down again. "When she died two years
ago. Stupid, wasn't it? To blame a piece of wood for not
protecting your wife?"

"Grief makes us do things," I said. "Will you put this
one back in the same place? In your shop?"

"Yes. It's time for me to get on with my life. I've wal-
lowed in self-pity long enough."

"It takes time." I looked down the hill and spotted
Willem Leclercq. It looked as if he was discussing a large,
black table that sat in front of a restaurant, under a grape
arbor. I suspected from his gestures that he might be dick-
ering to buy it. I asked Malcolm.

"Right. It's not old, but he decided he had to have it for
the garden of the house he's furnishing. It'll cost him more
to ship it to Belgium than he's paying for it."

"Did you advise him against it?"

"It's not my concern. I'm only here to advise him about
antiques."

I stood up to leave. "I'm sorry to hear about your wife."

"Thank you." Without looking at me, he added, "If I
could ask a pretty woman such as yourself to dance with
me some evening, it might be a good next step. Would
you?"

"Of course." I think I blushed. Well, what else could
I say?

FOURTEEN

As Marco helped Ollie off the launch and back into our ship, I saw FBI Special Agent Bondurant standing immediately inside the security checkpoint. Ollie jerked around when he saw Bondurant and, for a moment, I was afraid he'd bolt. But Bondurant took Marco aside while Lettie and I steered Ollie to his room.

After we deposited the big lug on his bed and removed his shoes for him, I left and went in search of Luc Girard and/or his new assistant, Sophie. I found her but not Girard in the library, where she was surrounded by books and by what appeared to be a number of pages downloaded from the internet. Girard's sandbox of pottery shards still sat on a side table, illuminated by a gooseneck lamp.

"Dotsy, it's terrible! We've found four items in the display cases are stolen, and we haven't checked them all yet. They haven't all been stolen from the same place, though, and they aren't all in the LAMBDA book. We have limited references with us on the ship but we're finding some help on the internet. Dr. Girard is taking photos of the ones we can't identify and emailing them to people he thinks might help us."

"What about the identity numbers? Aren't the museum pieces supposed to have black numbers on them?"

"We'll have to get the cases unlocked in order to see. But the amphora on the Zeus deck, a krater in the case outside the show lounge, in fact, all the pottery items are probably bolted through their bottoms to the case itself."

"You mean they drilled a hole through them to bolt them down?"

"Yes. Otherwise, when the ship rolls, the pottery would break."

"And the drill hole would likely remove some or all of the ID numbers." I cringed at the thought of using a drill on any of these relics.

"Dr. Girard is trying to get someone with a key to open the cases for him."

"Sophie, can you leave for a few minutes? I'd like you to show me your room."

"Now? Why?" Sophie frowned, and then her face softened. I think she realized I was really asking to see Brittany Benson's room, which also happened to be her own room. "I suppose I can leave. Let me put away some things first." She moved the sandbox into a cabinet, closed its doors, and looked around the library. "Let's go."

The crew slept in the bowels of the ship. Luxury, I found, ended with the Athena deck. Below it was the Demeter deck with crew quarters, metal grid stairs leading down to the engine room, and noise. The engine noise on this level was overwhelming.

Sophie slipped her key card into one of about fifty doors on the left side of one hall and ushered me into her tiny room. She and Brittany had somehow managed to cram two narrow beds into an L shape along two walls in a manner that must have made it nearly impossible to change sheets on the one in back.

"Most of the rooms have the beds stacked up, but Brittany and I decided to do this because neither of us wanted to sleep on the top. It puts you so close to the ceiling, if you sit up in the middle of the night, you crack your head."

"I understand." They each had a small desk and a closet no more than two feet wide. "Where is your bathroom?"

"Down the hall."

"Would you mind going into the bathroom and getting me a paper towel?"

Sophie looked at me questioningly, and then said, "Of course."

Sophie was a bright girl.

"How long do you want me to take, getting this paper towel?"

"Ten minutes ought to do it. But keep an eye on the hall, too." It wasn't hard to figure out which bed, closet, and desk were whose. Sophie's had Greek language magazines under it, and Brittany's were all in English. Near the foot of Brittany's bed was a clipboard with an unfinished letter tucked under an envelope addressed to her, care of this ship. I pulled the envelope out and looked at the letter beneath. It professed true love for the recipient. In English. I pulled a notepad from my purse and jotted down the name and return address on the envelope.

Under Brittany's bed, I found two flat garment boxes. One was full of costumes, the other, street clothes. Her desk yielded little but nail polish, a curling iron, and makeup. Brittany wasn't much of a reader. Or much of a writer, either, I decided.

The closet with the longer clothes and the size nine shoes had to be Brittany's. On its floor I found two cardboard cartons, wedged in so they couldn't shift with the roll of the ship. I pulled both out and opened them. The first contained a geometric-style krater, probably the one Stone and Leclercq had tried to buy from her yesterday. With repeating black patterns on a red background, it had no identifying numbers anywhere on it and it was in excellent condition. If it was a genuine fifth century B.C. krater, it had weathered the millennia well.

In the second carton I found a footed stone box with a carved scroll design that looked similar to pictures I'd seen of finds from the Cyclades. The carton also contained a lid, wrapped separately and tucked in on top of the stone box. Returning both cartons to the floor of the closet, I turned my attention to Brittany's desk drawers but I knew my time was running out. I hoped to find some paperwork: a receipt, a certificate of authenticity, anything that would shed light on these two items and how they came to be in Brittany Benson's closet.

The doorknob turned and I caught my breath. I still had one drawer open and both hands in it. Thankfully, it was Sophie. I could breathe again.

"I need to get back to the library," she said. She didn't ask what I'd been doing or what I'd found, and I didn't offer to tell her. She handed me a paper towel.

FIFTEEN

CHIEF LETSOS, FBI Special Agent Bondurant, Marco, and Villas, the policeman from Mykonos, were in Letsos's office once again, each sitting in the same place as last night but this time Marco had been awarded a chair. Young Demopoulos, who was scheduled for night duty, wasn't there.

"Update on the George Gaskill affair." Bondurant started without referring to the notes on his lap. "We have a report from Pennsylvania on him. He's a registered sex offender and the young lady he was convicted of abusing just happens to be a member of the crew on this very ship. The odds that this is a coincidence are vanishingly small.

"He was employed at a used-car dealership in Elkhart, Indiana. Wife works at a department store. No children. Gaskill was definitely not Employee of the Month. According to the manager, he hadn't sold a car in ages.

"Health problems." Bondurant went on in his staccato fashion. "Heart bypass surgery scheduled for July. He'd already been granted leave from work for the operation."

At this point, Bondurant referred to a page of his notes. "Brittany Benson. Sixteen at the time Gaskill was convicted of abusing her. Born in Philadelphia, Pennsylvania. After high school she worked as a flight attendant for Delta Airlines for two years, then quit. Moved to Miami and worked in a bar. Shared an apartment with a Peter Davis. Moved to Lima, Peru. We have an address for her in Lima, but our men are still checking on whether she was living alone or if she had a roommate. Started work for this cruise line two years ago. Gives her current address as 1253 rue de Lausanne, Geneva, Switzerland."

"Busy young lady," Letsos said, then turned to Villas. "What have you got for us today?"

Villas, his elbows on his knees, read from his notepad. "We have a list of everyone who went ashore in Mykonos yesterday. Both passengers and crew. We've created a database of their identity cards. This includes their photo, country of origin, passport number, and cabin number.

"We have identified and talked to the owner of the shop where the knife that was used to kill Papadakos was sold. He is certain it is the same knife that was purchased by a man shortly after this ship docked. He remembers the man spoke English, was neither tall nor short. He wore sunglasses and a tourist-type shirt. Flowers or leaves or something all over it."

"Does he recall the color of the shirt?"

"Unfortunately, he is color-blind, he told us."

"Anything else?" Marco asked. "Did the man who bought the knife speak English with an American accent, or what?"

"I don't know, but if the shop owner is like me, all accents sound the same in English. I faxed the photos of all the men in our database to the Mykonos police station, and the shop owner is coming in to study them and, hopefully, recognize one."

Marco cleared his throat. "May I make a suggestion?"

Chief Letsos tapped a pencil against the edge of his desk and paused a second before saying, "Go ahead."

"There is a woman on the ship—Lettie Osgood—who was on the scene yesterday and who walked up and down the streets on both ends of that alley yesterday, moments after the murder. In fact it was she who first recognized that it was Papadakos. This woman has an unusually good, what they call photographic, memory. If you will talk to her, she will probably be able to tell you everyone who was in the area."

"Osgood?" Letsos frowned and leaned so far forward his wheeled chair zipped backward. He caught himself by grabbing the lip of the desk as his chair hurtled out from under him. He pulled the chair forward by its arms and reseated himself. "Is this the wife of our prime suspect in the murder of George Gaskill?"

"Well, yes."

"Can we expect her to tell us the truth?"

"You will have to ask her."

Letsos tossed the pencil he'd been playing with across his desk. It bounced off the phone. "Yes. Well, our best bet is still the shop owner who sold that knife. Hopefully he'll recognize either the man or his shirt."

"Do not forget the identification photos were taken at boarding time. Our man was probably not wearing the same clothes again yesterday." Marco leaned back and slung one arm over the back of his chair.

"Good point, Captain Quattrocchi," said Bondurant.

Villas nodded and wrote something on his notepad.

Letsos glowered.

MARCO SLIPPED OUT of the security office and tracked Lettie down. Returning, he tapped on the door and ushered Lettie inside, where he found Letsos, Villas, and Bondurant, still sitting in the same chairs as when he had left them. He introduced Lettie to the men and waved her into the lone empty chair, retreating, himself, to the wall opposite Letsos's desk.

"I'll tell you all I can remember," Lettie said. "Where do you want me to start?"

"The alley where Papadakos was found joins two streets filled with shops," Officer Villas said. "Both of these streets lead up and through Little Venice and down to a plaza on the waterfront."

"That's right."

"Tell us about everything you saw in the area. Start with the first time you were there."

"The first time was when I walked up from the waterfront because I was tired of listening to my husband trying to talk to Greek fishermen who didn't speak English. I went into a shop called, well, I don't know what it would be in English but in Greek, it said…" Lettie grabbed a notepad off Letsos's desk and wrote ηλιoζ, held the paper up, and turned it around for all the men to see.

"I know the place," Villas said.

"It was two fifty-five when I walked in. I looked at my watch. Inside the store, I saw four people from the ship. A man, a woman, and two children. The man was wearing a tan-and-green shirt and black shorts. White gym shoes, no socks. Reddish hair. The woman wore a red-and-gray striped sundress with spaghetti straps and a straw hat. Straw sandals. The children, now…"

Marco leaned over and touched Lettie on the arm, but Villas looked up from his frenzied note-taking and shook his head at Marco. Lettie stopped talking.

"Go on, Mrs. Osgood."

"Well, next I went to the bar up the street to see my friend Dotsy, and Marco here. I didn't know there were two pelicans following me, but maybe they smelled fish or something on the sponges. I had a big bag of sponges with me."

"Stop." Letsos held up one hand like a traffic cop. "How did you know they were in the bar?"

"When Ollie and I went down to the waterfront to begin

with, I saw Dotsy and Marco walking in. That was at two-twenty."

"You forgot to tell us about that, didn't you?" Letsos leaned back, tilting his head accusingly. "You forgot to mention you and Mr. Osgood were, in fact, on that street earlier."

"But it was a long time earlier! More than an hour before we found the body."

Letsos held up both hands and shook his head.

Lettie, her feet not quite touching the floor, wiggled in her chair, jammed both hands, palms downward, under her thighs, and sighed. "When I came out of the shop, at three-ten, I saw Brittany Benson walking down toward the plaza. She was wearing a white tank top, pink Capri pants, and straw espadrilles with red leather ties. There was no body in the alley at that time, because I looked when I went past. There was only a large tabby cat sitting on a box. A blue box."

Twenty minutes and ten pages of notes later, Villas flexed his writing hand and thanked Lettie for her help. Bondurant appeared to have slipped into an altered state. Letsos had executed an elaborate doodle on his green blotter. Marco's mouth quivered in a barely suppressed grin.

Thanks to Lettie, they now knew Dr. Luc Girard, Sophie Antonakos, Brittany Benson, Willem Leclercq, a family of four from the ship, Dotsy, Marco, Ollie, and herself were all in the area at or around the time of the murder. On her way up the other street as she, Ollie, and Dotsy returned to the ship, they had walked past the crowd gathered at the entrance to the alley and Lettie required another ten minutes to enumerate the gawkers and what each of them was wearing.

"Thank you very much, Mrs. Osgood," Villas said. "I may need to talk to you again, but you have been most helpful."

SIXTEEN

THE SHIP DECLARED the evening Formal Night. Why all cruises do that, I don't quite understand. I think it's a holdover from the glory days of the *Titanic* when scions of American industry rubbed elbows with British lords and dukes in the first-class dining hall while lesser folk ate in second-class, and refugees from the famine in Ireland stuck it out in steerage. But I went along with it and wore my size eight black dress with my Swarovski crystal necklace.

Two women from America sat with us at dinner. I'd seen them several times already, one being the squash-shaped woman I'd seen flirting with Marco the night before, and again that morning, barging out of the internet café, incensed the ship had no high-speed cable connection. Ernestine Ziegler introduced herself and her daughter, Heather, adding that they were both nurses. Ernestine worked in med/surg at a large Chicago hospital, she told us, and Heather was a pediatric nurse for a private practitioner. Ollie was unable to attend due to his excesses earlier in the day, but Lettie was there. Kathryn Gaskill also ate with us, and that made Marco the lone man at a table with five women.

Marco, incidentally, looked good enough to eat in a charcoal suit, obviously hand-tailored, a light gray shirt, and diagonally striped tie. Italians do know how to dress.

I found myself musing at the relationship between the Zieglers, mother and daughter. Ernestine dominated the dinner conversation but Heather spoke only when spoken to. Ernestine's round face, framed by an extra chin and hair that reminded me of a doll I'd once had—the one I'd tried to give a permanent using glue and bobby pins—was accented by too-red lipstick, too-small glasses, and too-thin hoop earrings.

Heather Ziegler reminded me of Robert Burns's description of a mouse: "Wee sleeket, cow'rin beastie." She was twenty-five years old, unmarried, and lived with her mother, who, having expunged all traces of her second husband after he joined a doomsday cult, had resumed use of her first husband's (Heather's father's) name. Marco and Lettie listened in silence while I, with perverse glee, dug into the Ziegler family history. Heather, I discovered, had not been allowed to go away to college because her mother wouldn't let her. She had taken her nursing degree from a nearby community college.

Not only did Marco look irresistible tonight, he turned out to be a good dancer, too. After dinner we went dancing in the mid-section of the Hera deck where a five-piece band cranked out tunes from the forties and fifties. Both Lettie and Kathryn declined our invitation to join us, but as a waiter seated us at a small table near the dance floor, a martini-swilling Ernestine burbled coquettishly at Marco from a nearby table. I quickly shoved one of the two empty chairs at our table away, ostensibly for more leg room, but actually to make it difficult for her and Heather to join us without moving furniture.

After placing our drink order, Marco led me to the dance floor. The band played "Perfidia." He swirled me into the center of the floor with an easy grace that left no doubt about who was leading. I tried to recall the last time I'd danced with a man. It might have been with Chet, in fact. My ex-husband. It would have been more than three years ago at a Christmas party where the girl/woman with whom my husband was destined to run off had stood icily by, waiting for her chance to cut in. I shivered at the memory.

"You are the prettiest woman here, Dotsy."

"Oh, shucks. You're not so bad yourself."

"You do not like me without a beard, do you?"

"Of course I like you, with or without a beard. How silly."

"You are very…"

"Very what? I'm having a lovely time, Marco. Don't try to analyze me, okay?" I looked at him, smiled, and winked in a way I hoped would convey simple fun.

At a table on the other side, Brittany Benson sat, her body turned at an angle that gave the entire room a good view of her long dancer's legs. She was leaning forward toward the man who was sitting with her, smiling, running her finger around the lip of her wine glass. When he turned his head slightly I saw it was Willem Leclercq.

"Dotsy?"

"Huh?"

"You are not listening to me."

"I was looking at Brittany Benson over there. When did she and Leclercq get together?"

Marco turned his head and followed my gaze. "Interesting."

"We know he wants the krater she picked up in Mykonos." I paused a moment and thought about that.

"And we know he played cards with the man who was convicted of abusing her, only a few minutes before that man was killed."

"Coincidence?"

"Coincidences do happen, Dotsy."

I scanned the rest of the room as Marco swirled me

around. Nigel Endicott was sitting alone at a table in the back, Malcolm Stone and a couple I didn't know had a table near the bandstand, and Ernestine Ziegler was studying Marco's backside with obvious relish.

We returned to our table and found our drinks waiting for us. Marco raised one eyebrow at me tilting his head toward the music, but the band had lit into a song that sounded way too tango-like for my skill level. I shook my head. Leclercq, I noticed, clasped his hand over Brittany's and his left leg was touching hers.

"I wish you could have been in the security office when Lettie was telling us what she remembered from the time of the murder." Marco laughed and slapped his forehead. "She remembered everything! The name of the shop she went into, even though it was in Greek, the color of the cat in the alley."

"How did Chief Letsos react to her?"

"Like he could not believe his ears."

"Did you learn anything new?"

"Yes. Papadakos, the photographer. He is from Crete, you know. From an olive-growing part of central Crete where his family still lives. Now, what is important about that?"

I shook my head. "I have no idea."

"Many of the illegal artifacts of Minoan origin come from central Crete. We get them coming through Italy on their way to the rest of the world. Bronzes and pottery of all sorts are smuggled out and they find their way onto the international market."

"What could Papadakos have to do with that? He was a photographer."

"I do not know, but it seems to me that working on a cruise ship which stops off in Crete, in Rhodes, in Turkey, in Santorini…" Marco planted his right hand in spots around the table as if it were a map of the eastern Mediterranean. "It would be a way to pick up goods in one place and drop them off in another."

"What about customs? How would he get things through customs?"

"I do not know, but they would only have to go through customs if they were brought to shore in Athens, I think, and I do not believe customs in the port of Piraeus is very strict. There are planes, you know. Little private planes, all sorts of planes fly between Santorini, Rhodes, Rome, and Athens every day."

"So Papadakos could have been killed by a fellow smuggler?"

I felt a tap on my shoulder. It was Malcolm Stone and he bowed slightly as he asked me to dance. The band was now playing "Bésame Mucho." I glanced at Marco, unsure of whether I should accept or decline, and saw a look of irritation—almost anger—flash across his face. But he nodded assent as Stone took my hand and led me toward the dance floor.

He wasn't nearly as good a dancer as Marco. Stiff as a robot. But then, I told myself, he probably hadn't danced since his wife died some years ago. He was tall enough so that, even in my high heels, I found myself staring at his bow tie.

"Your friend, Captain Quattrocchi, isn't it? Have you known each other a long time?"

"I met him two years ago when Lettie Osgood and I went to Italy together."

"And since then?"

"Since then, what?"

"Has he come to America to see you? Have you seen him since your trip to Italy?" He stepped on my foot and apologized more than necessary. "What I'm trying to find out, quite clumsily, is whether the two of you consider yourselves a couple?"

"No, we're not a couple, but we did plan this trip together."

"He's in on the investigation into George Gaskill's murder, isn't he?"

"In an unofficial capacity, yes."

"Are they making any progress? What a horrible thing it was! I mean, Willem and I were with him an hour before his death." Stone shook me with his shiver.

"We don't know he died an hour after your card game ended, do we?" I realized it sounded like an accusation and I hadn't intended it that way but, now that I'd said it, I wasn't sorry. I drew back and looked up at his face.

"Well, no. I mean, yes, I believe I heard someone say it happened at about one or two A.M."

"They only know it was before four A.M. That's when Kathryn Gaskill and I found the…when we went out on the back deck."

"Perhaps I misunderstood." Malcolm turned his head.

Nigel Endicott had slipped up behind him and tapped on his shoulder. He was cutting in.

Malcolm handed me off to Nigel with a polite but grudging, "Certainly."

Nigel Endicott's hand was cold and damp and he held me as if I were made of whipped cream. Searching for something to say, I came up with, "Kathryn said you're from New Hampshire, right?"

"Vermont."

So much for that. Over Nigel's shoulder, I located Marco, still sitting at our table. Ernestine had moved in and now stood a few feet away from him, gushing and flouncing like a teenybopper. Heather still sat at their table, staring at the dance floor.

"When I met you yesterday, I'd been talking to Kathryn for a few minutes but I didn't know she was the woman whose husband was murdered," Nigel said.

"I see. Yes, I was surprised to find her on deck that morning. The day before, she'd stayed in her room and only came out for dinner at my insistence."

"How is she doing now?"

"It's hard to tell. I had dinner with her tonight, but she didn't say much."

"You were just dancing with the Englishman I heard was playing cards with Kathryn's husband that evening. Does he have any suspicions?"

The abruptness with which he changed the subject startled me. "Well, no. Security has talked to him, I'm sure, but I've no idea what he told them."

"And what a shame about the poor photographer being killed. Didn't your friend, the man you're with tonight, help the police with it?"

"We both happened to be in the area at the time. So Marco, being a police officer himself, stayed behind to help. Just with crowd control, though." I wondered how he knew about Marco helping them. Maybe Nigel had been in the group gathered at the end of the alley. The group Marco had been pushing back when Lettie, Ollie, and I walked past them on our way back to the ship.

"So he didn't talk to them about the crime itself? Do they know what the motive was?"

"If they do, he didn't tell me about it." I felt Nigel's right hand quiver against my back. *This poor man is scared to death,* I thought.

The song ended before Nigel could ask me any more probing questions, but as we turned to leave the dance floor, Malcolm Stone, again, popped up behind and tapped me on the shoulder.

"Dotsy? One more dance before the band takes a break?"

"I'm sorry, Malcolm. I think I'll go back to my table now." I'd been away from Marco too long, basking in the glow of my sudden popularity. Marco would probably have something pointedly sarcastic to say and I told myself to take it gracefully.

But he didn't. He was gone.

I sat at our table and waited for fifteen minutes. Long enough to be certain he hadn't simply gone to the men's room. Ernestine Ziegler watched me, I noticed, by cutting her eyes my direction without turning her head. Malcolm joined Brittany and Willem at their table and Nigel Endicott disappeared. The band left for their break.

I took the elevator down to my room, phoned Marco's room, and let it ring seven times. Leaving him a message to call me back, I stood in the middle of my room and tried to think what I should do next. Check the other bars and lounges? The casino? The security office? Marco might have dropped in there to see if there was any news. Using the elevator again, I checked every public gathering-spot I knew of, ending up in the observation bar on Zeus deck. No Marco anywhere.

I'd really done it now.

I walked around the bubble-top gymnasium, from which the plonk of bouncing balls still emanated, to the aft rail and looked down on the outdoor pool of the Poseidon deck. The wind blew my hair across my face. A half-dozen children still cavorted in the bottom-lit pool, playing Marco Polo. Ouch. That name. Parents sipping drinks at tables and shivering children wrapped in towels watched the game in the water as white-jacketed waiters wandered around, picking up glasses from abandoned tables.

How could I have been so stupid? Marco had given me

plenty of warning he was losing patience with me. You can't expect a man to put up with cold shoulders forever. I had turned away from his kiss this morning on the launch boat to Patmos, slipped away like some kind of scared rabbit that first evening on the promenade deck when all he'd done was try to hold my hand, and now, tonight, I'd acted cozier with every man who'd asked me to dance than I had with him.

From Marco's point of view, this would make no sense. I'd never discussed my past with him. He might really think it was all about the beard. I was ashamed of myself. *Stop it, Dotsy! You're acting like a victim. Now, lighten up and let Marco touch you. Unless he's had it with you already.*

With nowhere else to check, I decided to make one trip around the promenade deck and turn in for the night. I took the elevator down, considered knocking on Lettie and Ollie's door, then thought better of it and shoved open the heavy teak doors to the outside deck. Greek Bouzouki music drifted down from somewhere above.

I turned left and walked toward the back end of the ship. A few wooden lounge chairs were still out, the rest stowed away for the night. In the daytime, the bulkhead was lined with cushioned chairs. Most of the ship's outside lighting was directed toward the water, leaving the deck itself in dim shadow. I stepped carefully to avoid tripping over a chair.

As I turned the corner, the churning water from the engines glowing green and white in the floodlights, I heard a voice behind me. I turned. It was Brittany Benson, alone now, and she was on a cell phone. Her voice shook as she almost shouted, "I know someone went through my room! I put those boxes in my closet with the arrows pointing

toward the wall, and when I came back, they were pointing the other way!"

I froze.

"Sophie says she knows nothing about it."

I slipped back a little, into the deep shadow at the corner
of the bulkhead. From here I could actually see Brittany
if I moved my head a bit forward, but remain hidden from
her as long as I stayed plastered to the wall. I prepared to
hold my breath and pray as she walked past me. I might, I
thought, pretend to be having a dizzy spell if she saw me.
I'm afraid I've used my diabetes more than once to get me
out of tight spots. I grab my head, wobble around, and call
out for orange juice. Call it the "juice excuse."

Luck was with me. Brittany stopped before she rounded
the corner, spun around as if the person on the other end
of the conversation had said something outrageous, and
plopped down on a deck chair. She turned, her back to
the wind, facing my direction. Ideal, as long as she didn't
see me. I decided to risk it and hang around, even though
the longer I lurked in the shadow the harder it would be
to explain if she caught me.

"No, nothing's been taken…I have my suspicions…
This woman I've seen talking to Dr. Girard and Sophie.
She's from Virginia… No, I haven't. I talked to her for one
minute before we went ashore in Mykonos. Why? Because
she's friends with the Carabinieri captain from Italy, and
because she's been checking out the stuff in the display
cases. She's got some sort of book…and she's the one who
hooked Sophie up with Girard. Sophie's his assistant now."

There followed a long silence before she said, "Yeah,
okay. She's an older woman, salt-and-pepper sort-of hair.
Kind of short, but not too short."

To whom was she describing me and why? I felt a
sudden need to go to the bathroom. My heart pounded

so loudly I could hardly hear Brittany. There was another long pause.

"Well, I'm sooorrry! My God! Please forgive me for getting a little upset when the FBI accuses me of murdering the slime-ball!" I peeked. She had jumped up and was waving her free hand at the sky. "Oh, Sophie backed me up… His name is Bondurant. He's stationed at the U.S. embassy in Athens, but he's staying on the ship until… well, I really can't control that, now, can I?…Sophie told them I came out here to make a call and said she was with me the whole time…I don't know…I don't think so… They showed me the boarding photo of Gaskill and his wife…I'd never have recognized him but she hasn't changed a bit… So what are you saying? What am I supposed to do now?"

Brittany snapped her cell phone closed, yelled, "Shit!" to the sea, and tramped back the way she had come. After she had disappeared, I allowed myself a deep breath. Marco might not be my biggest problem now.

Back in my room, the phone's message light was dark. I tried Marco's room again. Still no answer and it was after 1:00 a.m.

I saw my travel clock's hour hand creep past every numeral from two through seven. I hashed over the George Gaskill situation and tried to tune in to the intuitive side of my brain for guidance. I don't really believe in that left-brain–right-brain stuff they talk about, but if I tell myself to look at the big picture and forget the details, I often get a sensible answer to my question. The answer I got this time was strange. My intuition said, "Kathryn Gaskill knows more than she's telling." Kathryn was doing a fine job of playing the bereaved widow. She'd packed plenty of black clothes, hadn't she? Had she known Brittany Benson was on the ship when they'd planned the trip? It was possible.

Was George a card shark? Ollie said George didn't seem to be very familiar with the game of Texas hold 'em, but he did take Malcolm, Willem, and Ollie for about two grand apiece in a game Ollie said was primarily psychological. In Texas hold 'em, no player has any choice in the cards from which he makes his hand. Ollie said it was all a matter of estimating odds, psyching out your opponents, and maintaining your own "game face." Had George cheated? Did any of the other three men find him out?

What about Brittany Benson? The cell phone conversation I'd overheard sounded threatening to me. Why had she given the caller a physical description of me? Was I on a hit list now? She knew somebody had snooped through her stuff and she suspected me. Being friends with the Italian Carabinieri made me suspect. I could understand that. But how did she know I'd been checking out the antiquities in the display cases and refer ring to that LAMBDA book? Did she know Dr. Girard?

Who killed Papadakos? I tried to recall him to my memory and got a picture of a friendly, round-faced man. Rather nice-looking, always chiming, "Say tsatziki!" instead of "Say cheese." He'd most likely been killed by someone from the ship because the knife had been bought by a man in a tourist-type shirt shortly after we docked. That didn't mean the killer was necessarily one of the passengers, though. The ship's staff, those not required for domestic or navigational duties, had been free to wander around Mykonos wearing whatever they wanted. I recalled seeing Brittany Benson in her capri pants and skimpy shirt. Was Papadakos tied up in smuggling? Did he discover something about the smuggling that made it necessary for someone to whack him? He was, it occurred to me, always stationed with his camera wherever folks were embarking or disembarking, ideally positioned to see everything as it came and went.

What was I going to say to Marco tomorrow? I could: a) give him hell for leaving me alone at the dance, b) beg forgiveness for leaving him alone too long while I danced with other men, c) bare my soul to him, d) act flippant and say, "Can I help it if everyone wants to dance with me?", e) play it off and act like I assumed he'd left for some sensible reason or other. He hadn't responded to the message I'd left him, so option e was pretty weak.

At 5:30 a.m., I decided to handle it by saying, "Good morning, Marco," and let him take it from there. I got up, washed my hair, tried to pay attention to the closed-circuit TV that ran the same stuff all day and all night with captions in the language of your choice, turned the TV off, and reviewed the info in my guidebook about Rhodes, today's destination. At seven, I power-walked three loops around the promenade deck, worked up a sweat, and went back to my room to repair my face.

My phone light was blinking.

But the message was from Lettie, saying she and Ollie were going to breakfast at seven-thirty and asking if I would join them. It was still too early to call Marco, so I traipsed up to the dining hall alone.

Ollie, looking quite recovered from his hangover, stood as our waiter seated me. "We had an interesting visit last night. About nine, wasn't it, Lettie?"

"Nine-fifteen," Lettie answered. "Brittany Benson. She came to our room and tapped on our door shortly after I got back from dinner. Ollie was lying on the bed. Dressed, fortunately."

"That's because I was incapable of undressing myself when you and Lettie dumped me there," Ollie said, pressing his sausage-like fingers to his chest. "Dotsy, for whatever I may have said or done yesterday, I humbly apologize."

"No apology needed. I didn't even talk to you yesterday. Now, go on with your story."

"Brittany suggested she and I are now brothers-in-arms. *Compadres,* don'cha know, because we've both been accused of killing George Gaskill. She told me she had been raped by Gaskill when she was in high school and he'd been convicted of the lesser offense of sexual abuse of a minor."

"She cried a lot," Lettie said.

"Told us she had almost put the nightmare behind her, and here it comes again. When they called her into the security office, they made her go over the whole thing again and it brought it all back. Then Bondurant, the FBI man, asked her if she'd had a little peek at the passenger list before the trip." Ollie leaned over his omelet and lowered his voice. "Asked her when, exactly, she found out Gaskill was on the ship."

Lettie took over. "So Brittany told us, she said, 'I told them I didn't know George Gaskill was on the ship at all.' And Bondurant said, 'Then you must be the only one on the ship who didn't. He was paged numerous times on the speaker and everyone on the ship was talking about nothing else all day.' Brittany said she felt like they were trying to trap her because what she meant was, she didn't know he was on the ship until she heard about the murder and even then she didn't know it was the same George Gaskill."

I ordered an omelet with feta cheese because Ollie's looked good and grabbed a roll to nibble on until the omelet arrived. I glanced around the dining hall to see if Marco was there, but avoiding me. Bright morning sun poured through the plate-glass windows.

"Then, about midnight, guess who else came to visit us?" Lettie wiggled in her seat and fluttered both hands. "Marco!"

I sucked a mouthful of coffee down my windpipe and grabbed my napkin, catching the coffee spray as it came out of my mouth and nose.

"Marco called first. Said he needed to talk to Ollie. So I woke him up and…"

"No you didn't. I was already awake."

"I woke him up, and put him on the phone. He told Marco to come ahead, so I grabbed a bathrobe and washed the overnight rejuvenation cream…"

"Green goo."

"…off my face. When Marco got there, it was a little after twelve."

"He asked me what I knew about Malcolm Stone." Ollie said. "Wanted to know how he'd been acting the night we played poker. Wanted to know if George Gaskill had ever mentioned Brittany Benson to me."

Lettie touched my hand and whispered, "Wanted to know if you were dating anyone back home."

"You're kidding."

"Now, Lettie, we promised we wouldn't tell that," Ollie said.

"Oh, I forgot. Forget I said that, Dotsy." She winked at me and added, "I told him you've been going out with the governor of Virginia. And George Clooney."

Ollie cleared his throat and glared a warning at Lettie. He turned, looked at a spot behind and above me, and said, "Good morning, Marco."

Marco had slipped up behind me. He walked around behind Lettie and took the chair opposite me. "*Buon giorno,* all." He looked at me, "Good morning, Dotsy."

He'd stolen my opening line so I just nodded. He asked

the waiter to bring fresh fruit and another basket of rolls and snapped his napkin across one knee.

"We told Dotsy about seeing you last night," Ollie said, omitting the fact that Lettie had spilled the beans about his inquiry into my life on the western side of the Atlantic.

"What happened to you last night, Marco? I came back to our table and you were gone."

"I looked at my watch and remembered I needed to talk to Ollie, so I left. Sorry, I did not leave word and let you know where I had gone."

"At least I knew you hadn't gone off with the squash-shaped woman. She was still there with her daughter when I left."

Lettie and Ollie laughed.

Marco said, "Do not be ridiculous."

"What do you want to do in Rhodes today?" I asked him.

"Oh." Marco's face reddened. "I forgot to tell you. I am not going to tour Rhodes today. I am returning to Italy. I have booked a flight from Rhodes to Milano."

"Oh, no!" Tears rushed out and spilled over. I couldn't help it. "I'm so sorry, Marco! Please don't go."

Marco ripped open a hard roll. "It is not you, Dotsy. I am taking the blood sample I collected from the deck to our forensic laboratory. I want to know for certain if it is George Gaskill's blood, and I also need to meet with the team that has been investigating the smuggling of antiquities. I have an idea, but I cannot discuss it with them on the phone."

"Isn't the FBI doing DNA tests?"

"Yes, but who knows how long it will take? I can at least get preliminary results quickly."

I turned to see what my three breakfast companions were looking at, and found Kathryn Gaskill behind me, looking rather more chipper today in a little yellow head scarf, tied behind her neck, and a yellow shirt. "Don't get up," she said. "I see you have a full table. I'll sit somewhere else."

"No, no, Kathryn," Lettie said. "I'll move around to Ollie's side. We've already eaten. We're just having our coffee." Lettie vacated her chair and dragged another from a nearby table to the corner between Ollie and Marco.

"Kathryn, do you happen to know George's blood type?" Marco asked.

"Why, yes." Kathryn seemed baffled by the question. "It's type AB positive. I know this because of the blood-work they did a couple of weeks ago to get him ready for bypass surgery. I told you about his surgery, didn't I?"

We all nodded. Kathryn explained it was a fairly rare blood type and asked Marco why he wanted to know. Without mentioning he'd surreptitiously collected his own sample, Marco explained that, while the DNA tests would be definitive proof of whether or not the blood on the deck had been George's, it took a while to get those results, and a quick-and-easy blood type test could at least tell us if the blood wasn't his. If the type proved to be A, B, O, or Rh negative, they wouldn't know whose blood it was, but George would be eliminated and another scenario for what happened on that deck would have to be proposed.

"I see," said Kathryn. "Would you tell me as soon as they do the test? I mean, I know it was George's blood. I knew it the minute I walked out on that deck. Dotsy will tell you." She turned to me. "Didn't I tell you, Dotsy?"

"You did, indeed."

"And the sooner we know for certain, the better." Kathryn paused and sighed. "Mr. Bondurant told me that if they can't prove George is dead, I'll have to wait seven years before they officially declare him dead! Seven years! Of course, I'd give anything to see George walk in here, right now." Kathryn raised her eyebrows and looked toward the ceiling. "That would be the most wonderful thing in the world, but, realistically, it's not going to happen, and if I have to wait seven years for George's life insurance to pay out, I don't know how I'll live. My job doesn't pay enough to even cover the mortgage." She lowered her eyes. "I may have to sell the house, anyway."

Lettie reached around the bread basket and touched Kathryn's hand.

Marco swiped his napkin across his mouth and pushed back from the table. "You will all excuse me, please? I have to go to the purser's office and I have to pick up my passport before we dock."

I jumped up, too, and dashed out beside him. "Marco, please. Do you have to go? I don't want you to go! Are you mad at me?"

Shoving through the dining room doors, he turned and growled, "Am I mad at you? Mad at you? I am not a child. I do not buy a plane ticket to Milano just to get away from you. No! I am going home because there is something important going on on this ship and the information I need is in Italy."

"What information?" I asked, walking sideways so as to keep facing him.

The elevator doors opened, unbidden by either of us, and Marco hopped in, but I was right behind him. He punched the button for the Poseidon deck. "I talked to Dr. Girard," he said, his eyes trained on the blinking buttons. "They have identified four stolen items in various display cases around the ship. Most of the other items they can find no records for. The Carabinieri have a database that should help us."

The elevator doors opened. I intended to follow Marco,

begging all along the way, but I was hijacked by a voice from down the hall.

"Mrs. Lamb?" It was the woman who ran the internet café. "I have an email message for you."

SEVENTEEN

THE INTERNET ATTENDANT had caught me while she herself was in the process of unlocking the door to the computer room, opening up for the day. She flicked on the overhead lights and slipped around the room, hitting buttons. As computers booted, one by one, they sounded like an orchestra tuning up. "It came in last night, but it was too late to call you." A minute later, she brought up my message on one of the screens and pointed to the line below the subject with a crimson-nailed finger. "There's an attachment. If you need to print it out, let me know. There's a one-euro charge for printing."

"A euro per page?" I asked and got an indifferent nod in answer. That was highway robbery, but on a ship like this, they didn't deal in loose change. Almost everything was covered in the price of the cruise, but anything that wasn't, I had observed, was priced at a round number.

The mail was from my son Charlie, responding to the message I'd sent him yesterday morning. He certainly hadn't worked very long at the task I'd given him. I clicked on the appropriate inbox line, expecting nothing much.

Dear Mom,
What kind of unsavory people are you hanging around with? A pervert and a pole dancer? I may have to fly to Greece and drag you home by your ears! George Gaskill, as you said, is a registered sex offender, who

lives at 8108 Lonesome Pine Rd. Elkhart, Indiana. He's married to Kathryn Peterson Gaskill of the same address. Employed by the Altoona, PA school system from 1989 through 2001. Principal of Mann High School from September 1998 to May 2001. They are members of Gethsemane United Methodist Church in Elkhart, and I managed to find their church pictures online. I've attached a photo of George and Kathryn, taken in February of this year. George is not involved in any community activities other than church, because I found nothing about him in the Elkhart local news. I got several articles from April 2001, describing the rather juicy trial in which Mr. and Mrs. Benson, parents of Brittany Benson, charged him with child abuse, rape, sexual abuse of a minor, etc. I've attached a photocopy of one article. Let me know if you want more.

Brittany Benson, her innocence perhaps compromised at this point, dropped out of college three weeks into her first semester, and went to work as a flight attendant for Delta Airlines. Quit two years later and moved to Miami where she worked as a dancer at the Sandy Jug (I checked their website, Mom, and I don't think it was ballet).

I couldn't find out anything about her high school record because those files are confidential, but her next move after the job in Miami is strange. She ups and moves to Lima, Peru. The next address I found for her was in an exclusive part of the city, where most of the residents are American expats and international jet-setters. The house at this address is currently on the market, for an asking price of $3 million, U.S.!

That's the latest thing I found on Brittany, but you say she's working on your cruise ship now? Okay, I'll believe you. Do they have a pole for her to use? Or do they fill the pool with Jell-O?
Love,
Charlie

I smiled at the screen. This was about as flippant as Charlie ever got, and I was happy to see this levity. Maybe it meant the atmosphere at his school wasn't as tense as it had been the last time I talked to him. Charlie had always taken things too seriously and since his dear wife was diagnosed as manic-depressive, his life had been nothing but stress at work, alternating with gray clouds at home. Maybe he was learning to laugh at the human comedy.

While the photo Charlie had attached was printing, I studied it on the screen. Kathryn Gaskill sat with her left shoulder toward the camera, her hands folded in her lap. George stood behind her with his hands on her shoulders. I'd only seen George once, that first night at dinner. Strange to think how my trip to Greece had been hijacked by a man with whom I'd shared only a few sentences of innocuous, pointless small-talk.

The photo brought him back to me. The slicked-back dark hair, the trim little goatee, the prominent front teeth. I recalled how he whistled his Ss. Was this the face of a child-molester? I tried to wipe my mind free of what I now knew and look at him with objective eyes. What I saw was a beaten man. Shoulders drooping, eyes without luster, a man upon whom life had dumped more than he could bear.

I wondered how Kathryn had reacted to his conviction. Had she recoiled, avoiding his touch? Hated him secretly while sympathizing with him openly? Did she blame him for their plummeting social position? From professional, upper-middle class, probably with a home in a nice part of town, to used-car salesman and wife living in a town where nobody knew them?

My photo lay on the floor in front of the attendant's desk, having been spit out with great vigor by a printer that had apparently had a good night's rest. I walked over, picked it up, and signed the billing sheet with my cabin number and number of pages I'd printed. On regular cheap copy paper, the picture wasn't as clear as it had been on the computer screen.

"Mrs. Lamb?" Luc Girard walked through the door. "Good. I've been looking for you since yesterday. May I speak to you for a minute?"

I wanted to chase Marco down, but "speak to you for a minute" sounded like such a reasonable request, I said okay.

He took my elbow and led me out into the hall. "Have you seen this?" he asked, stopping in front of a display case that held a lovely gold bracelet. "No known provenance. As far as I can tell, this has never been photographed, catalogued, or described anywhere, by anyone."

"Thessaly?" I bent down and read the brass plaque inside the case with the bracelet.

Girard stepped back from the display case and looked at me over the top of his black-rimmed glasses. "Thessaly's a big place. Where in Thessaly? When was it found? By whom?"

"Why haven't I noticed this before?" I wondered aloud. "It's right outside the dining room."

"But it's between the door to the dining room and the men's room. You probably don't go to the men's room often." Girard turned toward the open double doors to the dining room. "Could we have a cup of coffee and talk for a few minutes?"

"Well," I said, hesitating. Most of all I wanted to catch up with Marco, but if that couldn't be done, I hated to pass up this chance to pick Luc Girard's brain. "Could you wait here a second? I have to check on something. Won't be a minute."

"I'll be in the dining room. I'll order coffee for you."

The main desk around which the offices, including security and purser's offices, were arrayed was on the same deck so all I had to do was run down a hall past the casino and into the vast open space, roughly circular and three stories tall, designed to afford guests every opportunity to spend yet more money on land excursions, jewelry, sweaters, and photos of themselves. Photos now being taken by Nikos Papadakos's replacement.

Marco was nowhere in sight. I asked about him at the main desk, but the attendant on duty didn't know who Marco was. I talked the man into ringing the security office for me. He shook his head after a minute. "No answer," he said.

I walked around to the security office door and knocked. No answer.

Girard had taken a table near the entrance to the dining room. Two cups of coffee had already been served. As I took my seat, he pushed his chair back from the table, crossed his legs outside the linen cloth and threw one arm across the back of his chair. "Sophie and I have checked every display on the ship and we've found four items stolen from museums, ten with no known provenance, and five that were legally purchased through a dealer or an auction house."

"So they weren't all obtained the same way," I said. "Interesting."

This was the first time I had noticed how truly sexy Luc Girard was. Way too young for me, more's the pity, but a serious threat to a younger woman's heart. His mouth was almost feminine but strengthened somewhat by a roughly shaven jaw line and a sparse goatee that divided itself into three isolated parts: mustache, small tuft under the lower lip, and a few chin whiskers. Behind his black-rimmed glasses, his dark eyes smoldered with what was—to be totally honest with myself—no expression at all. Any message a woman got from those eyes was one she read into them herself. I checked his left hand. On his ring finger was a hefty gold job with an inlaid onyx. It could have been a college ring.

"This cruise line is owned by a Geneva-based company called Helvetia Shipping, but the directors of the consortium are actually Italian, for the most part, with some Americans, Greeks, and others thrown in for good measure. You dig?"

"So who acquired the things we see in the display cases?"

"That's not going to be easy to find out. But Sophie and I are working on it from several angles." Girard uncrossed his legs and leaned forward, his hands around his coffee cup. He looked straight at me, then quickly down at his cup. "Sophie, by the way, is a very…astute woman. She is incredibly bright, you dig? I thank you for introducing her to me."

Oh, please. He couldn't fool me with that "astute" business. The man was falling in love. I shook my brain back to the subject we were allegedly talking about. "Wouldn't it be a matter of finding out who's in charge of purchasing?"

"The ship was overhauled and renovated three years ago. I've talked to the purser about who did the buying at that time and where they bought from. I've talked to Chief Letsos. Have you met him? He's no help at all."

"He's not the most amiable man I've ever met."

"Letsos keeps reminding me, subtly, that he and I are

both employed by the company I'm suggesting we investigate. If we value our jobs, you dig, we shouldn't rock the boat…no pun intended."

French accent notwithstanding, Luc Girard had firm command of English idiom.

"I don't care about that myself," he said without a hint of bravado in his tone, "but I wouldn't want to ask Sophie to risk getting fired. She needs her job more than I need mine."

"How can I help?"

Girard turned his face toward the windows and, without looking at me, said, "Did you visit Sophie and Brittany's room yesterday?"

This caught me off-guard. I took a long sip of coffee to give myself time to think. "Yes. I assume Sophie told you. There's no other way you could know."

"It doesn't matter. What did you find?"

When I didn't answer immediately, he reached across the table and clasped my hand. "We are speaking in total confidence here. I promise you I won't even tell Sophie anything you tell me, but if I'm to make any progress, I need to know."

"Of course." I had the uneasy feeling this whole thing might get out of hand, but Girard was right. I had opened this up, myself. Gone to him with what I'd discovered, and I couldn't hold out on him now. I squared my shoulders and told him about the krater and the carved stone box. On a scrap of paper, I drew the pattern I had seen on the box, as nearly as I could remember it. "I looked for paperwork. Anything that would tell me where she'd got these things and whether she'd paid for them. I found nothing."

"Was there anything else inside the boxes? Anything written on the outside of the boxes?"

"No." I slipped my napkin onto the table. "And if you'll excuse me…"

"Thank you, Mrs. Lamb. And if you see Captain Quattrocchi before I do, ask him to come see me, will you?"

If I see Captain Quattrocchi before you do, I thought, I've got some other things to ask him first.

I WENT TO THE disembarkation point fifteen minutes early, hoping to be the first off the ship so I could catch Marco before he got away. The ship docked beside a concrete bulkhead in the Rhodes harbor, close to the city wall. Entrance into old Rhodes town is restricted to eleven widely spaced gates in the medieval wall, and from the window in my room it looked as if there was only one gate close by. It stood to reason that if I went ashore quickly and stood by the gate, Marco would have to walk past me. But if he was heading for the airport, he'd probably catch a taxi and I could see several cars that might or might not be taxis parked along the outside of the wall.

At the bottom of the gangway, a new photographer was set up to snap everyone as they set foot on Rhodes, the island of roses. *How easily we can be replaced,* I thought as I walked past him, shaking my head. I was in no mood to have my picture taken. *If I died today,* I continued thinking in that maudlin vein, *how long would it take my college to replace me?* No time at all. They'd just open their bulging applications files and call a few numbers.

Passengers from the ship were directed down a rather narrow concrete strip between the city wall and the harbor in order to reach the aptly-named Marine Gate, the entrance to the old town. I stepped aside, out of the continuous stream of foot traffic, when I found a grassy spot some twenty yards from the gate. Turning, I scanned the heads and faces behind me for Marco. I wished he were in the habit of wearing distinctive headgear or something that would help me pick him out of the crowd, because his dark hair and medium build made him extremely average from a distance. Instead, I spotted Lettie, sans Ollie.

She joined me on the grassy strip. "Ollie had to run back to the room for his sunglasses," she said. "This looks like a good place to wait for him."

"I'm hoping to catch Marco before he leaves the island."

"Oh, right. He told us at breakfast, didn't he? He's flying back to Italy? What's going on with you two?"

"He says it's about George Gaskill's murder, but I'm afraid it's really because he's fed up with me. I didn't mean to ignore him last night, but Malcolm Stone and Nigel Endicott kept asking me to dance, cutting in and all, and I'm afraid I…"

"What else did you do?" Lettie glanced up at me, frowning.

"He asked me what was wrong, and I told him not to psychoanalyze me."

"You done screwed up again, Dotsy. I told Ollie yesterday, I said, 'Marco's too good for Dotsy, but she'll find a way to screw it up. Never fear.'"

Brittany Benson approached us and, not far behind her, Malcolm Stone and Willem Leclercq. She waved in our direction, slipped on her sunglasses, and would, I'm sure, have walked past us without speaking if Lettie hadn't pulled her aside.

"Are you all right, Brittany?" Lettie asked. "After you left our room last night, Ollie told me he knew exactly how you felt. It's such torture to be accused of something you didn't do."

Brittany shot daggers at me through her sunglasses. I held my breath, my mind racing, deciding what I would say if she confronted me with my invasion of her room.

Instead, she said, "Right. And I know how your husband feels, too. This cruise can't be over soon enough for me."

"Brittany!" The call came from Willem Leclercq, who nodded goodbye to his companion and headed toward us. "Join me for a drink, Brittany? I heard there's a nice little taverna inside the gate." Brittany looked as if she'd rather not, but she let him take her arm and lead her away.

"I saw them together last night at a table near Marco and me. I wonder if that was before or after she came to your room."

"If you and Marco were still together, it must have been before."

"Oh, dear, there's Malcolm Stone," I said. "If Marco walks by now and sees me talking to him, that'll really do it." I turned and examined the scruffy bit of a tree behind me, reminding myself Marco insisted he wasn't mad at me, but was flying home to confer with his forensic people.

"He's walking on by, Dotsy. You can turn around now. Gee, he looks like a lonely soul, don't you think so?" Lettie and I watched Malcolm stop and wait his turn to pass through the Marine Gate. With Leclercq hitting on Brittany over a cappuccino, Malcolm would probably have to see Rhodes alone.

"Lonely? Yes, probably. His wife died a few years ago, he told me. But there's something else going on with him. I can't put my finger on it."

"Maybe it's the George Gaskill thing. He's been questioned, too."

"He's always looking around. As if he's expecting someone. I noticed it yesterday, too, when we were in Patmos."

Luc Girard rushed up, greeting me as he came. I introduced him to Lettie. "What good luck to find you here," he said. "Are you, by any chance, planning to visit the Palace of the Grand Masters today?"

Until an hour ago I had planned to tour the Palace with Marco but, since then, I hadn't thought about anything except finding Marco before he left. I stood, stupidly forgetting to answer Girard's question, until Lettie nudged me. "Yes, of course," I said. "And the Street of the Knights. They're close together, aren't they?"

"They're adjacent to each other. When you go through the gate here, turn right and right again. That'll be the Street of the Knights, and at the end, you'll see the Palace. How about meeting me there? There's someone I want you to meet."

We agreed to rendezvous in the central courtyard inside the Palace, and Girard left, joining the throng at the gate.

"Why does that man always carry a backpack?" Lettie said. I saw she was looking at Nigel Endicott, hip Nigel, trekking up the walk. Today, his hair was gelled up like a bird's nest, his T-shirt's advertisement for some brand of surfboard peeked out between the padded straps of his backpack.

"There's another man with something on his mind. When I danced with him last night, I got the feeling of… oh, I don't know…fear. The man is frightened of something, Lettie."

Nigel nodded to me as he approached us. I introduced him to Lettie, who, with her customary reticence, said, "Why do you always carry that backpack, Mr. Endicott?"

He blinked and took a small step back. "I don't always carry it, but, since you ask, I'm on my way to the hammam, and one has to bring one's own towel and toiletries."

"Hammam. You mean a harem?" Lettie's eyes widened. "Where they have girls?"

I laughed and Nigel explained, "A hammam is a Turkish bath. There's a famous one that's been here since the seventeen-hundreds. So that's why I'm carrying my back-pack. Would you like to see?"

"No, it's okay. Have a nice…bath, Mr. Endicott."

After Nigel had walked on, I caught Lettie staring toward the pier. She touched my arm. "Agent Bondurant is following Nigel Endicott," she said, her voice low. "He was right behind him until Nigel came over here and talked to us, then Bondurant stopped and pretended to be inter-ested in a piling. When Nigel left, he followed."

That would explain why Nigel acted frightened, but why was Bondurant interested in him? Was he another suspect in the murder of George Gaskill or could it be something else entirely? The whole situation was beginning to make me dizzy.

The ship had nearly emptied by this time, a few strag-glers still ambling down the gangway. It looked as if Marco had given me the slip. Did he do it on purpose? Had he been picked up by a boat or something on the other side? Perhaps I'd missed him while I'd been talking.

"There's Ollie," Lettie said, jumping and waving at the bald head sticking out above the crowd. She and Ollie left me to explore Rhodes on my own.

EIGHTEEN

I WANDERED THROUGH shops along Socrates Street and noticed that nearby streets were named for other ancient Greek scholars like Pythagoras and Aristotle. Although inhabited since before Christ, the medieval period gave the city its character because Rhodes served as a base for the Knights of St. John during the Crusades. All over the town, jewelry, clothing, and souvenir shops, tucked into narrow, arched, cobblestone streets, competed with mosques and fourteenth-century towers for the visitors' attention.

It was while I was thumbing through a stack of scarves in an alley off Socrates Street that I caught a whiff of something unpleasant. I moved around the rickety table on which the scarves were displayed and the smell got stronger. Like old cheese. No, not exactly. More like stinky feet. No, that wasn't quite it either.

Glancing around and making a couple of moves to narrow down the source, I discovered it to be a man at the other end of the scarf table. He was studying the post-cards on a four-sided rack. Dirty hair with traces of the last fingers raked through it, baggy woolen trousers, and an old tweed jacket that might have originally been more colors than brown. I couldn't see his face and didn't really want to. Goats! That's what he smelled like. I hate goat cheese because, to me, it smells like the goats my grandfather used to have. *This man must have goats living in his closet,* I thought.

I left the shop without buying and turned down Socrates

Street toward the Mosque of Suleiman the Magnificent. I had hoped to see the inside, but found it closed to the public, and a good thing, because it was crumbling so badly it probably wasn't safe. More than content to study it from the outside, I stepped to the opposite side of the street and stood.

Malcolm Stone breezed by right in front of me. I called his name, loudly. He must have heard me, but he kept walking. In fact he quickened his pace, almost running, into the intersection in front of the mosque. His left hip grazed the fender of a little delivery truck as he ducked out of my sight. The truck driver tooted, swore, and eventually drove on, but by that time Malcolm was nowhere to be seen.

My watch said it was almost time to meet Dr. Girard, and the Palace was nearby, so I located the main entrance, bought a ticket, and climbed a couple of flights of stairs into a medieval exhibition room. I needed to find the Central Courtyard.

The Palace, a labyrinth of square rooms with mosaic tile floors and tiny doors leading off in various directions, gave me vertigo. After trying several doors that led nowhere, or back where I'd come from, I asked a guard whose explanation for how to find the courtyard was completely unintelligible, but did involve some pointing, which helped.

The courtyard was huge and empty and open to the sky. On the opposite side near an exterior staircase, Luc Girard stood, talking to a woman. I recognized Girard's dark khaki bush jacket and shorts. They both watched me as I trekked across the marble tiles and joined them. Girard introduced me to the small, dark woman, curator of the museum under the stairs. She led us through a dozen rooms devoted to the ancient city of Rhodes, dating from the fifth century B.C. We saw a scale model of the city as it would have appeared back then, and the tiny hooks-and-eyes they used to fasten their clothing.

The curator gave me some literature and photos I knew I could make use of in my classes back home. She took us into a little back room and dug through a pile of books and periodicals, leaving Girard and me with nothing to do but watch.

"She's looking for some publications on the theft of antiquities in this part of the Mediterranean—the Dodecanese and Turkey. I told her about our little problem on the ship."

Without turning from her search, she said, "We have been fortunate at this museum, probably because of our location inside the fort, but the Archaeological Museum down the street has lost quite a number of items to thieves. Gold, mostly. Small and easy to get away with, you know." She yanked a dusty soft-cover book out of the stack and handed it to Luc Girard, then pulled out several more publications and gave them to me. They were in Greek.

Girard flipped through the book she'd handed him. "May we take these on loan for a few weeks? They'll be safe in our ship's library and I can bring them back the next time we dock here."

The curator nodded assent and told me, "You may keep the things I gave you. I have copies."

I thanked her and bade goodbye to Girard, who was leaving the Palace immediately. I intended to get my money's worth from my ticket and there were many rooms I hadn't yet seen. The fortress consisted of two, in places three, floors of chambers in a square around the Central Courtyard. Some of these chambers held furnishings like statues and thrones, some were empty, and most had tile mosaics from the island of Kos imbedded in the floor.

I had ambled through perhaps twenty rooms, some of

them twice, when I realized I was lost. I'd met only a few other visitors on my ramblings and in this part of the Palace I seemed to be alone in a section of the second floor that consisted of six rooms with doors that led from one to the other but nowhere else. None led out. I made the circuit three times before I stopped, my heart pounding, and gathered my thoughts. Find a window, I told myself. If you can see outside, you can get your bearings. Walking clockwise through three rooms, none of which had a window, I stepped through a fourth door and stopped dead in my tracks.

In the next room, Brittany Benson stood near the window I'd been hoping to find and she was talking to a man in a tweed jacket. "Hi there," I said, but they both slipped through another door as I said it, leaving me to wonder if they'd heard me, if I should follow them, or what. I stepped to the window where they'd stood a moment earlier, and caught a pungent whiff of—goats. Brittany's companion had left an aroma in his wake that was thick enough to put out a fire. I was sure it was the same man I'd seen at the scarf shop and he was following me. Recalling Brittany's cell phone conversation I'd overheard last night on the promenade deck, I wondered if this man had been given my description and told to follow me. Why? What did he plan to do to me?

The window looked out onto the Central Courtyard, and, although the thickness of the wall kept me from seeing more than a thin vertical strip of it, it seemed the door on my left could start me on a clockwise path to the exit. It looked as if I had one more wing to go before I reached the big twin towers that flanked the ticket office. If I stuck doggedly to a clockwise path, I reasoned, sooner or later I'd find a way out.

Before opening the door, I steeled myself for another encounter with Brittany and friend, but there was no one in the next room. As I closed the door, I thought I heard voices behind me, perhaps someone entering the room I'd left. I kept walking. Straight, then right, then straight again, through four more rooms, all of which had windows telling me I was on the right track.

Then I came upon one of the strangest puzzles I'd ever encountered. The next room was long and rectangular and on the far end stood a large sign with an arrow. EXIT. I'd have kissed the sign, but I couldn't reach it because the floor between the sign and me was covered, patchwork style, with wonderful late Hellenistic mosaics, perhaps thirty of them. They were separated from each other by borders consisting of a single row of plain tiles. I read the sign, printed in three languages, at the entrance to the room. DO NOT STEP ON THE MOSAICS.

I certainly didn't want to step on the mosaics, committed as I am to preserving antiquities, but how could I get from here to the other side without doing so? Only one way I could think of. I slipped my purse over my head so it hung diagonally across my chest and spread my arms wide, like a tight-rope walker.

Putting one foot carefully in front of the other, I picked my way between the nearest two mosaics, turned sharply at the corner of the one on my right, and minced along another border. Occasionally, I stopped and planned the next few legs of my journey, careful to stay away from the walls because there'd not be enough room to keep my balance. It took me a few minutes, but I did it.

I reached the EXIT sign, resisted the urge to kiss it, and wished a security camera had been watching me. I'd love to know if I'd met their expectations. Glancing over my shoulder, I saw Brittany Benson and the goat man, arms extended, teetering along the same path I'd taken and a good three minutes behind me. I had plenty of time to make my getaway.

NINETEEN

BACK ON THE SHIP, I headed for the middle of the Hera deck for a mid-afternoon snack. I hadn't eaten lunch and, being diabetic, I have to guard against hypoglycemia. Here, they served drinks and simple food like gyros, burgers, and pizza practically all the time. I grabbed a slice of pizza and a glass of mango juice and looked around for a table. A bingo game was in progress on the port side so I headed for the starboard.

Kathryn Gaskill, sitting at a table by herself, waved me over to join her. A cell phone and a cup of tea on the table in front of her, she marked her place in her notepad and closed it as I put my food down. "The purser very kindly gave me a cell phone to use so I can call anywhere in the world. It's set up for easy international dialing, and the bill, he told me, would be paid by the cruise line, no matter how much calling I do."

"Nice of them."

"Not really. A small price to pay for keeping me happy, and they're trying to accommodate me in any way they can so I won't sue them."

"Sue them?"

"I'm not planning to sue them, of course. What happened to George, as far as I know, was not due to any negligence on their part but if they failed to offer me anything I need I could make trouble for them later." Kathryn flipped through a couple of pages on her notepad.

I bit into my pizza. "What else have they offered you?"

"They offered to fly me home immediately, but I don't want to go. With the investigation going on here, why would I want to be anywhere else? We have no children to rush home to." She turned the notepad toward me. "I've called all these people today. George's sister and brother, my own family, our pastor, the car dealership where George worked—now, that ticked me off."

I raised an eyebrow and trapped a large gush of tomato sauce with my napkin.

"The owner of the dealership says he's halting all fringe benefits immediately. Is that legal? We have medical and dental insurance through them. What am I going to do about that? I can't afford an individual policy." Kathryn tapped the table with her forefinger. "And they'd better come through with the sick leave and vacation pay George had built up. They're supposed to be paying him right up through the surgery he had scheduled after this trip."

"I think you'd better talk to a lawyer as soon as you get home."

"I will. I may have to sell the house, Dotsy. I don't think I can afford it on what I make, but where can I find a place I can afford? Everything's so expensive these days."

"Didn't George have life insurance?"

"Yes, but what if they make me wait seven years before they pay out? That's what Mr. Bondurant told me. He said without a body, a person isn't declared dead until they've been missing for seven years."

"In a case like this, I think they could declare him dead immediately. I mean, look at the circumstances. In fact, I read about a case recently not all that different from this one. A woman—she was apparently three sheets to the wind—fell off a cruise boat and drowned. She was declared dead shortly thereafter even though they never recovered the body."

"Oh, I do hope that's the case." Kathryn nodded toward a table near the bingo game. "There are the Zieglers, the mother and daughter who were at our dinner table last night. Have you talked to them much?"

"No," I said, opting not to mention the older woman's obvious flirtation with Marco.

"The daughter, Heather. How does she strike you?"

"She strikes me as being firmly under her mother's thumb. Ernestine, the mother, told us Heather hadn't been allowed to go to a college away from home. I can't imagine any of my five children accepting that. They all went away to college when the time came, and if I'd told any of them they couldn't, they'd've gone bananas. I mean, if Chet and I had said we couldn't afford to send them away it would've been one thing, but if we'd said you simply can't go, can't leave home because we won't let you, any of the five, I'm sure, would have left anyway, even if they had to pay their own way."

"But Heather stayed home and she still lives at home. Heather wears no makeup and her mother wears tons of makeup." Kathryn took a sip of her tea. "And she steals."

"Steals? Ernestine?"

"No, Heather. Did you notice the silverware on their side of the table last night? The waiter did. He didn't say anything but he looked all around, under the table, and everywhere for the silver that was mysteriously missing. I saw Heather slip a fork into her handbag under the table."

I glanced toward the table where Ernestine and Heather sat, Ernestine scanning the room while Heather stared blankly at her own glass. "Repressed, I'd say. Heather may be asserting herself in the only way she's allowed to do. Surreptitiously."

"Excuse me. Mrs. Gaskill?"

"Oh, Mr. Bondurant, isn't it?"

I turned and found the handsome FBI Agent Bondurant standing behind me. He nodded to me and, to Kathryn, said, "I wonder if you'd mind coming with me to the security office."

Kathryn seemed to freeze. She looked at me, then back at Bondurant. "Sure. You mean now?"

"Yes, now." He looked at me again. "You're Mrs. Lamb, aren't you? You were with us the other morning when we…"

"That's right. Captain Quattrocchi asked me to be there when you, after you found the note."

"Perhaps you'd better come with us again."

Kathryn slid her chair back with a skittering screech against the deck and wobbled as she stood up, but she said nothing. Bondurant escorted us to an elevator and pushed the button for the Dionysus deck. He made no eye contact with either of us, holding the door open for us to exit, pointing toward the security office as the elevator door closed behind us. As she stepped onto the carpet, Kathryn stumbled slightly and looked at me—a helpless, vulnerable look.

I put my arm around Kathryn. Her bra, I noticed, was cutting into her fleshy back, creating sizeable rolling hills at the top and the bottom of the elastic back.

"I'm afraid they've found something I don't want to see!" she whispered to me as Bondurant ushered us into the security office. Chief Letsos was inside, sitting behind the room's only desk. Kathryn and I took chairs on the other side.

"I suppose we'll need to take it out of the bag," said Bondurant.

"She'll need gloves." Letsos reached for a box of latex gloves on the floor behind him and handed two of them to Kathryn. He looked toward Bondurant as he jerked his head slightly in my direction.

"She won't need them," the FBI agent said. To me, he said, "You won't need to handle this so you don't need gloves. You're here for moral support."

The suspense was killing me. Kathryn pulled on the stretchy gloves with difficulty, first getting the thumb of one on the wrong side. Letsos got up and walked to his filing cabinet, pulled out a plastic bag, cut it open, and laid a gold watch on the desk in front of Kathryn.

"It's George's watch," she whispered. "Look." She picked up the watch and turned it over. "Look at the inscription on the back. 'To Mr. Gaskill, our mentor and friend. From the Junior Class of '95.'" She turned to me, her eyes glistening with tears. "George was Junior Class sponsor that year. The class officers thought enough of him to hold a car wash and a bake sale, plus they all kicked in their own money, to buy him this watch." She turned it face up and touched the crystal with her gloved thumb. "I was there the night they presented it to him. They even wrote a song about him, 'We Love You, Gaskill,' it was. A lot like the song from *Bye, Bye, Birdie,* the musical." She glanced at Bondurant and added, "You're too young to remember."

"I remember," I said.

"Where did you find this?" Kathryn asked.

"In the room of a member of our staff," Letsos said. "Someone I believe you already know, Brittany Benson. The room is also shared by another one of our dancers named Sophie Antonakos, but the watch was found on the floor of Miss Benson's closet."

I heard nothing more after that. In my mind, I saw the floor of Brittany Benson's closet and the two cardboard cartons. The cartons, I knew, contained valuable artifacts—or fakes—but I couldn't say anything without confessing to snooping through her things. That would implicate Sophie, my enabler, and open up the whole issue of the stolen antiquities. Bondurant and Letsos already knew about it, because Luc Girard told them. They may also have known that Girard and Sophie were researching the display items on the ship, trying to find out where they came from. But Kathryn knew nothing about it, so I decided I'd better keep my mouth shut. I was, quite frankly, relieved to be able to justify, to myself, saying nothing. I needed to think this through before I went any further.

Kathryn slid the watch across the desk toward Letsos. "I guess that tells us who killed George. But why did she keep the watch? That was stupid."

"Perpetrators often like to take a souvenir," Letsos said, with an air of authority.

FBI Agent David Bondurant flashed him a look that said, *Shut up, you fool.*

I WALKED KATHRYN BACK to her room and asked her if she wanted me to come in, but she said she needed some time alone. That made sense to me, so I trekked down to Marco's room and pecked on the door on the off-chance he might be there and his leaving merely a bad dream. Then I stopped by my own room, freshened up, and decided to call on Lettie and Ollie.

As I turned the corner leading to their hall, I caught the backside of Brittany Benson rounding the next corner down. I recognized the yellow jumpsuit I'd played "Spy vs Spy" with in the Palace of the Grand Masters. Lettie opened her door within a few seconds of my knock.

"You just missed Brittany Benson. She's getting to be a regular in our room."

"Why did she stop by again?"

"Well, more of that compadre stuff, you know. She says she and Ollie have to stick together because they're both being accused of a murder they had nothing to do with."

Ollie, lying on top of the bedspread, was reading a very large book, titled *Fishes of the Mediterranean Sea*. "Hi, Dotsy. Marco's cut out on us, huh?" He rolled his oversized frame into a half-upright position, resting on one elbow.

I didn't feel like answering him.

Lettie said, "Brittany told us why Bondurant was following Nigel Endicott this morning. Do you remember?"

"Yes. Nigel told us he was going to the Turkish bath, and you noticed Bondurant waited for him and then followed when he left. Why?"

"Because!" Lettie put the back of one hand up to her mouth as if she was whispering a secret, but continued on in a loud voice. "They think Endicott killed Mr. Papadakos! They showed a bunch of pictures to this man who owns the shop in Mykonos where they think the murder weapon, the knife, was bought. The man said he can't be sure but, of all the photos, Nigel Endicott's looks the most like the man he thinks bought the knife."

"They're looking for the shirt," Ollie butted in.

"Right. The shirt. The shop owner remembers a brightly colored shirt, and Bondurant wants to have a good look at the one Endicott wore when he got off the ship in Mykonos. I told Ollie about the backpack Endicott told us was for the towel and stuff he was taking to the harem."

"Hammam." I corrected her.

"Whatever. I wonder if it really was towels or if he was sneaking off the ship with the…" Lettie waved her fingers in front of my face in what I think was supposed to be a scary manner. "Bloood-staaained shirt!"

"That sounds like a bit of a stretch to me."

"But possible."

"Possible. But the thing I came by to tell you is, they've found George Gaskill's watch on the bottom of Brittany Benson's closet." I waited for that to sink in. "Kathryn and I were taken to the security office a few minutes ago and she positively identified the watch as George's. There's a personal inscription on the back."

Ollie sat up with a jerk and planted both feet on the floor.

Lettie stood there, mouth open. Ollie said, "Oh, my God. The little fox!"

"She has the best motive of all," Lettie said. "Revenge."

"They've already questioned Brittany. She told them she was with her roommate, Sophie, from the time she finished her last performance until the next morning, and Sophie backed her up." I realized I was sorting out my own thoughts as I was talking. "I told Bondurant I'd seen both of them on the deck at 3:00 a.m., soon after George was killed."

"So Brittany and Sophie are in it together?" Lettie sat beside Ollie on the edge of the bed and stretched an arm around his shoulders. "That makes sense. Two young women could do it more easily than one. One could have distracted him, lured him out to that little deck. And the other could have slipped up behind him with a knife."

"They could've been pretty sure the stern deck would be deserted at that time in the morning," Ollie added.

Lettie frowned. "But would the time work out? You left George a bit after midnight. He was on his way back to his room then, and the murder didn't take place until…"

"That's just it," I said. "We don't know when it took place. We only know it was after midnight and before four."

"Right. And I don't know whether he was on his way back to his own room or not," Ollie said, folding Lettie's free hand in his. "I assumed he was. He could have been heading for a secret meeting with Brittany."

"Or Sophie."

I threw both hands up. "Wait a minute. Now we're going too far. I don't know Sophie Antonakos very well, I admit, but she strikes me as an honest girl. She has an innocence about her."

Ollie exhaled loudly. "Innocence can be faked. There's innocence and then there's good acting."

I didn't feel like going any further with this conversation. I'd let Ollie and Lettie hash it over between themselves and I'd think it over alone.

TWENTY

I SHOWERED AND CHANGED for dinner, without much thought for what I'd wear because it didn't matter how I looked anymore. Glancing over the evening's offerings in the "Oracle" bulletin, I found nothing of interest. Maybe I'd go to the library after dinner and read. I hoped Dr. Girard had put the material the museum curator had given him today on the library's shelves and I wondered what language it was in.

I put on my makeup robotically, but stopped when my blusher brush scratched my cheek. I examined the brush and found the culprit was a clear, slightly concave, disc. Less than half an inch in diameter. It wasn't particularly brittle because it yielded a bit when I squeezed it. Could it be a contact lens? If so, what was it doing here, in my blusher brush? Only one way to find out, I thought. I filled a glass of water from the bathroom sink and dropped the disc in. I stuck it up high, on top of my TV, so I wouldn't forget and drink it. Then I remembered I'd plucked the little disc off the sink that morning after we found the pool of blood. It was in the bathroom at the end of the hall, near the door to the stern deck.

Before dinner I took a stroll around the promenade deck. I stopped in at the library but no one was there. The sandbox Dr. Girard used for supporting pottery shards while the glue dried was still under the gooseneck lamp. Sophie's notebook and a couple of catalogs were stacked neatly on a table, pens laid alongside. I wondered if and when this room was ever locked. It seemed to me they trusted passengers a lot, but then it would hardly be worth it to steal big, heavy things like books and sneak them off the ship in your luggage. Anyone with a mind to steal something could find richer pickings elsewhere. Such as in the dining halls. I remembered what Kathryn had told me about Heather Ziegler. Was Heather really swiping the silver?

I walked around the bow of the ship and down the port side. Most of the round porthole windows on this side had curtains drawn, I assumed, because the late afternoon sun was pouring in. Some of the portholes were open, the breeze rippling the curtains inward. My own window, I had discovered, didn't open, obviously because my room was on a lower deck and positioned so that, in rough seas, waves could splash in.

I wondered which of these was Lettie and Ollie's window. *Theirs would be about halfway down,* I thought. Not meaning to spy on anyone, because most of the curtains were drawn anyway, I happened to look through a porthole whose curtain was not drawn and saw Kathryn Gaskill. She stood, facing the window but apparently she didn't see me. I stopped, turned toward the railing, and a few seconds later, glanced over my shoulder at the window again. The sun bouncing off the water had contracted my pupils so that I now saw nothing through the window, but it must have been slightly open because I heard Kathryn's voice.

"It had to be done," I heard her say.

I stepped aside, out of the line of sight through the window, and closed my eyes to give my pupils time to dilate. It occurred to me Kathryn hadn't seen or at least hadn't recognized me because the setting sun was in her eyes. Then, as casually as I could, I ambled back past the porthole window, turned, and looked inside.

I saw Kathryn in profile. Her head was down, resting on the chest of the man who held her in his arms. The man holding her was Nigel Endicott.

I WAS THE LAST to arrive at our dinner table. Lettie, Ollie, and Kathryn were already there, as were Ernestine and Heather Ziegler. I'd intended to tell Lettie and Ollie not to mention anything about George's watch before they talked to Kathryn because I wasn't sure we were supposed to be blabbing that around. While I studied the menu and placed my order, I stayed mum, hoping the conversation around me would tell me who'd already said what. Had Kathryn told them George's watch had been found? Had Lettie mentioned Agent Bondurant following Nigel Endicott? Had either she or Ollie mentioned Brittany Benson's visits to their room?

"Where is our friend, Captain Quattrocchi?" Ernestine asked me. She virtually salivated when she said the name.

"He was called back to Florence," I said, handing my menu to the waiter. "About some case he's working on."

"Oh, dear me. Is he coming back?"

"I don't know."

"I'll bet he's tracking down an international jewel thief!" Ernestine bent forward until her left breast swiped the butter off her roll. Lettie pointed at the problem and Ernestine applied her napkin to the greasy blob. "Or maybe he's cracking a spy ring! What do you think?"

"I really couldn't say."

It was as if we'd all been warned to shut up. Throughout the meal, we talked about families back home, our impressions of Rhodes, other trips we'd taken, but nothing related in any way to the murders, until the dessert plates were cleared and coffee was served. Then Kathryn said, "They found my husband's watch today. It was in the closet of that bitch, Brittany Benson."

"Who?" asked Ernestine.

"One of the dancers on this ship who also just happens to be the girl who got my husband fired from his job ten years ago!"

Heather Ziegler's eyes widened. It was the first expression I'd seen on her face. She'd sat, more or less silent throughout the meal, glancing frequently at the rest of us as if she assessed our alertness and her own chances of successfully filching the salt shaker. What I saw in her countenance now was glee. Excitement. An awakening.

Ollie rose. "Careful now, Kathryn. I know how Brittany feels, being accused of murder. I'm in the same boat she is." Ollie, I felt, could afford to be magnanimous now that the fire wasn't so hot under his own feet.

Kathryn spluttered and mumbled something I didn't catch.

Heather said, "Exactly when was your husband killed, Mrs. Gaskill? I understand they found a pool of blood on the deck at about three in the morning and it was still liquid."

We all stared, open-mouthed. For a girl who had been as silent as a Carmelite nun until now, this was quite a debut. Kathryn looked at me, her eyes saying, You take it from here.

"It was Kathryn and I who found the pool of blood, in fact. It was sometime after three in the morning, and yes—I suppose it's all right to say it—the blood was still liquid."

"So it must have happened between two-thirty and three," Heather continued, her words now tumbling over each other. "Exposed to the air, the blood wouldn't have remained liquid for more than a few minutes. I know. I'm a nurse. Blood clots really fast in the presence of oxygen. Otherwise, we'd all bleed to death every time we cut ourselves!"

Kathryn, her mouth tightly shut as if she was about to vomit, got up and, without a word, left the table. I ran after her, dodging around tables and waiters carrying loaded trays, across the dining hall and out through the double doors at the entrance. There I stopped and looked around, but Kathryn had already given me the slip. Perhaps not, I thought. The last time she did this, I'd found her in the bathroom down the hall on the left. She could have gone there again.

I didn't get the chance to find out, however, because at that moment a hand grabbed me firmly by my elbow and dragged me down the hall to the right. Dragged me toward the display case. It was Sophie Antonakos.

"Dotsy, look! Look at the bracelet. You've seen it before, I hope."

It took me a second to get my bearings. Then I remembered. "Yes. Dr. Girard showed it to me this morning. We talked about how it has no known provenance and, as far as he knows, it's never been photographed or described."

"Too late now," Sophie said. "This is not it. Someone has stolen the real bracelet, the one he showed you this morning, and replaced it with this fake!" Sophie's dark eyes flashed.

"Are you sure?"

"Of course, I'm sure. Look at the workmanship." The bracelet was a gold spiral that would have wound around the arm twice ending in a serpent's head on one end, its tail on the other. I couldn't tell about the workmanship because I'm no expert, but Sophie said, "This spiral is thicker, probably because it's not solid gold like the real one was. The scales on the snake's body are different and the carving isn't nearly as fine. Do you see the stones that are set into the curve of the tail?"

"Yes."

"They're green, aren't they?" Sophie backed up and let me get a closer look at the tail. "This morning, they were blue!"

"Uh-oh."

"This is probably a copy from a museum gift shop. Some of the copies are quite good, you know."

"But if the bracelet that was here this morning had never been photographed or described, how could it have been copied?"

"This particular bracelet, as far as we know, had never been described. This *type* of bracelet, with the coils and the snake head and tail, has been found perhaps a dozen times. I've seen some, very similar, in the big museum in Athens."

I looked at the display case on all sides. On one side, between the base and the Plexiglas top, I found a key hole. I ran my fingers around and over it. "I see no damage. It looks as if the thief had no trouble breaking in."

"Someone had a key," Sophie said.

"Someone also had a really good substitute handy. This makes no sense. Are we saying the thief is someone on the ship who travels with duplicates of the display case items?"

"I'll bet you could find something like this in one of the shops in Rhodes. There must be a hundred jewelry shops in Old Rhodes." She was right. I'd walked past more than a dozen myself today.

"Before we get too upset, Sophie, let's ask Luc Girard if this is his doing. I know he was concerned about it, and it's just possible he made the substitution himself. He may have tucked the real one away in the safe."

Sophie told me she had to dash off and teach a dance class to a group of passengers, explaining that the class wasn't supposed to run over into the time for the second dinner seating. I checked the bathroom (no Kathryn) and decided to give it up. Kathryn could mull over what Heather had said, alone. I took the stairs to the promenade deck and slipped out the starboard side doors. The sweet night air and the lights on the dark water lured me to the rail. Looking up, I found the Big Dipper and, following the pointer stars, the North Star. So we were headed west. Somewhere, over the horizon ahead, was Italy. And Marco. I wondered what he was doing tonight, and if there was any chance he'd come back. One side of my head said, *That's wishful thinking.* The other side said, *But that Italian temper of his is as volatile as water on a hot griddle. He can get mad in a flash, but he can also get over it in a flash. Maybe…*

I tugged at the library door and found it was now locked. Sophie was teaching a dance class and I had no idea where Luc Girard was, but the night was far too beautiful for me to go to my room, so I took the elevator to the top deck, the deck with the observation bar on the bow, the gymnasium in the middle, and the small open deck where I'd first seen Kathryn and Nigel Endicott together, on the stern.

A couple of deck tables were occupied. I found one for myself at the stern rail overlooking the pool three decks below, steeling myself to endure calls of "Marco" and "Polo" from the children I saw cavorting in the water. A waiter appeared out of nowhere and asked me if I wanted a drink.

"Ouzo, please. My room number is three sixty-five."

As the waiter walked away, I thought: *Who killed*

George Gaskill? At this point, the easy answer would be
Brittany Benson. She had motive and she had the victim's
watch, but did she have opportunity? I rejected Ollie's
suggestion that Brittany and Sophie might have done it
together. I couldn't believe Sophie would be involved in
anything so heinous, but Ollie did have a point. I didn't
know Sophie that well, and innocence could be faked. It's
hard to fool me, though. After raising five children, I'm
pretty damn near foolproof. I couldn't believe Sophie was
involved, but she may have gone too far when she gave
Brittany an alibi for the entire night. Her roommate could
have slipped out when Sophie was asleep and slipped back
without awakening her.

But how could Brittany have known where George
would be and when? If she had contacted him earlier, letting him know she was on board, would he have consented
to a wee-hours meeting? I doubted it. Suppose he'd contacted her? He might, after all, have found out she was
on the ship's staff, contacted her and...oh, golly! What
if George intended to kill Brittany? He could have ren-
dezvoused with her, or simply bumped into her that early
morning, tried to kill her, and Brittany, being younger and
more fit than George, could have turned the tables on him.
The idea had a certain appeal.

The waiter brought my ouzo and a glass of water. I
wished the deck lights were brighter because I love to see
ouzo turn blue when you add water to it. I poured about
an equal measure of water into the liquor.

Now, what about Malcolm Stone and Willem Leclercq?
Like Ollie, they could've been angry enough over their
poker losses to have followed George, accused him of
cheating, and then what? Killed him when he refused to
give them their money back? No. The amount they lost,
though hefty, didn't call for such drastic measures. More

likely, it would have had something to do with antiquities. Malcolm was an avid collector. He'd obviously been up to something today when I ran into him near the Mosque, and his interest in me might be sincere or it might be a way of finding out what Marco did or didn't know.

It looked as if Willem Leclercq and Brittany were getting together. Brittany, I knew, was up to her—well, at least her knees—in some sort of funny business with ancient artifacts and Willem was actively seeking the same. Whatever was going on, I knew it had something to do with antiquities. There were too many connections to believe otherwise.

I turned my thoughts to Nigel and Kathryn. What was going on between them? When did they really meet? I'd bet that morning on the deck wasn't their first meeting. The scene I'd witnessed earlier this evening wasn't between two people who'd simply shared a table for coffee. To what had Kathryn been referring when she said, "It had to be done"? Did she mean George had to be killed? I shivered at the thought.

Did she mean Nikos Papadakos had to be killed? Had Nigel, in fact, been Papadakos's killer and did Kathryn know all about it? The owner of the shop where the alleged murder weapon had been purchased picked Nigel out, from all the photos he was shown, but had admitted he couldn't be sure. Kathryn couldn't have witnessed the murder in Mykonos because she hadn't set foot off the ship that day.

The waiter dropped by my table and I ordered another ouzo.

I remembered what Marco had said about Papadakos. Everyone on the ship liked him, or so they said, but he was from Crete. Marco seemed to think that fact might be important because Crete was the source of much of the looted antiquities. We'd be docking in Crete tomorrow, near the town of Heraklion. The Palace of Knossos was one of the main reasons I'd wanted to go on this trip, but now I found myself wondering how far Papadakos's home might be from Heraklion. If it were possible, would it be instructive to drop by and visit? Forget it. I couldn't talk to them, anyway. I knew the country folk who lived outside the regular tourist spots rarely spoke anything other than Greek.

Nigel Endicott bothered me. He had a British accent but he was from Vermont. No, he'd told me he was retiring to Vermont, but had he told me where he was retiring from? Somehow, I had the impression he was leaving a big city. I needed to look into that. Did Nigel Endicott and Kathryn know each other before this trip? If they did, they'd both lied to me from the beginning.

What motive could Nigel have had for killing Papadakos? I'd originally thought the photographer had been killed because he saw something he wasn't supposed to see. His position at the foot of the gangway at both embarkations and disembarkations made that a likely possibility. But now, I wondered if he, too, mightn't have been tied up in smuggling.

The waiter walked by and I ordered another ouzo. My third.

Lettie had been sure Nigel's backpack held something like a bloody shirt, and he was sneaking it off the boat, but it seemed to me it would be simpler to toss it overboard when no one was looking. Why go to the trouble of smuggling it off the ship? I now thought it was more likely the backpack contained stolen artifacts. The bracelet? How would Nigel have managed to get a key to the display case?

If I was on the right track it would mean that, of the men at the poker table the first night, only Ollie Osgood was uninvolved in the antiquities market. Weird. But which of the others were smugglers and which were honest buyers?

My third ouzo having hit my brain, I finally ventured into the thought territory I'd been avoiding. I made myself consider the possibility it was Ollie. Ollie was the last person known to have seen George Gaskill alive. He had motive. Perhaps not a sufficient motive in terms of the amount of money he'd lost to George, but he would've also been angry if he thought George had cheated. Where was he at the time of the murder? We had only Lettie's statement that he was in bed with her, but a wife's testimony is virtually useless. And the murder could have occurred before he came to their room and went to bed, unless Heather Ziegler was right about the liquidity of the blood pointing to a much later time. Ollie was in the vicinity when Papadakos was killed, but he hardly looked like the man the shop owner thought bought the knife. And how did the Mykonos police know the knife they found was the knife that killed Papadakos? It was found, Marco said, in shallow water, so both blood and fingerprints would have been washed off.

"Another, Madam?"

"Huh?"

"May I bring you another ouzo?"

"No, but I may need help getting back to my room."

TWENTY-ONE

I WOKE UP WITH a thumping headache. My eyeballs shot
darts of pain through my head as they scraped against the
insides of my eyelids. I couldn't bear to think of sitting up,
so I lay in my bed, swearing never to touch ouzo again.

One of my first lucid thoughts, after finding a rela-
tively comfortable position for my head, was about the
main thing I'd intended to think about last night. That is,
I needed to talk to Agent Bondurant and tell him—what?
I had to decide. Should I confess I'd been snooping in Brittany Benson's room? That Sophie had helped me? That a
fake old bracelet now lay in the case where the real one
had been until yesterday?

If George Gaskill's watch had been on the floor of Brittany's closet at the time I'd pulled those boxes out, how
could I have failed to see it? I couldn't have, so it hadn't
been there. Bondurant needed to know that, so I'd have to
confess. Could I do it without getting Sophie in trouble?
I decided I'd say I sneaked Sophie's room key out of her
purse when she was absorbed in her work in the library
and sneaked it back in later without Sophie ever knowing.

If Bondurant had really been following Nigel Endicott
yesterday, should I tell him what I'd seen through the porthole window last evening? I'd be ratting on Kathryn, but
was that a problem? I had no moral obligation to support
Kathryn, and if what I saw cast doubts on her truthfulness,
so be it.

But if Bondurant confronted Kathryn and happened to mention me, I wouldn't get any more information out of her.

I turned my head and opened my eyes to a swirling mass of bright spots. I forgot what I was thinking about. I tried to recall, knowing it was something important, and then realized I'd better check my blood sugar.

Stumbling to my dressing table, I found my glucose meter, did the test, and found my sugar level was so low that by rights I should be comatose. No time to dress and go to breakfast, I grabbed one of the little cartons of orange juice I always have with me, jabbed the straw through the foil hole, and sucked in a mouthful. Somehow, I managed to sit down and lean against the table until the juice kicked in and the room stopped spinning.

I was in the shower when I remembered what I'd been thinking about that was so important. I needed to tell Bondurant about the theft of the bracelet from the display case outside the dining room. According to Marco, the United States FBI was, along with Scotland Yard and the Italian Carabinieri, on the front line in the war against the black market in antiquities. Luc Girard had talked to Bondurant and Chief Letsos already, but that didn't mean Bondurant was up to date on everything now.

My phone rang.

I wrapped a towel around me, dripped across the carpet, and picked up the receiver. It was Agent Bondurant. "Mrs. Lamb? I need for you to come to the security office."

"Now?" I looked at the clock. It was only 7:35.

"Yes, now." His tone scared me.

LETSOS AND BONDURANT WERE BOTH there when I walked into the security office. Bondurant showed me to a chair in front of the desk, directly opposite Security Chief Letsos who sat and stared, stone-faced, at me as I took my seat. The whole atmosphere was icy.

Letsos spoke first. "We talked to Miss Benson about the watch soon after Mrs. Gaskill identified it as belonging to her late husband. We told her we'd found it in the bottom of her closet and asked her to explain how it got there."

"What did she say?"

"She said you must have put it there. Did you?"

All the blood in my body rushed to my stomach, leaving my extremities cold. My first response, I think, was an incoherent bunch of syllables obliterated by the ringing in my ears. When I got control of myself, I said, "I did go to Brittany Benson's room when she wasn't there, but I did not put George Gaskill's watch in her closet. I'd never seen that watch until yesterday and I had no idea it even existed."

"Tell us why you went to her room when she wasn't there."

"Do you know Dr. Luc Girard? Of course you do, how silly of me." I was still stumbling over my own words. "I teach ancient and medieval history back home in Virginia and because of that, I made Dr. Girard's acquaintance soon after the cruise began. In fact, I introduced him to Sophie Antonakos who is now working as his assistant and who also happens to be Brittany's roommate.

"So my friend Lettie Osgood and I discovered that one of the display case items, the Panathenaic amphora in the Zeus deck lounge, had been reported as stolen from a museum. We had a catalog of stolen antiquities Dr. Girard had given me. I told Dr. Girard and my friend Marco Quattrocchi about it, and I understand Dr. Girard reported it to you."

Letsos fidgeted with a pencil, still glaring at me. Bondurant tilted his head a little to one side. Neither man said anything to help me along with my story.

"Well…" I stopped and took a deep breath. "I'm a rather nosy person, and I had already noticed Brittany had picked up a vase in Mykonos that Malcolm Stone, an antiques dealer from England…" I paused until I got a nod from Bondurant indicating he knew Stone and further identification wasn't necessary. "Mr. Stone said was quite valuable. He and his friend, Mr. Leclercq, had both tried to buy it from her and had offered her a large sum, but she wouldn't negotiate. I thought that was odd. I mean, especially with the other things we'd found out. And being the nosy person I am, I sneaked a room key out of Miss Antonakos's purse while she was working in the library. I went to her room and looked through Brittany's things. I found a couple of very interesting artifacts in cartons in the bottom of Brittany's closet, but there was definitely no watch there."

Bondurant said, "It defies all logic, Mrs. Lamb, to propose that you, who happen to be Mrs. Osgood's best friend, also happen to break into Miss Benson's room on the day after Mr. Osgood is questioned in the disappearance and murder of Mr. Gaskill, who also happens to be the man Miss Benson accused of raping her when she was in high school!"

When he put it like that, I had to agree.

"We know that you and Mrs. Osgood have taken several trips together, and that you booked this cruise together as well."

"How did you find out I'd snooped in Brittany's room?"

"Another staff member happened to see you leaving that afternoon. He recognized that you were a passenger, not staff, followed you to your room, and wrote down the number."

"I see."

"So here's what it looks like to us," Letsos leaned back in his chair and casually, almost insolently, threw his legs across the corner of his desk. "It looks very much as if Mr. Osgood gave you Mr. Gaskill's watch and told you to deposit it among Brittany Benson's things. Mr. Osgood killed Gaskill over the poker game in which he'd lost his shirt, and stole the poor man's watch before tossing him overboard. He discovered there was someone else on board who harbored a grudge against Gaskill and, after we turned the heat on him, decided to use the watch to implicate Miss Benson."

"Oh, you mustn't think…I have to admit your theory makes sense, Chief Letsos, but I promise you, that watch was not in Brittany Benson's closet two days ago."

"So you said." Bondurant's tone told me he didn't believe me.

"Can't you look for fingerprints on the watch?" The suggestion popped, unbidden, out of my mouth. "I promise you won't find my fingerprints on it."

"Strangely enough, Mrs. Lamb, there are absolutely no fingerprints on the watch. It's as if the last person who handled it wanted to remain anonymous."

Letsos glanced toward the door. "Did you find any other stolen items in our display cases, Mrs. Lamb?"

"Yes. Didn't Dr. Girard tell you?"

"We'd like to hear it from you."

That was strange. Didn't they trust Luc Girard's information? They certainly didn't trust me, so why did they want to hear it from me? Nevertheless, I told them we'd identified four stolen items and several that had been bought from reputable dealers. "So they aren't all stolen. I guess that's the good news. However, there was a bracelet in the case outside the dining room that's been swiped in the last twenty-four hours and replaced with a copy."

"Is that a fact?" Bondurant said in a tone of feigned interest. I searched his face, expecting to see a sarcastic smirk, but all I saw was a dead-pan look that required me to go on with my story.

"Yes. Miss Antonakos pointed it out to me last evening. The authentic bracelet had blue inset stones and the new one has green stones. So you see what that means, don't you? Someone on the ship is stealing things right now. This isn't about something that happened when the ship was furnished years ago, it involves someone or ones on this cruise. Whether this last theft was for the purpose of smuggling the bracelet to a buyer or to keep you guys from tracking down who put it there to begin with, I don't know."

Bondurant and Letsos looked at each other. Why were they asking me these things? Surely they could get better information from Dr. Girard. The light dawned. They were stalling for time.

"Tell us what you found in Brittany Benson's closet," Letsos said.

I heard a knock at the door.

"Come in."

Ollie Osgood's big burly frame filled the doorway. "My wife said you wanted to talk to me."

So that was it. They had made sure I had no chance to fill Ollie in on what I'd told them by keeping me here until he arrived. Now I knew how Ollie felt.

I HAD TO GET SOME solid food in me soon but I was still without makeup or brushed hair, so I sneaked through the breakfast buffet line at the outdoor pool on the Poseidon deck and into a table along the rail. As I sat down, I glimpsed the north shore of Crete, coming up on our port side. I'd have given anything to stay in the security office and find out what they were saying to Ollie, but Bondurant had ushered me out before I could even give Ollie a nod. Someone had left a copy of this morning's "Oracle" bulletin on my table so I looked it over while I ate.

It said we would be asked to wait on board for a brief time after we docked in the Iráklion harbor of Crete to allow time for the formation of a funeral cortege for Nikos Papadakos. Until that moment, it hadn't occurred to me to even wonder where his body was being held. Had they kept it on our ship since we left Mykonos? I thought not. In fact, I was pretty sure Marco had told us the body was still in Mykonos, awaiting autopsy, after we left. Perhaps they had transported it by ferry from Mykonos to Crete.

One whole column of today's "Oracle" was set off by a black border. Inside the border, a photo of Nikos, the smiling baby-faced photographer, and this announcement:

Many members of our staff and crew and, perhaps, some of our guests will want to attend the funeral service, which will be held in our dear friend Nikos Papadakos's village today at 11:00 a.m. A cortege of hired vehicles will form near the dock and make the 13 km trip to the church. Local taxi services have been notified and all have agreed to make the round trip and to wait near the church until after the service, for a flat fee of €50 per vehicle. Up to four passengers may share one vehicle. If you wish to attend, please wait at the dock until a vehicle is made available to you. Please do not telephone the taxi companies as they are already prepared for this event.

The family and friends of Nikos Papadakos request that you respect the traditions of Cretan village life by dressing conservatively and remember their grief with appropriate conduct and decorum.

I finished my coffee and trekked downstairs to my room. My wet towel still lay on the floor where I had dropped it after Bondurant's phone call. I smeared on some makeup and changed clothes, now donning the somberest clothes I had with me, a navy T-shirt and a denim jumper.

I couldn't find my water glass until I looked at the top of the TV and remembered I'd dropped the little glassy disc into it yesterday. Pouring out the water through my fingers into the sink, I trapped the thing, which had become more like a jellyfish after sitting in water all night. It was, as I had suspected, a contact lens. Now, why would a single contact lens have been stuck to the side of that sink in the bathroom at the back end of the hall? It might be one of those disposable lenses, so whoever lost it might have thought it not worth the effort of looking for it. Someone with dust in his or her eyes had probably popped in, used the mirror and the sink to rectify the problem, and lost a lens. Big deal. He or she probably had extras. I stuck the lens back on top of my TV, this time without water.

Our ship was nearing the dock when I walked out on the promenade deck. I pulled on the door to the library and it opened. Luc Girard and Sophie Antonakos were inside, Sophie reading from a sheet of notes as Girard checked the contents of a leather satchel.

We greeted each other and Sophie said, "Dr. Girard has a lecture today at the Archaeology Museum in Iráklion. Fortunately, most of the items he wants to use for illustration are already at the museum, so we're just packing a few little things."

"Are you going, too?" I asked her.

"Sophie gets the day off." Girard looked up from his

satchel. "Today's lecture will be in English, so I can handle it by myself."

"Good," I said. "Because I want to go to the funeral for Nikos Papadakos, and I would love for Sophie to come with me." I turned to her. "Could you please, please come with me? Otherwise I won't be able to talk to anyone."

Before Sophie could answer, Girard said, "Cool! Look for a man named Spyros Kontos. He owns a sort of hardware store there. I know, because I talked to him many times when I was working with Dieter Matt on the excavation I told you about. It was only a mile from Papadakos and Kontos's village. I used to buy shovels and trowels from him.

"This guy Kontos, you dig, is one of those illegal excavators who sells whatever he finds to the smugglers. Mind you, I don't know the names of any of the smugglers, but I certainly tried to get him to tell me. Maybe you and Sophie can turn on your charm and get something out of him."

"Oh, I…I don't think so," Sophie stammered.

"I explained to him a million times why it's wrong—what he's doing—but I could never make him understand. As far as he's concerned, whatever is buried in Crete belongs to Cretans, and he's Cretan. So if he finds it, it belongs to him!"

"Sophie, will you come with me?" I asked again. I had to promise to pay for the taxi and to buy her lunch but she finally agreed.

SOPHIE AND I SNAGGED the very last taxi in line. At the front was a dark blue Mercedes station wagon, its hood covered with a large swag of white flowers. Six men, toting a black coffin from the ferry boat docked near our own ship, paused while another man opened the Mercedes' hatchback to receive the casket. Sophie nodded at passengers in several of the cars as we walked toward the back of the line, mumbling things to me like, "That's the maître d," and, "She runs the gift shop." I gathered that the first few cars carried family members who had come down from the village to meet the ferry.

In the fifth car back, Captain Tzedakis, wearing enough medals to sink the ship, sat stiffly beside another uniformed man who may have been his first mate. Agent Bondurant and Officer Villas, the policeman from Mykonos, stood beside a car about halfway down the line, obviously scrutinizing the attendees. Was Papadakos's killer in this line?

When the line started to move, Sophie dashed toward a taxi that was maneuvering to back up and leave, having picked up no passengers. She halted the driver and waved at me to hurry up. As our car pulled out, I spied Brittany Benson on the promenade deck high above the dock. She was on her cell phone again, and waving her free hand in apparent frustration.

WE ROLLED OUT OF Iráklion and into rocky hills peppered with olive trees. A winding road narrowed to a single paved lane, and then the pavement gave out altogether as we climbed higher. Our taxi had to plow through the dust kicked up by all the cars ahead of us. Sophie and I alternated between rolling our windows up to keep out the dust and rolling them down to keep the back seat from overheating. At ten A.M. the sun was already beating mercilessly on the roof of our unair-conditioned cab. I fanned myself and Sophie held a scarf over her nose and mouth. In Greek, she asked our driver if he knew a man named Spyros Kontos and was met with a negative shake of the head.

"Do you speak English?" I asked him.

"Ochi," he answered, meaning no, so I felt free to tell Sophie about my morning's grilling in the security office, confident the driver wouldn't understand what I was talking about.

"They know I snooped through Brittany's stuff," I said. "But I told the FBI man and Chief Letsos I stole your room key out of your purse, so they don't know you had anything to do with it."

"Thanks, but Brittany already knows how you got in. Did they accuse you of putting the watch in her closet?"

I stopped fanning myself and looked at her. "So you know about that, do you? Yes, they did."

"How did the watch get there?"

"I have no idea."

"Brittany thinks you put it there. I had to tell her everything, including the fact that it was I who let you in, and I had to tell her why."

"Gulp! So Bondurant and Letsos knew I was lying about stealing the key from your purse."

"Don't worry about it. They can figure out for themselves that you were doing it to protect me."

We both stared out our windows for a long time, in silence. The rocky slopes, I noticed, were pockmarked with holes, some of which were surrounded by rude scaffolding. Like the entrance to a cave or something.

"There was no watch in her closet when I was there," I said.

"I certainly didn't put it there."

"So it must have been Brittany herself."

"I don't think so." She looked at me hard, and then added, "I truly don't think Brittany knew anything about it."

I turned back to my window. By now, there was a thick layer of dust on everything including my denim jumper and my navy T-shirt. I studied the holes in the terrain, to get my mind off the chill that had suddenly come over us. I had an idea. "Sophie, do you think these holes are places where people have been digging for loot?"

"I'll bet you're right! I was wondering what they were." Sophie rolled her window down a bit lower and coughed as more dust poured in. "I see a little village ahead of us."

TWENTY-TWO

NIKOS PAPADAKOS'S home town was straight out of *Zorba the Greek*. Narrow streets, whitewashed shanties with red tile roofs, sheep assuming the right of way wherever they happened to wander. The funeral procession stopped when, I assumed, the lead car reached the church. Since there was nothing resembling a place to park, the rest of the cars simply stopped and disgorged their passengers.

Sophie talked to our cabbie and told me he and the other drivers were going to take their vehicles out of town where they would wait for us until the service was over, then drop back around to pick us up. He showed her how the cardboard sign in his windshield would help us find him again, without which, of course, he couldn't collect his fare.

I stepped to one side of the street and slapped a cloud of dust off my clothes. Some fifty yards ahead of us stood a small stucco church. From the car behind the hearse, a young woman in the black of deep mourning and a boy of about seven climbed out and were led off toward the church. The little boy looked back toward me before they led him away. Big dark eyes and a mouth that looked as if it had already been tightened by manhood thrust upon him too soon. He was, I assumed, Papadakos's son, and he was now the man of the family.

Sophie took my arm and we headed up the street, following the crowd. "Nikos had two children. That's his wife and son you were looking at. His baby daughter, I would imagine, is at home and being tended by another member of the family."

"Did you know Nikos well?"

"I hardly knew him at all, but I live in the crew's quarters, so I've heard the talk. There's been talk of little else since he was killed."

"Have you heard anything that would indicate a motive?"

"Nothing. Everyone who knew him liked him."

It was the umpteenth time I'd heard that. How exceptional, I thought, for a man to work and live with these people for two years, and for everyone to still like him. Either Nikos Papadakos was a most amiable fellow, or somebody's fibbing.

Sophie had covered her head with the scarf she'd been using to cover her nose earlier. I looked around and realized I was the only woman with a bare head. "Is there a shop or something nearby? I need to buy a scarf."

We found a sort of tobacconist shop that also carried odds and ends. While I looked for something scarflike, Sophie talked to the girl behind the counter. She learned today's service for Nikos was not to be his only funeral. This one was for the foreigners, people from the ship, but another funeral, tomorrow, would be for the village. This close-knit community, hardly changed for hundreds of years, would suffer the indignities invariably inflicted on their church and their customs by the outsiders for an hour or two, saving their own mourning for later. Sophie also learned the location of Spyros Kontos's store. It was about three blocks away.

My head now properly covered by a purple something with a Greek key border, I noted we were more than a block behind the end of the line heading to the church. "Sophie, let's not go to the funeral. I'd rather look around and find that hardware store."

"Okay. I'm only here because you promised to buy my lunch," Sophie reminded me with a little grin.

We found the store, but we didn't find Kontos. The store was being tended by a man who told Sophie that Kontos was at the funeral. I looked around the store, craning my neck to see around the counter and into their back room. Might it hold some of Kontos's recent diggings? I tried to think of an excuse to go back there. I watched the attendant for a minute and saw that he was so completely absorbed in flirting with Sophie, he wouldn't notice me if I stripped naked and danced on the counter. I simply walked into the back room and looked around. I saw nothing that looked the least bit incriminating. No artifacts. Nothing. When I returned to the front room of the store, I found Sophie edging her way toward the door and the attendant trying his best to keep her from leaving. I rescued her by calling out, "Let's go, Sophie."

Sophie exhaled loudly and rolled her eyes as she joined me outside the store. "Dotsy, why are we here? If you didn't want to go to the funeral, why did you want to come here at all?"

"We're here because I'm looking for a connection between the murders of George Gaskill and Nikos Papadakos. My best friend's husband and your roommate are suspects in the former, and, other than a possible smuggling operation, no one has come up with a reasonable motive for the latter. But I believe they were connected."

"The woman at the first store told me where Papadakos lived. Would you like to go there?"

"Sure, but only to walk by. I wouldn't dare impose on them."

Sophie led me off the main street and up a winding dirt lane that terminated in a cluster of tiny stone-and-stucco dwellings. "This is it," she said, stopping in front of the one with green shutters.

From inside the hut came a baby's cry. An old woman dressed in black wobbled by the open door, one hand on a quivering cane. She glanced out toward us, shielded her eyes with her free hand, and stopped.

"Kalimea!" Sophie said brightly.

The old woman said nothing, but she waved us in. The next thing I knew, we were inside Nikos Papadakos's home talking to his mother, and Sophie was holding the crying baby, which the old woman had unceremoniously handed her, then tottered to a cane chair beside a spinning wheel. She seated herself with the utmost care, and swept one hand around toward a table loaded with nuts, bread, small glasses, and a bottle of Metaxa.

Sophie bounced the baby into silence. It made me a little nervous, knowing her tendency to drop things, but she shushed into the baby's ear and the baby seemed happy enough. "She says, 'Help yourself.' The food on the table is the traditional funeral offering."

Feeling like a terrible intruder, I grabbed a handful of peanuts, and smiled at the woman. She and Sophie lit into a long discussion of something, while I studied the simple room, its plain cement floor, smoke-stained hearth, and simple wood-framed windows. I didn't know whether I should sit down or not so I stood quietly and ate my peanuts. My gaze fell on a stack of black pottery bowls on the floor. They looked exactly like something I'd seen in the back of the LAMBDA catalog of stolen antiquities. Stolen items painted shiny black to make them look like cheap tourist junk. They could be slipped through customs easily with officials never suspecting they were real artifacts. So Papadakos was a smuggler, after all! I must get one of those bowls. I faked a coughing fit as if I had peanuts stuck in my throat and walked out the door, still coughing.

Sophie followed a minute later, sans baby. "Are you all right, Dotsy?"

"I'm fine, but I want one of those black bowls on the floor in there. You have to help me get one."

"Are you crazy?"

"They've been painted black so they can be smuggled out of the country, Sophie. I saw a photo just like them in the LAMBDA book."

"Oh, Dotsy. They're probably just cheap bowls."

"I don't think so. Please. Go in and offer her money. Here." I dug in my purse and pulled out a wad of Euros. "Give her whatever it takes."

Sophie spun around and threw her hands up. "This is silly. Okay, how much should I offer her?"

"A hundred Euros."

"She'd laugh at me. They probably cost less than five."

"Do whatever you have to."

With a loud sigh, Sophie slipped back inside and said, *"Na sas rotiso kati?"* I saw her shuffle her feet self-consciously as she listened to the old woman's answer. A few minutes later, she emerged with a black bowl and handed it to me. "That sweet old woman is now certain all tourists are crazy. I paid her ten Euros for a two-Euro bowl."

"You're a good girl, Sophie."

We arrived outside the church when the service was ending and watched as the mourners left. No surprises, really. Nigel Endicott, Malcolm Stone, Willem Leclercq, Brittany Benson—none of them were there. Bondurant, Officer Villas, and Captain Tzedakis were the only people I recognized, and I already knew they were here. The hired cars were waiting for us, now heading the opposite direction. We located our cab and hopped in. We were at the back end of the line again but our driver, rather than wait his turn to move out, shoved the car into reverse and drove around behind the church and out of the village by a different route.

I looked at the black bowl on my lap. Out of the corner of my eye, I caught Sophie's grin. "Laugh all you want. You and Dr. Girard will thank me when you see I've rescued a priceless antiquity."

"Are you still going to buy me lunch? I'm hungry." Sophie grabbed the bowl and turned it over, examining the bottom.

"Sure. Do you know a good place to eat in Iráklion?"

The cab was sweltering and the sun beat in on my side of the back seat. I rolled my window down and watched the barren hills roll by. We weren't returning by the route we'd come, but we were going downhill, so I figured it had to be all right. Sophie told me about the work she was doing for Dr. Girard and her tone of voice confirmed my belief that a fondness was growing between them.

"I love the work," she told me, "even though it means working full time as a dancer and working with Dr. Girard in my free time."

I looked out the back window. A silver car, a lot like one we'd passed back in the village, was behind us. Sophie turned as well, and looked back. "Are we going the right way?" I said.

Our driver swerved left onto a smaller side road and a big puff of dust flew into my face. I rolled up my window and leaned forward to ask the man if he knew what he was doing. I smelled—GOATS.

"EXCUSE ME," I SAID, tapping him on the shoulder. "Aren't we going the wrong way?"

Sophie leaned sideways and looked across the seat back. She was in a better position than I was to see his profile. I could see only the back of a greasy head and, in the rear-view mirror, his eyes. Sophie turned to me and mouthed something that looked like, "Oh, shit."

We careened around a hairpin turn and the car speeded up, hitting a boulder on the side of the road that nearly turned us over. The road descended more steeply on the other side of the turn. Like a sidewinder rattlesnake, our cab slid and slipped down the hill and from the window on my side I saw that the goat man, our driver, was heading for a grove of trees. Once inside the grove, both we and the car would be hidden from view in all directions. My door was on the downhill side. I had to risk it. The lock button on my door was up. Unlocked.

I grabbed Sophie's wrist, popped my door open, and rolled out, pulling Sophie along with me. We both hit the ground hard. My left side landed on a thorny bush, my left leg twisted up under me. Sophie, I think, must have fallen flat on her back because I heard a pained "Uunh."

Without a word, we both scrambled to our hands and knees. Stumbling and crawling, we struggled toward a large boulder some twenty yards away. I heard the crunch of tires on gravel behind and above us. Then shouts.

Then the crack of gunfire.

I heard the ping of a bullet that grazed the boulder Sophie and I were headed for. Sophie had fallen. I heard her say, "Go on, Dotsy. Save yourself."

I slid an arm around her and pulled. Pulled her toward the boulder, inch by inch. Sophie regained her footing, sort of, and we stumbled on.

More shouts. Another shot. Thuds. I hit the dirt and flattened myself out against the ground, waiting for the next shot, which I fully expected to enter my left temple at any second. Two arms lifted and turned me over, pulled me up, and held me tightly. I smelled a clean, soap smell. Clean? Not goat?

I drew back and looked up. It was Marco.

TWENTY-THREE

"I THOUGHT YOU WERE in Italy."

"I came back." Marco stood up rather abruptly and I fell back, my elbows scraping against the ground. "Excuse me. I have to see about this man who was shooting at you and make sure he does not escape."

To Marco's retreating back, I said, "Find out who he is."

I sat up and looked around. Sophie lay face down, a few feet downhill from me, her arms and shirt streaked with blood. My heart thudded in my chest. As I scooted over toward her, she raised her head and looked around. "Oh, thank God, Sophie, I thought you were a goner."

"A goner? No, I'm still here, I think." She sat up, groaned, and plucked a triangular black shard out of her right arm. "I broke your priceless antiquity, though." She examined the broken edge of the shard and said, "Plaster. What did I tell you?"

Even I could see the white interior was nothing but plaster, painted black. We checked ourselves for injuries. Sophie had numerous cuts, and a right arm she thought might be broken. It was numb, she said, and it did have a funny angle to it.

I had too many cuts and scrapes to count, especially on my left side, but everything seemed to move properly. Except my neck. It only wanted to turn right. I had left my newly purchased scarf, which was probably meant to be a tablecloth, around my shoulders and I found it now, a couple of yards uphill and ensnared in a thorny bush. I retrieved it and made a sling for Sophie's arm with it.

"Who is that man?" Sophie asked, so casually it made me laugh. She had no idea what was going on. But then neither did I.

"I don't know who he is, but he's the same man who was following me in Rhodes yesterday. I realized he wasn't our driver when I leaned forward to talk to him and smelled goats."

"Goats?"

"Yes. I smelled that same smell at a shop in Rhodes, thought nothing about it at the time, of course. But when I saw Brittany in the Palace of the Grand Masters a little while later and smelled goats again, I realized they were together and they were following me. I still have no idea why."

"That's your friend from Italy, isn't it? The man who saved us?"

"Right. Marco Quattrocchi. He's with the Italian Carabinieri."

"I know. He and Dr. Girard have been comparing notes. Why is he here?"

I looked up the hill and saw Marco now had the goat man firmly in hand, up against the car, and was tying him up with a necktie or something. Behind the cab we'd been riding in, which was now angled precariously on the verge of a steep drop, sat a silver Mercedes, obviously the car I'd seen behind us a few minutes ago.

Sophie and I struggled to our feet and picked our way gingerly up the hill, Sophie wincing as she cradled her right arm with her left. I got a sharp pain in my collarbone region when I tried to turn my neck again.

Marco jerked his prisoner around to face us. "Do either of you ladies know this man?"

"I know he was following me yesterday in Rhodes, but I don't know why," I said.

"I need to take him to the jail in Iráklion but I also need to take you two back to the ship. I do not think you will want to ride in the same car with this man because he smells like goats."

"It's okay. I just want to get back to the ship."

"Me too," Sophie said.

Sophie and I climbed into the back seat of the silver Mercedes and Marco tucked us in carefully, adjusting the position of Sophie's arm before he closed our door. He threw his prisoner into the front seat, and slipped behind the wheel himself. Turning to me, he said, "Put this on the floor and try not to kick it." He handed me the gun, still warm from having been fired.

On the way back to town, I filled Marco in on what we'd been doing in the little village while we were not attending the funeral of Nikos Papadakos. I explained all I knew about the events in Rhodes yesterday, but didn't say anything about George Gaskill's watch, the accusations and the counter-accusations that had kept us busy on board the ship since he'd left. There'd be time for that later. Our would-be assassin, his hands tied behind his back, stared glumly out the side window.

"I rented this nice car to impress you, Dotsy. Are you impressed? I went to the ship this morning and Dr. Girard told me where the two of you had gone. He said you had gone to the funeral and he told me how to find the village. So I thought I would pick you up in this nice car, like a knight on a white horse, you know?"

"I'm impressed." I tried to give him a playful punch across the back of the seat, but was stopped by another stabbing pain in my collarbone. "Anytime you save my life, Marco, I'll be impressed. You could have ridden up on a donkey and I'd have been impressed."

"Thank you for saving my life, sir," said Sophie.

MARCO HELPED US into the lobby of the hospital in Iráklion, keeping one eye on the prisoner in the car as he did so. "I am sorry to leave you here, but…"

"We'll be fine, Marco. Take Goatman to the police station before he figures out how to escape."

Sophie took care of the red tape at the admissions desk, spending far more time dealing with my American insurance than with her own. If I'd been alone, I couldn't have done it. As it was, I'd have to pay them for my treatment today and settle up with my insurance company when I got home. I nearly cried when they took Sophie away to x-ray her arm. This was all my fault. If I hadn't practically forced her to go with me, she'd have spent a happy day in the ship's library, sorting things for Dr. Girard, and none of this would have happened.

Eventually a nurse led me to another room, helped me take off my clothes and don a hospital gown. After they'd x-rayed me front, back, and sideways, they parked me in an alcohol-scented hallway between an old man and a whimpering child on his mother's lap, neither of whom seemed to care about my lack of clothing. A half-hour later a nurse who spoke broken English came around and led me into a little examination room. Under her arm, she held a large envelope. She asked me questions about how this all happened.

"I fell down a hill about ten miles south of town." That's all she needed to know.

She poked around, made me lift my arms and turn my head as far as I could. Left, right, up, down. Noting my scrapes and cuts were still bloody and dirty, she went to work with a towel and antiseptic until most of my left arm and leg were painted mustard yellow. She pulled my x-rays out of the envelope and stuck them up on a light box. She touched the ghostlike shadow of what was obviously my collarbone. "See the little black line here? And the point here? It is what we are calling a…"

"A break?" I tried to help her out.

"No. Not a break…a…crack. Is this a good word?"

"It's a better word than break."

"Ah, yes. So we will not operate on you. There is nothing that will fix it but time. It hurts, yes? We will make over to you a…support." She crossed her arms over her chest, mummy style. "You can wear it until your crack is better."

I think it's good to find humor even in adversity.

The nurse gave me a sort of straplike device and a sling for my left arm. The padded strap thing looked as if it should be attached to a space suit. She showed me how to put on both items and told me I didn't have to wear them all the time. "But at least when you sleep, you should wear the brace to hold your shoulder when you turn over," she said.

I was free to go after I signed a bunch of papers that, for all I knew, gave them title to everything I owned. I let them make an imprint of my credit card and returned to the area from which they had hauled Sophie away, thinking I'd stay there and wait for her. I had no idea how long it would take but I realized it might be hours. A white-uniformed nurse approached me and touched my shoulder. She looked familiar. After a few seconds, I recognized her as the nurse from our ship, the one who'd been trying to help Kathryn Gaskill that morning when they showed her the ersatz suicide note. Kathryn had rebuffed her, saying,

"I'm not sick. I don't need a nurse," and that's when Marco had brought me in.

"Mrs. Lamb?" she said. "Are you all right?" When I assured her I was, she said, "I'm waiting for Miss Antonakos. When she comes out of the operating room it will still be some time before they release her. I'll take her back to the ship, so you can leave if you wish. I'm sure you could use a little rest."

"How did you know we were here?"

"Mr. Quattrocchi telephoned from the police station and explained. I believe he's waiting in the front lobby now."

The nurse pointed me in the right direction and assured me she didn't mind waiting alone. In the lobby, I found Marco sitting in a plastic chair, but he wasn't alone. In the plastic chair next to him sat Luc Girard, both men staring straight ahead as if they were waiting for word their babies had been delivered.

Marco jumped up when he saw me, rushed over as if to hug me, then stopped. "I should not give you a hug, I think."

"I'd appreciate it. But I'm okay. Only a fractured collarbone. Nothing's broken." I smiled at him and he smiled back. The panic now over, I really looked at him for the first time today. He hadn't shaved in a while and black stubble cast his lower face in shadow. The effect was not unattractive.

Luc Girard came forward and joined us. "Where's Sophie?"

I explained, and assured him her injuries weren't life-threatening. Marco said he'd drive me back to the ship and Girard said he'd stay there and wait for Sophie. I told him about the nurse waiting for her down the hall.

Marco walked me to his rented prestige car, opened the door, and set my purse on the floor beside my feet.

I discovered it was impossible to straighten my twisted denim jumper without using the neck muscles attached to my collarbone. How else to raise one's hips and thighs off the seat? I was stuck with the twist.

"What's the story on the goat man?" I asked, after Marco had fastened my seat belt for me. Fortunately the seat belt crossed my right shoulder and the fracture was in my left collarbone, so it didn't hurt.

"The goat man is not talking. They got a name and address out of him and that is all. He is waiting for his lawyer but I did not have the time to wait. I will call them later this evening and find out what is going on."

"He's connected to Brittany Benson. That's all I know."

"You told me that she has a boyfriend."

"With all due respect to Goatman, I don't think he's Brittany's boyfriend."

"I know." Marco glanced toward me briefly before he swung the prestige car out into traffic. "Because I know who her boyfriend is. I know where he lives and I know the Carabinieri are looking for him."

"You're kidding!"

"The address Brittany listed on her employee data form. I checked it out at our offices in Milano, and it is the address of Robert Segal, who is suspected of being the kingpole of antiquities smuggling in Western Europe."

"Kingpin," I corrected him.

"What?"

"It's kingpin, not kingpole. So what else did you learn? Tell me everything."

"That will take a long time," he said, swinging into the dock and around to the ramp beside the *Aegean Queen*. "You go now and get some rest. I have to return this impressive car before it turns into a melon. Can you get to your room by yourself?"

"Of course." I slipped carefully out of the car, reaching back in to pick up my purse with my right hand. Huh? Turns into a melon? Oh. He meant pumpkin.

ENOUGH HILL COUNTRY DIRT poured off me in the shower to clog the ship's drains. I would've liked to wash my hair but, being able to raise only one arm to my head, I figured it would be smarter to tackle that job after a good rest. Better yet, how about a visit to the ship's salon? Across the hall from my bathroom hung a full-length mirror on the outside of a closet door. I stood and stared at my unclothed self and laughed. With mustard-yellow patches of antiseptic, scrapes now darkened with scabs, and purple bruises—especially a real beauty on my left shoulder—developing rapidly, I looked as if I were wearing a camouflage body suit. Dressing myself with great care, I struggled with the criss-cross brace the hospital had given me. Do you wear it under or on top of your clothes? With or without a bra? I started with a nightshirt and fastened the brace on top of it, then considered the likelihood I'd have visitors dropping in as folks returned to the ship and my nightshirt, bunched up by the brace, was awfully short. What if I got called out to go somewhere? Did I really want to go through the dressing ordeal again? I settled on a cotton shirt and a pair of shorts. Buttoning the shirt one-handed proved impossible, but I found I really could use both hands enough to do the buttons. It only hurt when I raised my left elbow sideways.

I clicked my TV on, grabbed a package of cheese crackers and a carton of orange juice, and stretched out on the bed. A message was crawling continuously across the bottom of the screen: Any passenger or crew member knowing the whereabouts of taxi #930, last seen near the village of Aghios Minos, please call the main desk immediately.

I reached for the phone and hit the button for the main desk. I explained that I had been riding in taxi #930 until a couple of hours ago, but I had only the vaguest idea where we had left it. That took a bit more explaining.

"The driver of the car is waiting on the dock. He can't come aboard, so could you go out and talk to him?"

I sighed and said, "Of course, but I'll need someone who speaks both English and Greek to go with me. If it's the same man who drove us to the funeral, he speaks no English."

"We'll send someone down to accompany you, Mrs. Lamb."

I was glad I'd decided to get dressed before strapping myself into the brace. While I finished my snack and waited for someone from the desk to come to my door, I remembered the poor cab driver still hadn't been paid his fifty Euros, the agreed-upon fare. I had no Euros. I'd given the whole wad to Sophie to buy that bowl, and she hadn't given me any money back. As I was wondering if there was an ATM on the dock, someone knocked on my door. It was a man I'd seen at the main desk several times earlier.

"Oh, my!" he said when he saw my brace.

It took a few minutes to explain the events leading up to the abandonment of a car from the funeral procession and my standing before him now in a figure-eight clavicle brace. He said, "Oh, my" several more times.

"I'm afraid I won't be able to tell the man where his car is now, because I don't know where I was when I last saw it." I remembered its precarious position at the edge of a cliff. "But the car's okay, as long as its hand brake holds. When Captain Quattrocchi comes back from the car rental place, he'll be able to give better directions, since he was driving."

We met the driver on the dock near the foot of the

gangway. His face was only vaguely familiar to me because I'd seen mostly the back of his head on the trip up to the village. The man from the desk, our translator, listened as the driver gesticulated and shouted in rapid-fire Greek. He turned to me. "He wants to know what you did with his car."

"Tell him what I've told you. Explain why I don't know exactly where his car is, but if we could find a map, I think I could show him the general area." There was a tourist information kiosk I thought would probably have maps, on the dock only a few yards away. "Also, tell him I'll give him his fifty Euros as soon as I find an ATM."

After another conference with the driver, the translator turned to me. "He says he's already been paid. While he and the other drivers were waiting for the funeral service to end, a man came up to him, gave him a hundred Euros, and told him to ride back with another driver. Told him he could pick his car up here, on the dock, when he got back."

"I see!"

"The man told him he was taking you and your companion to a surprise party in Iráklion."

"It was a surprise, all right."

While the cabbie and I waited for our interpreter to buy a map at the kiosk, an Iráklion police car pulled onto the dock and Marco hopped out. He waved at me, then stuck his head back into the car and said something to the driver. After I introduced Marco and the cabbie to one another, they launched into a bilingual gesturing frenzy that included a good bit of forehead-slapping. At length, Marco called out to the policeman, still sitting in the squad car. He got out and approached us as the man from the front desk loped over from the kiosk with a map.

It didn't take the policeman and Marco long to locate on the map the approximate area where the action had taken place. Although I only understood bits and pieces of the discussion, I gathered we all had to go back to the site. The policeman needed more information from me about what led up to Sophie and me jumping out of the moving vehicle, and I could do that most effectively on the actual site. The cabbie, of course, needed to pick up his car, and Marco could fill in the parts of the story I'd missed when Sophie and I had been facedown in the dirt.

"Do I really need to go with you?" the desk clerk said as he refolded the map and handed it to the policeman. "You speak English, don't you? I'm supposed to be on desk duty now, and you already have four people going up in the same car."

"We'll be all right. Mrs. Lamb can write out a statement for me, in English." The policeman looked at my brace. "Can you write, Mrs. Lamb?"

"I'm right-handed. I should be able to."

The cabbie took the front passenger seat, leaving the back of the squad car to Marco and me. Following several exchanges in Greek between the men in the front seat, the policeman turned around and asked if either of us had the keys to the taxi. We didn't, so that meant we had to swing by the police station and see if Goatman had them.

The keys, Goatman told them through the bars of his cell, should still be in the ignition.

As we wound southward, back to the hill country and to the scene of the crime, I tried to write my statement on the yellow pad the policeman handed me, but I couldn't. Not because of my fractured collarbone, but because we bumped and bounced along the rutted road, like so many balls in a Lotto machine. I gave up and held my left arm tight against my stomach with my right. Marco looked over at me, and winced in sympathy. He reached over and touched my hair, lifting a wisp off my face. He touched my cheek with the back of his hand.

"You haven't shaved in a while, have you?" I said.

"Not since I left Rhodes."

"Why?"

"You did not like me without a beard."

"It was just a shock when I first saw you. I'd never seen you without one."

Marco called out to the policeman, "Sorry, I didn't see the road. Back up a little and turn down this road on the right."

The taxi was still there with the keys in the ignition. The cabbie kissed its hood and drove away immediately. Marco and I walked the policeman through the events surrounding the shooting, using tire tracks and skid marks as our guides. The shrub I'd landed on still waved a few purple threads it had ripped from my scarf, and the rocks I'd dragged Sophie over in our desperate rush for cover still bore traces of her blood or mine. Did I break Sophie's arm when I pulled her out of the car? Did it break when she hit the ground? It occurred to me I'd rather not know.

I sat under an olive tree and wrote my statement while Marco and the policeman trekked back to locate the place where Goatman had veered off the main road. I filled only a page and a half, realizing as I wrote that parts of the scene were a blur in my mind. Rolling down the hill, for instance. How far had we rolled? It could have been a foot or a football field. All I recalled was a swirl of rocks and thorny bushes. Looking up at the slope now from my seat under the tree, I could see it had been about a twenty-foot slide. I signed and dated the statement, rested my head against the trunk of the tree behind me, and dozed off.

THE POLICEMAN DROPPED US off at the ship. I went straight to my room, kicked off my shoes, and lay down. Less than a minute later, Lettie knocked at my door. She worked herself into an awful snit when she saw my brace, so I took it off to prove it wasn't holding me together.

I went back to my bed and explained the day's happenings from a reclining position while Lettie sat at my dressing table, her hands clasped so tightly her knuckles were white. When I finished my harrowing tale, I asked her how she'd spent her day.

She shook her head as if she was waking from a nightmare. "Nothing as exciting as that, I can assure you. Ollie and I went to the Palace of Knossos and so did Nigel Endicott and Malcolm Stone. I watched them carefully every chance I got, but they didn't do anything suspicious. Agent Bondurant wasn't following Nigel today, but the security man, Chief Letsos, followed us the whole time."

"They had all their bases covered. Bondurant and Villas were with the group at the funeral. Did you notice who, in particular, Chief Letsos seemed to be watching?"

"Ollie and Malcolm. He didn't seem to care about Nigel Endicott, but he watched every move Ollie or Malcolm made."

Lettie was on her way out when we heard a knock at the door. Lettie opened it and gave a little squeal when she saw Marco. She pinched his cheeks. "Welcome, back! Dotsy told me everything about being kidnapped by a goat man and bullets flying and you riding up in a silver car to rescue her in the nick of time."

Marco glanced from Lettie to me and blushed.

"I must say, you certainly know how to make an entrance," Lettie continued. "Like Dudley Do-Right."

"Who?"

"Oh I forgot. You probably didn't have the same cartoons in Italy."

I butted in because I knew Lettie could go on for hours

about Rocky and Bullwinkle and Boris and Natasha. "You didn't leave the gun in the back of the Mercedes, did you?"

"It is at the Iráklion police station. Bagged and tagged, as they say." Marco came over to the bed where I lay and touched my forehead, as if he was checking for a fever. "I am going to the purser's office and return my passport to the safe."

"Oh. May I go with you?" I had an idea. While I had been analyzing things last night, through an ouzo-induced haze, it had occurred to me George and/or Kathryn Gaskill's passports might shed some light on whether or not they had truly come on this trip for a simple vacation. I'd also wondered about Nigel Endicott. Where was he from? Was he even American? "I'd like to see where they keep the passports."

"I doubt they will let either of us go into the safe. The purser will probably take my passport and lock it up for me."

"Marco, I want to go into the safe. Please. Make up some reason why you and I have to go in there ourselves. Can you please do this for me?"

"Probably not. If they do not want to let me go in, I cannot go in. It is that simple."

"Can I at least go with you to the purser's office?"

He turned around, looking for Lettie, but she wasn't there. She'd slipped out while Marco and I had been talking. "If you will give me a kiss, I will let you go with me."

He kissed me. It was the longest and best kiss I'd had since Rome.

THE PURSER, THE OFFICER IN CHARGE of monetary transactions, wasn't in, and a young assistant was on duty. We were in luck. He sat behind a tall counter, swiveling back and forth on a tall stool as he talked to Marco. Behind him was a small officelike room with file cabinets, a desk, and a computer. By stepping to the right, I could see a polished steel door with a combination lock on the front. It had to be the safe and it looked as if the door might be ajar. Could I be so lucky? From the size of the door, I figured it had to be a walk-in type safe.

"Sorry, sir," the young man said. "I don't know anything about the passports. Could you come back when the purser is in?"

Here was Marco's chance. But would he take it?

"I do not want to walk around with it, because you never know. I might drop it overboard and then where would I be?" Marco glanced quickly at me and winked. "I know how they keep the passports. They put them in a drawer inside the safe. I have been in there. I know."

"Well, sir, I'm not sure…"

"Look. Call your purser on the phone. Tell him it is Captain Marco Quattrocchi. I am a police officer from Florence." Marco leaned conspiratorially over the counter and lowered his voice to a whisper. "He knows me, and he knows I am helping Chief Letsos with his investigations. The murder investigations." He flipped his passport open, showing that he was, indeed, Marco Quattrocchi, and slipped his hand inside his jacket as if searching for his police ID.

The young man didn't wait for Marco to actually pull out any additional identification and didn't make the suggested call, either. "All right, sir. If you're sure you know where to put it, go on back. The door's open."

Marco rounded the counter and I slipped through with him, attached to his side like a leech. I didn't look at the attendant or give him a chance to stop me. He could, after all, watch us so we wouldn't have been able to steal anything. The safe wasn't really big enough to walk into.

Inside were three walls of shiny metal drawers, most with keyholes, some without. The whole floor area was no more than three feet wide and two feet deep. From the counter outside, the attendant could watch us as we worked. On the wall in front of us and about halfway down, I saw two drawers, conveniently labeled Passports A—M and Passports N—Z. Marco pulled the second one open and I did likewise to the first.

I turned to the assistant, who was swiveling rather nervously on his tall stool, and said, "My name is Lamb. I'm just checking something on my own passport." I fingered through the *G*s until I found the two Gaskills, pulled them out, and looked. They were both United States passports, recently issued. The photo of George looked like the man I recalled having dinner with that first night. Both documents bore only one stamp each, indicating they had immigrated into Athens, Greece, on June fifteenth.

The assistant slipped off his perch and came toward me. Marco was pretending he couldn't find the *Q*s in the second drawer. "I'm sorry madam, but I must ask you to wait on the other side of the counter." I guess he figured I'd had enough time to check something on my own passport.

"Oh, dear," I said. "I'm keeping a journal, you see, and I've forgotten exactly when I entered and left each country on my tour. It's so confusing. One day I'm in Germany, and the next day it's Switzerland. Or is it Hungary? Or Greece?" I laughed. "If I don't get it straight now, I'll never be able to sort it out when I get home, because I write an entry in my journal every day and…"

He left and returned to his stool.

I found the *E*s and pulled out Nigel Endicott's document. The photo showed the man I knew as Nigel. He was, after all, a U.S. citizen because he had a U.S. passport. His had also been issued recently, within the past year, but he had two immigration stamps and one visa stamp. On June fifteenth, Nigel had entered Istanbul, Turkey, an immigration that also required a visa, and on June seventeenth, Athens, Greece.

Marco nudged me with his elbow. "We must go."

Thanking the young man, and holding up both my hands so he could see I hadn't swiped anything, I made my exit and headed for the elevator. "Thank you, Marco. That worked perfectly."

"Did you find out what you wanted to know?"

"I found out Nigel Endicott didn't come here straight from America. He went to Istanbul first, then here."

"Very interesting! Who is Nigel Endicott?"

The elevator doors opened and we stepped inside. "Oh, dear. You're so far behind. We really need to talk."

TWENTY-FOUR

SHORTLY AFTER I RETURNED to my room, Sophie dropped by, proudly displaying the cast on her left arm. I showed her my multicolored arms and legs, and she pulled up her pants legs to show me she had as many mustard-yellow patches as I had.

"I thought you were going to buy me lunch," she said. "I go through all this and I still don't get lunch!"

We both laughed. I said, "Was Luc Girard still at the hospital when you got out of surgery?"

"Yes. He and the ship's nurse brought me back."

I filled Sophie in on the parts of the day she had missed, up to the time when I fell asleep under the tree. "That reminds me. The police may need a formal statement from you. Marco and I both gave them our versions."

"They'll have to ask quickly because the ship is getting ready to pull out, and I'm going to the clinic. The nurse is making up a bed for me because she wants to watch me until tomorrow morning. The anesthesia, you know. The hospital let me go sooner than they normally would, because the nurse told them the ship was leaving." Sophie stared out my window for a minute. "And besides, I don't want to go to my room, anyway. I don't know what to say to Brittany."

"How were things this morning before you left?"

"Strained. Very awkward. Brittany is practically under house arrest. Letsos told her she'd have to have an escort if she left the ship today. And, although we didn't talk about it, she knows I let you into our room that day."

"And, if she didn't leave Gaskill's watch in her closet herself, she obviously believes I did. The watch, Sophie, is the key to everything. Do you suppose I was the only person who sneaked into your room? Might there have been someone else who wanted to throw suspicion on Brittany?"

"Maybe Willem Leclercq? He's been hanging around with her lately. Perhaps he's flirting with her as a way of getting into our room."

"An interesting thought. We have to find out how that watch got into Brittany's closet because whoever put it there either killed George Gaskill or knows who did. And that includes Brittany herself."

I walked Sophie to the clinic, aware that she was still woozy from the anesthesia. The nurse I'd last seen in the hospital waiting room took over and said she'd have Sophie's dinner sent up from the kitchen. Hearing the thunk of gears engaging somewhere deep in the ship, I hurried down to the promenade deck to watch us pull out of the harbor. From the rail, I scanned the horizon, knowing the Palace of Knossos, number two on my list of things I most wanted to see, would have to wait for another time. Maybe. Would I ever be back? Number one on my list, the ruins of Akrotiri on the island of Santorini, was yet to come. It was the 3,500-year-old Minoan town, excavated in the late twentieth century. Buried under volcanic ash in antiquity, it had emerged beautifully preserved, wall frescoes of boys fishing and children boxing still brightly colored. From my reading at home I knew excavators had covered the entire town with a sort of canopy, but I didn't know if the site was open to the public now. If not, I would miss seeing both of my top two places.

Crewmen on the dock below started to drag the ramp away from our ship and shouted to each other in preparation for dropping the dock lines wrapped around huge cleats on the dock. A man came flying across from the street that ran along the harbor, waving his arms, shouting, "Wait! Wait!" Two dockhands called out something to the bridge high above me, and the engine shifted to a deeper rumbling sound.

Malcolm Stone, carrying a large package, dashed up the ramp, yelling, "Don't close the door!" and leaped across a foot-wide gap from the top of the ramp to the ship. The ship, still moving away due to the inertia, would have been out of jumping range if he'd been a tenth of a second later. From all along the promenade deck, from the dock below and the deck above me came a chorus of "Crazy!" and *"Proséxte!"* and "Who is that nut?"

THE CONVERSATION AT DINNER that evening was revealing, if hardly appetizing. We mostly talked about blood. Lettie, Ollie, Marco and I joined Kathryn Gaskill and the Zieglers who were already seated. I figured Ernestine Ziegler had discovered Marco was back and had wangled a place for herself and Heather at our table, because their earlier assignment had been elsewhere and our table only seated six comfortably. Tonight we were seven.

Marco brought up the subject. "Kathryn, you said your husband's blood type was AB positive, didn't you?"

This, I believe, was Marco's very first use of a contraction. I could have proposed a toast to this big linguistic step forward but I didn't want to change the subject.

"Yes. His doctor at home told him that was good because it made him a universal recipient," Kathryn said. "In other words, he could receive blood from most anyone, but he couldn't donate it except to another person with AB blood."

"It's not quite as simple as that," Ernestine Ziegler, who I recalled telling us she was a nurse, butted in. Her gaze shifted around the table. When it came back to Marco, her eyelashes fluttered. "Blood has a number of factors other than the A, B, O, and Rhesus factors. Not to mention the fact that it needs to be screened for hepatitis, HIV, and a lot of other things. But you're right, generally speaking."

Kathryn looked at Marco, quizzically. "Why do you ask that again?"

"Because," Marco began, then paused and took a sip of water as if he wasn't sure how to proceed. "Because I took a small sample of the blood from the deck. I collected it that morning after you and Dotsy called me out there. I took it to our laboratory in Milano yesterday and I asked them to do a DNA test on it. That test takes a while, but the A,B,O test is fast. It only takes a few seconds. They told me immediately the sample I gave them was type AB positive, and only three percent of the population has AB positive blood."

"Now you know what I knew already." Kathryn didn't appear shocked that Marco had surreptitiously collected a blood sample. "I knew it was George's blood. Didn't I tell you?"

"Well now, wait a minute. Three percent is three percent. It is not a certainty. It would not hold up in court as proof the blood was George's. For that you need the DNA." Marco swept his hand around, taking in most of the dining room. "How many people are here right now? About three or four hundred? So there are probably ten or twelve people in this room with AB positive blood. Not good enough."

"When the DNA tests come back, they'll prove it was George's blood."

"Don't you need some of George's DNA to compare it to?" Ollie asked.

"I am afraid I must confess. I also took a few hairs from George's brush. The FBI collected George's toothbrush and hairbrush as well as blood samples from the deck but it will take them a long time to get the results. I have connections so I can get it done faster."

I hope the hairs you pulled from George's brush were from his hair and not from his hairpiece. I forced myself to keep a straight face as I flashed on an image of a lab worker yelling out, "It's not even human!" or "This hair is from a woman of Tahitian ancestry."

"And another thing," Marco added. "They told me the blood has a high level of a chemical called EDTA. I thought that was strange."

"That's a blood thinner. They use it to keep blood from clotting. Don't you remember the big to-do in the O.J. Simpson case?" This came from Ernestine. "The defense tried to say it meant the blood on the back fence had been planted there from a lab sample."

Kathryn put her fork down and wiped her mouth with her napkin. "George was taking a blood thinner. There was so much plaque in his coronary arteries, the doctors were worried about a blood clot. That's why he was scheduled for heart surgery this summer."

Ernestine Ziegler almost shouted, "If he was scheduled for surgery, why was he on blood thinners? Doctors always take a patient off that stuff, weeks before surgery."

"No they don't. Not always." This came from Heather Ziegler in the form of a tiny croak.

Her mother rounded on her as if she were about to strike. I caught my breath. Ernestine seemed to consult her plate for instructions on how to respond. She patted the tablecloth and shifted a spoon. "When you've been a nurse as long as I have, young lady, you'll know that when a doctor keeps a patient on a blood thinner regimen right up until…"

Lettie cut her short with, "Did you know Dotsy got kidnapped and shot at today?" That was brilliant. Nothing short of a bombshell like that would have been sufficient to divert the conversation onto a less contentious path. All heads turned toward me and I, looking pretty unscathed because I hadn't worn my clavicle brace, launched into a lengthy and, if I do say so myself, entertaining account of my narrow escape from the goat man.

The waiter brought our desserts and coffee.

Should I bring up the watch? I tossed it around in my mind while the waiter corrected the placement of the desserts, giving the lemon tart to Lettie and the baklava to Heather. Kathryn and I hadn't been told not to talk about it so I decided to go for it, but not actually reveal that it had been found in Brittany's closet. "The investigators are asking questions about George's watch. A beautiful gold watch Kathryn said was given to him by a high school class he sponsored when he was a principal."

"Actually, it was when he was still a teacher. Before he became principal," Kathryn said.

"Do any of you remember if George was wearing it that first evening after we left Athens?"

Ollie and Marco shook their heads. Ernestine reminded me she and Heather weren't with us that evening. Lettie, the little human data bank, closed her eyes, licked a blob of lemon tart off her upper lip, and appeared to go into a trance. After several seconds she said, "I don't believe he was. At dinner he was wearing a long-sleeve shirt and jacket so a watch could have been hidden by his sleeves. But when he reached to the center of the table for the creamer, I remember, his jacket sleeve crept up and there was no watch on his wrist. Not on his left wrist, anyway."

This phenomenal display of total recall got wide-eyed stares from everyone at the table, except me and Ollie. We were used to it.

"George was left-handed. He wore his watch on his right arm," Kathryn said.

HEATHER ZIEGLER caught up with Marco and me in the hall outside the dining room. She tugged at his sleeve. "Captain? About what Mother was saying in there about the blood thinners and all."

"Yes?" Marco said and we both stopped to listen.

"I didn't say anything at the table because Mother is… well I didn't want to contradict her, you know." She pulled Marco out of the flow of traffic, people heading for the elevators, and I followed. "You said a large amount of EDTA was found in the blood sample you collected, didn't you? Well, if it was from receiving EDTA as a blood thinner, it would have been a small amount. A large amount would likely mean it came from a drawn blood sample. EDTA is sometimes used to keep it from clotting in the test tube."

MARCO AND I WERE invited to a summit meeting in the library. I was to be, at least temporarily, admitted to the inner circle of the investigation because I had now acquired combat equity by virtue of being fired upon by a man who was somehow connected to the smuggling business, even if we hadn't yet figured out how. On our way out to the promenade, Marco told me he'd phoned the Iráklion police station and learned Goatman was now represented by an attorney with known connections to Robert Segal, big-time antiquities smuggler and, incidentally, Brittany's boyfriend.

Luc Girard was already there, as were Agent Bondurant, Officer Villas, and Sophie. Sophie looked alert now, greeting me with a little wave. We pulled a couple of chairs around, making a sort of conversation circle. Chief Letsos was conspicuous by his elsewhereness.

Bondurant spoke first. "It's a bit out of order, I know, having Mrs. Lamb with us, but Captain Quattrocchi and I felt that, although she was mentioned as having possibly had something to do with the placement of George Gaskill's watch on the floor of Miss Benson's closet…" He paused for breath and looked toward Sophie. "Mrs. Lamb has nevertheless become the target of certain denizens of the smuggling underground, and that's what we're here to talk about.

"The funeral of Nikos Papadakos was held today, as you all know, and Dimitris—Officer Villas—and I attended. Although Papadakos had never been suspected before, he did come from an area that's a known source of smuggled artifacts. Dr. Girard has even given me the name of a man he knows is involved, and he lives in Papadakos's village."

Luc Girard nodded, his hands tented beneath his chin.

"Our only suspect in the murder, so far, has been an American passenger named Nigel Endicott, and that's because a shop owner in Mykonos picked his photo as the most likely buyer of the knife that we think probably was the one used to kill Papadakos."

"It is not a lot to go on," Marco said.

"Exactly. And we can find no connection between Endicott and Papadakos, between Endicott and antiquities, smuggling, Mykonos, photography, or anything else. He has no criminal record. He is a retired insurance adjuster and a widower who has recently moved from New York to Vermont. But we mustn't forget this happened on the island of Mykonos, and it may have nothing to do with this ship. Dimitris? Would you talk about that?"

Officer Villas said, "There is not much to tell. We have talked to a hundred people on the island. Everyone known to have been in that part of Little Venice that day, all the usual suspects, as you Americans say." He nodded at Bondurant. "And we have come up with nothing. No one we have questioned seems to have ever heard of Nikos Papadakos, in spite of the fact that he has been on the island fifty times in the last two years.

"We have also considered the possibility the killer may have been someone from his own homeland, Crete, but there is simply no way to check that. Boats, ferries, small planes, come and go between Mykonos and Crete every day. Unless someone comes forward and tells us 'I saw this man who I know is from Crete and he was talking to Papadakos,' we have no way to follow up."

Bondurant looked around at all of us and said, "Right. Now let's talk about the artifacts on this ship that, thanks to Mrs. Lamb and Dr. Girard, we now know are stolen. How many of them are there and how did they get here? This is a subject Captain Quattrocchi and I have both been investigating for some time. Dr. Girard, be specific. How many stolen items are we talking about?"

Luc Girard, who had been staring unabashedly at Sophie throughout the whole discussion of Papadakos's murder, blinked as if surprised to find himself here. "There is the Panathenaic amphora, of course. The big vessel on display in the Zeus deck bar. It was stolen from a museum on the Greek mainland and it's very important because it dates from the earliest Athenian games. Then there is the gold serpent bracelet that, until yesterday, was on display in the case outside the main dining room. It's been stolen again, and a similar-looking copy has been put in its place."

Marco interrupted to ask him several questions about the bracelet. He had been in Italy when the theft occurred and knew nothing about it.

"There is a stone-and-gilt bull's head attached to a

wooden block for display purposes," Girard continued. "It's near the embarkation door on the Athena deck. It was stolen from the Iráklion museum some five years ago. And finally, there is a red-figure krater, a two-handled bowl, in the case near the entrance to the show lounge. It is about..." With his hands, Girard indicated it was about as large as a carry-on bag. "It is beautiful. It was stolen from a well-known private collection. So there are four items we know for certain were stolen and one of them, the bracelet, has been stolen again."

Bondurant turned to Marco. "Captain Quattrocchi, as I think you all know, has made a quick trip to Milan to check the Carabinieri files on known antiquities smugglers. Captain?"

Marco said, "It rang a bell in my head when Mr. Bondurant told us the address of Brittany Benson. All of the staff and crew are asked to provide a permanent address for the ship's records so they can communicate between touring seasons. Brittany Benson gave her address as 1253 rue de Lausanne, Geneva, Switzerland. I thought that sounded familiar and when I checked our files, I found that it is also the address of Robert Segal, the American man who used to operate a huge antiquities exchange in Switzerland."

"Used to?" Bondurant asked.

"Maybe he still does. We do not know. Interpol and the Swiss police broke up his operation three years ago and raided his warehouse, but he may have set up another. Agent Bondurant also discovered that when Miss Benson moved from Florida to Lima, Peru, she shared a house with the same man, Robert Segal. I think we can safely say she is up to her neck in the smuggling of artifacts.

"Mrs. Lamb says she saw Miss Benson talking on her mobile phone this morning as the funeral line was forming on the dock and Miss Benson seemed very upset. I have said to the Iráklion police this could be how the almost-assassin of Mrs. Lamb and Miss Antonakos knew where to find them."

Marco turned to Sophie who must have been nodding off because her head jerked up when he said, "Sophie, you will probably need to return to Crete to testify in a few months. Mrs. Lamb and I will be leaving Greece in a few days, and you will be the only witness left to testify against the man who kidnapped and shot at you."

"And I also need to write a formal statement, Dotsy told me. May I fax it to them?"

"I do not know. Perhaps you should do nothing until they contact you."

This was getting tedious, I thought. We had too many bits and pieces that didn't seem to have anything to do with one another. I'd heard unsolved mysteries described as jigsaw puzzles, but if this mess were a puzzle, what would the picture on the box look like? We'd got murder and smuggling, accusations of rape, stalking, late-night phone calls, secret meetings, theft, revenge, hatred, greed, and poker. The picture on the box in my mind looked like Picasso's *Guernica.* A mish-mash of slaughter and swords and severed legs and horse's heads. The fact that we also had four law enforcement bodies—if you could count ship security, Chief Letsos et al as law enforcement—with their fingers in this pie made things even worse. If only some-one could tell us which of these bits and pieces were key and which didn't matter so much. I tuned back in to what Bondurant was saying.

"Chief Letsos followed the group that went to the Palace of Knossos today, while Dimitris and I were attending the funeral. We split up that way deliberately so we could see who was interested enough in Papadakos to go to his fu-neral and also keep an eye on our other persons of interest."

The FBI man looked at the policeman from Mykonos and, almost grinning, said, "That's another American cop phrase for you, Dimitris. Person of interest."

It occurred to me these two men had forged a friendship. They'd met only three days ago, but had worked together almost constantly since then.

"Letsos watched Ollie Osgood and Malcolm Stone throughout the tour and saw nothing unusual, but Nigel Endicott was there as well. He was a good boy all day, too. We'd like to find the brightly colored shirt he was wearing when he got his embarkation photo made. It was that shirt or one similar to it that caused the knife shop owner to pick out his photo. Unfortunately, the shop owner claims to be color-blind, and we don't know what sort of shirt Mr. Endicott was wearing while he was ashore in Mykonos anyway, but the shirt he was wearing in the photo has mysteriously disappeared. Would that be because it was spattered with blood? We asked him to show us the shirt and we searched his room. He says he thinks he sent it to be laundered but the ship's laundry doesn't have it. So in Rhodes yesterday I followed Endicott to the Turkish bath and managed to check out the contents of the backpack he was toting. I thought he might be trying to get rid of the shirt by leaving it at the bath, but I was wrong. Towels and clean underwear. No shirt."

It was way past time for me to tell them about what I'd overheard between Kathryn and Nigel. I only hoped I could tell the story without inferring more than was there. "Excuse me, but I must tell you that last night, Kathryn Gaskill was in Nigel Endicott's stateroom. I happened to walk by on the promenade and I recognized her voice through the open window. She didn't see me, I'm sure, because the light would have been in her eyes." Plus, I was hiding against the bulkhead, but I didn't mention that.

"Now, I know I could be misinterpreting it, but he was holding her. They had their arms around each other. Of course, he might simply have been comforting her over the loss of her husband. It's what I heard her say that really bothered me."

"And that was?"

"She said, 'It had to be done.'"

"What did Endicott say?"

"That's all I heard. 'It had to be done.'"

Bondurant exhaled and rose from his chair. "Well, I hope something breaks loose soon. In two more days the ship will be back in Athens and our suspects will scatter to the four winds, because we don't have enough evidence to hold anyone."

Luc Girard caught up with Marco and me on the promenade deck when the meeting broke up. "Would either or both of you like to go to Akrotiri with me tomorrow? I could give you a special tour and show you some things they don't usually let tourists see."

A special tour sounded wonderful to me, and Marco, who, I imagined, didn't even know what Akrotiri was, said he'd like to go, too. We agreed to meet tomorrow when the ship docked in Santorini. It was only ten o'clock but I was exhausted, so I asked Marco to walk me to my room.

I asked him to come in because I wanted to show him the contact lens I'd discovered. I expected to find my water glass on top of the TV but found only a fresh, clean one on the bathroom sink. Then I remembered pouring the water out through my fingers and examining the jellylike disc that remained in my hand. What had I done with the lens? Oh, yes. I'd stuck it back on top of the TV. I ran my hand across the top of the wall-mounted set and the lens, now returned to its desiccated state, popped off.

"I found this in the little unisex bathroom at the end of the hall while you were out on the deck examining the pool of blood."

"Why did you think it was worth saving?" Marco leaned over my shoulder and took it from me. I felt his warm chest against my back. The lens on the tip of his index finger, he put his other hand on my waist.

"It probably wasn't. It's just that the bathroom was so clean. It smelled of pine, as if it had been scoured a few minutes earlier. It seemed like this thing couldn't have been there long or the cleaner would have wiped it off."

"Did George Gaskill wear contact lenses?" Marco stuck the silly thing on my dressing table and turned me around to face him.

"I don't know."

He kissed me. A long, slow kiss that now seemed to have lost its threat. I knew the threat had been completely and totally in my own head all along and had nothing to do with Marco. It was my problem. To shift this burden onto Marco, a good man, was simply wrong. I let myself enjoy the kiss. Except for the whiskers! He hadn't shaved for two days and his chin felt like sandpaper. It was sweet of him, deciding to grow his beard back so I'd like him again, but this could get painful in a few minutes.

"Marco?" I whispered in his ear. "When you decided to regrow your beard, did you throw your razor away?"

"No, it is still in my room."

"Go and shave. I'll be here when you get back."

TWENTY-FIVE

MARCO AND I JOINED Lettie and Ollie at their breakfast table. I couldn't resist the temptation to tease Lettie a little. "Are you ready for the Voodoo Island, Lettie? I've heard if you ignore zombies they won't bother you."

"Give me a break, Dotsy. I got two words mixed up. So what?"

Ollie explained to Marco, who hadn't been present for the voodoo discussion, "Lettie thought Santorini was Santeria. It's a religion in the Caribbean Islands that's also called voodoo. Lettie saw Santorini in the brochure and thought we were going to an island full of zombies."

Lettie shot a withering look at Ollie and then turned to me.

"How are you feeling today, Dotsy?"

"Great! I feel great."

Marco coughed and quickly covered his mouth with his napkin.

"Your collarbone doesn't hurt? You're not wearing your brace," she said.

"Oh. My collarbone. No, it's just a little sore." Now it was my turn to change the subject. "Dr. Girard has offered to take Marco and me to Akrotiri today. That's a Minoan town on the southern tip of the island. It was uncovered recently after lying buried under volcanic ash for 3,500 years, so the ruins are in great shape—for ruins, that is. Would you two like to come along?"

Lettie and Ollie looked at each other and Lettie answered

for both of them. "Thanks, but I'd rather wander the streets and hit a few stores. Ollie wants to locate the fishermen, of course. They may have some sponges he could buy." Lettie put her hand up beside her mouth as if she were whispering an aside to me and Marco, but continued talking in a voice loud enough for Ollie to hear. "He wants to make sure he buys every sponge in the Mediterranean before we go home."

The waiter brought my omelet and fruit and replenished everyone's coffee.

Ollie said, "Have you heard about the procedure for going ashore? You can't just walk off the boat and into the town because the town's on top of this huge cliff." He leaned forward, raising his eyebrows until his forehead wrinkled along a fault line that marked where his hairline used to be. "You can take the cable car, you can take a donkey, or you can walk. But the walk is up five hundred and eighty steps."

Lettie said, "The donkey sounds like fun, Ollie. Let's do the donkeys."

"Sweetheart, the donkey hasn't been made that can carry me up five hundred and eighty steps. That would constitute cruelty to animals. Plus, my feet would drag! No, dear, I'd need a mule."

"Or a Clydesdale," Lettie said.

"I'll definitely take a cable car," I said. "My collarbone doesn't need to risk another tumble like the one I took yesterday."

Having decided we'd all take the cable car, we finished our breakfast and agreed to meet again later.

ON MY WAY TO the Poseidon deck to watch for the first glimpses of Santorini, I walked past the internet café. The attendant must have remembered me from my earlier visit to email my son Charlie, because she waved me inside. As I approached her desk, she disappeared behind it and popped back up with a pink sticky note on her index finger. "You're Dorothy Lamb, aren't you? You have mail."

She led me to a nearby computer. "Came in last night. I'll pull it up for you." She clicked through several things, stopped when she got to a screen that had Charlie's email address on the "from" line, and walked away leaving me alone with my message.

Charlie had kept working at the assignment I'd given him. Since his last message, he had looked further into George Gaskill's trial for sexual abuse of the minor child, Brittany Benson. "Mom," he wrote, "everyone I've talked to is of the opinion it was a trumped-up charge. I met several school administrators from PA at a conference last summer, so I emailed them and asked if they remembered the case. Now that the furor has died down, all seem to agree Gaskill got railroaded by the Bensons." Charlie had also attached another photo of George, one that had appeared in the newspaper at the time of the trial.

I asked the woman at the desk to print it for me and a minute later I was looking at a George Gaskill ten years younger than the one I had dinner with last week. His hair was different. Of course it would be, wouldn't it? The thinning hair of a decade ago had been augmented later by a hairpiece. The hairpiece that had floated to the surface and been picked up by the police boat. I was shocked at how much he had aged in the decade between the taking of that photo and his tragic death. I folded the picture and stuck it in my pocket.

No one I recognized was on the Poseidon deck when I walked out, although I had rather expected to find Marco or Luc Girard. Did we say we'd meet on the Poseidon deck or the promenade? I couldn't remember. I nudged myself a space at the rail and looked to the north as the volcano that was Santorini rose from somewhere beyond the horizon. The morning sun bounced off tiny white cubes, probably houses in the town of Fira, along a section of its summit. I knew from my reading that Santorini was a crescent-shaped island, its hollow center a huge caldera out of which ashes and rock had been blasted in 1450 B.C., blowing most of the island into the stratosphere. Since then, a smaller island or two, still-active volcanoes, had popped up in the middle of the caldera. The tsunami spawned by the 1450 B.C. eruption had wiped out Minoan civilization on Crete, not to mention what the explosion did to life on Santorini.

A man standing beside me at the rail told me that, like the harbor in Patmos, our ship wouldn't be able to dock, so they'd send tenders out to pick us up and take us to shore. If these tenders were the same size as the ones we'd had in Patmos, they'd be capable of taking one or two hundred people at a time.

I dug in my pocket for my lip balm and felt the photo of George. Was the photo of George and Kathryn, the embarkation photo, back on display in the photo shop? The last time I'd seen it was when Kathryn and I had given it to Demopoulos, Chief Letsos's young assistant. He'd shown it around in an effort to locate the missing man. I decided to pop back around to the photo shop and compare that picture to the one my son had sent me. The photo shop was one deck down, between the main desk and the show lounge.

As I walked in, I stopped and did a double-take. The panels of pictures had multiplied by a factor of ten, until now there was barely room to walk between them. They were arranged like a maze with sections of Mykonos shots, formal night shots, dance floor shots, bingo shots, casino shots, and embarkation shots. Those last were the ones

I wanted. It still took a few minutes to locate the one of George and Kathryn because it had been posted on a board full of formal night shots. I pulled the photo from my pocket and studied them both. The past decade had put more than ten years on George's face.

In the embarkation photo, he stood beside Kathryn, one hand around her waist, the other holding a black carry-on. He was smiling broadly, his prominent front teeth glistening in the camera's flash. I recalled how George had lisped and wondered if it was because of those teeth. They may have been temporary caps, which would explain his enunciation problems. His black goatee covered his chin to where his mustache met it at the corners of his mouth. The rest of his jaw line was bare except for a small white patch in front of his left ear. I looked closely at his ear. Was that a hole? Did George have pierced ears? He didn't seem like the type. At any rate, there was no stud or ring in it in this picture.

I moseyed around, finding my own embarkation picture, and Marco's, and Lettie and Ollie's. I looked a couple of shades lighter in the photo than I did now. I searched up and down the board until I found Nigel Endicott's embarkation picture. This would, I realized, be the shirt all the hoopla was about. The infamous "brightly colored shirt" that had now disappeared off the face of the earth, or at least off the ship, and it was indeed a brightly colored shirt, with large flowers of yellow and red.

This was the man Lettie had called the "wrong-way man." I remembered seeing him dodging down the gangway against the flow of foot traffic. Why had he been going down? One of us had suggested he might have been seeing someone off, but Ollie said only ticketed passengers were allowed through security in the terminal building below. I recalled that he'd come back aboard toting a backpack a few minutes later.

I studied Endicott's face. His hair, in spite of the gel he used to make it stick up at odd angles, looked very sparse. Salt and pepper, more gray at the temples than on top. Sturdy but stylish black-rimmed glasses and, as always, one gold earring. But wait. On his jaw line, in front of his left ear, was a smallish white something. A bit of paper? It was too irregular to be a Band-Aid. Where had I just seen that?

I flew back to George Gaskill's photo. Oh, my God! It couldn't possibly be a coincidence. Back to Nigel's picture and back to George again. Then I recalled the round, flesh-colored bandage on George's jaw line at dinner that first night. Kathryn told us George had cut himself shaving. But does a man with a goatee and mustache use a straight razor? Doesn't he usually use an electric and move it in little circles along the sides? It looked as if Nigel Endicott had cut himself and stuck a piece of tissue on his face to stop the bleeding. So had George Gaskill. In the same spot. Coincidence? No.

Nigel Endicott was George Gaskill.

I found a wall to lean against before my legs collapsed under me. I let myself slither to the floor, not caring who saw me or what they thought. George Gaskill wasn't dead. Kathryn hadn't flown to the arms of another man, only to the arms of her husband. Who killed Nikos Papadakos? As the photographer, he, more than anyone else, would have had occasion to notice what I just had. I began to see a motive for murdering the jolly man everyone liked.

I have to find Marco. I have to find Bondurant. Officer Villas. Chief Letsos. Anybody who can nab Nigel Endicott before he jumps ship.

With my head still swimming in confusion, I slithered

back up the wall. Would it be smarter to have Marco, Bondurant—whoever—paged, or go and find them myself? The main desk was only a few yards away. But no. If they did a page that went out all over the ship, it might alert Endicott something was up. I'd try the security office first, even if it meant having to explain myself to the emotionally challenged Chief Letsos.

I didn't get the chance. Sophie Antonakos, her arm sling flapping like a sail in a stiff wind, rounded the corner from the direction of the show lounge. She skidded sideways on the slick floor and stumbled forward, barely managing to keep her feet under her until I grabbed her good arm and held her steady.

"The krater is gone! The krater is gone!"

TWENTY-SIX

LUCKILY, SOPHIE AND I were only a few yards from the security office but, unluckily, when we knocked on the door, we got no response. "Forget it, Dotsy. We can't wait for someone to show up. Come. I want to show you."

Down the starboard hall and around the corner we came to the entrance to the show lounge where Sophie and Brittany's dance ensemble performed. The display case opposite the door wasn't empty and open, as I was expecting, but was neatly closed as if nothing was wrong. The object on display was no longer the red-figure ceramic krater with dancing wood nymphs and satyrs. Instead, I found myself staring at a black glazed earthenware pot much like one I could buy at my local garden center back home for $39.95.

I stood, staring dumbly, until Sophie pointed toward an area near the show lounge doors where a small pile of dirt lay on the carpet. "See? They took the potted plant that was there, and put the pot in the case. I guess they threw the plant away."

On the other side of the doors sat a similar pot with a large snake plant, its robust spikes thrusting some four feet above the rim of the pot. "I suppose it was another snake plant they threw away," I mumbled, as if the sort of plant tossed out made any difference.

"This krater was the one Luc and I discovered had been stolen from a private collection. It was sold at auction by Sotheby's in 1998 for eleven thousand dollars."

I noted Sophie's use of her mentor's first name, but said nothing about it. "Is that legal? Selling it at auction?"

"Anything with provenance documenting that it was excavated before the 1970s is exempt from the laws against buying or selling antiquities. This krater's documentation goes back to the early 1900s. So, it was legal to buy it at auction." Sophie looked at me, her brown eyes flashing. "But it was not legal to steal it!"

"We need help. Let's go back to the main desk." We dashed down the port hallway to the big counter that curved around the foyer across from the security office. Having already decided an all-call wasn't a good idea, I snagged the girl at the phone bank and said, "Call Captain Quattrocchi in room 371 and call Dr. Girard in…Sophie, do you know Luc's room number?"

Sophie blushed, then stammered, "I…I don't know the number, but it's in the hall with the ship's officers' rooms. On the Apollo deck."

I relayed this to the desk clerk. This was no time for a lengthy explanation of how she knew where Luc's room was. I was delighted to know she did, but I didn't want to talk about it now. "When you locate either of them, tell them to meet Miss Antonakos and Mrs. Lamb right here, in front of this desk. It's urgent."

"Why here?" Sophie asked.

"Because it's an easy spot to find." I turned back to the attendant. "Also try to find Agent Bondurant, the FBI man. I haven't the vaguest idea where he is, but if you see anyone going into the security office, tell them to wait for us." From the main desk, the door of the security office was clearly visible.

"If Dr. Girard isn't in his room, try the kitchen. He might be there." Sophie turned to me. "He likes to have his morning coffee with the chef. They're both French, you know." Throughout this whole thing, Sophie had been waving her broken, cast-clad arm like a cricket bat. I unfurled the sling that had been flapping uselessly around her neck and slipped her arm back in it, giving her a stern, motherly look. "Oh, no!" she said. "What about the amphora on the top deck? Do you suppose it's been stolen, too?"

"Let's go check," I said. We made a dash for the elevator. It took a maddeningly long time for one to come. The lights on the panels beside each of the four elevators indicated they were all stopping on Athena deck, which meant folks were heading for the disembarkation point, probably lining up to catch a tender boat to shore. Had we dropped anchor yet? I hadn't felt the thunks from the ship's engine that normally accompanied a stop. Once inside the elevator, I punched the button for the Zeus deck. I couldn't imagine the amphora had been stolen. It was so large, over three feet tall, a thief would have a devil of a time sneaking it away, and to walk off the ship with it? Impossible.

I debated whether to tell Sophie what I'd just discovered about George Gaskill/Nigel Endicott. It was, after all, more important than our current quest for stolen artifacts. Smuggling and theft are bad but murder is worse. I decided not to mention it yet. There'd be time for that later and now was the time to find out what had been stolen and what hadn't. "Sophie, why do you suppose these things, the bracelet and the krater, were stolen at this particular time? They've been in these display cases for years, haven't they?"

"I think it's because they know we're onto them. They sold their illegal artifacts to whoever decorates and buys the furnishings for the ship, never thinking someone would go around with a LAMBDA book and compare. In fact, the LAMBDA book probably hadn't been published at the time the sales were made."

"And they didn't count on a woman like Lettie Osgood, with her amazing powers of observation, noticing that three little spots of missing glaze were identical on both the amphora and the photo."

When the elevator stopped, Sophie and I flew across the open deck to the Zeus bar, threw open the door, and skidded to a stop in front of the tall display case.

It was empty except for a sign in big red letters standing where the amphora had been: THIS ITEM HAS BEEN TEMPORARILY REMOVED FOR RESTORATION.

Sophie seemed to shrink several sizes as she looked. She buried her face in her hand and walked around in useless little circles, moaning something in Greek that sounded like "*den catalafa.*" Was there any point in checking the bull's head in the display case downstairs? Three out of the four were missing so it was a safe bet the head was gone, too.

I dashed through to the bar. The bartender wasn't on duty yet, and the only person I could find was a little man mopping the floor. With sign language, I persuaded him to drop his mop and come out to the entryway where he looked at the empty case and scratched his head. Sophie talked to him in Greek for a minute and then turned to me. "He says he never looks at that case. He only does floors. Let's go."

When we got back to the main desk, Agent Bondurant and Luc Girard were waiting for us. They said they hadn't seen Marco. Sophie and I blurted out our stories in two simultaneous avalanches until I caught the bewildered look on Bondurant's face and shut up. I decided to let Sophie go first, and then I'd tell them about George/Nigel after they'd had a chance to absorb the facts about the thefts.

Bondurant said, "The first tender is already loading. Let's go down to the security checkpoint. We need to stop that boat. Someone may be off-loading those pots right now."

"Stairs or elevator?" I asked, trying to be economical with words.

Sophie paused. "It's two floors down from here. The stairs would be quicker."

This turned out to be right because, as the four of us flew past the bank of elevators, I saw a crowd of at least thirty people waiting for a door to open. The next floor down was the Ares, or promenade, level and there we ran into a problem. The line to disembark stretched across this foyer and down the stairs to the Athena deck. Through the open doors here, I caught a glimpse of Marco on the deck outside. I started to call to him, but Bondurant grabbed my hand and pulled me around between the people and the stairway wall. Luc and Sophie followed.

"This is no time to remember our manners," Bondurant said, dragging me along. "Excuse us," he called out to a man who had taken it upon himself to uphold the rules of fair play by stretching out his arms. "FBI, United States. Let us through."

"Bande de chameaux!" the self-appointed traffic cop shot back.

We squeezed past the crowd and fought our way to the security checkpoint. Beyond the walk-through metal detector and the open door, the fully-loaded tender pulled out leaving nothing but open sky and sea in its wake.

"Too late." Bondurant said.

"Don't worry, sir. There will be another boat soon," one of the security men told him.

Meanwhile, Luc and Sophie had slipped down the hall to the case where the polished stone bull's head was supposed to be. Sophie looked back at me and shook her head, mouthing, "Empty."

I fought against the traffic to the case on the landing that held the little Cycladic fertility statue I loved so much. She was still there, thank heaven. I turned to Luc and Sophie, who by now had caught up with me, and gave them a thumbs-up. "I saw Marco on the promenade deck. I'm going up." People were much nicer about letting me go up than they had been about letting us go down. "Marco!" I called out as I ran to him. "Were you watching the tender while it was loading? Could you see who got on?"

Marco gave me a hug before he said anything. He was so far behind in terms of news, it seemed as if it would take me all day to fill him in. But before I started, I insisted on knowing if he'd recognized anyone leaving in that first boatload.

"I could not see the entrance to the boat because they use a covered walk for people to cross over. But the top deck of the tender was about even with where I am standing here. I saw Lettie and Ollie. They waved to me."

"Did you see Nigel Endicott?"

Marco frowned. "I do not know what Nigel Endicott looks like."

"Oh, I forgot. Anyone else?"

"Villas. I saw him."

"If Villas is on the boat, then Endicott is, too," said a voice behind me. It was Bondurant, and Luc and Sophie were right behind him. "Villas is tailing Endicott today. Letsos is staying here on the ship."

"What about Brittany?" Sophie asked.

"Oh yes, Brittany Benson. I think I saw her. She was carrying a very large potted plant."

Sophie and I looked at each other and, more or less in unison, shouted, "The krater!"

"She must have stuck the snake plant in the krater," I added. "Sneaky! How do you smuggle a stolen krater off a ship? Stick a four-foot-tall plant in it and no one will notice anything but the plant."

"Miss Benson isn't supposed to leave the ship without an escort. We have to catch the next boat," Bondurant said, waving us toward the door. "Hurry."

Bondurant took off down the stairs, leaving the four of us to make our own way. By the time we got to the security checkpoint, he had already flashed his badge at the guards and explained this was an emergency. The next tender pulled alongside our ship and we were the first aboard.

But we seriously needed to have a meeting. I was the only one who knew the whole situation, and I had no idea how to proceed from here.

THE FIVE OF US GATHERED in a corner of the tender's lower deck, in the covered cabin section beneath the upper deck. Both fore and aft of the cabin were open decks. Marco pulled a plastic chair into the V formed by the benches along two walls, so we could sit in a rough circle.

I began. "We have big problems. Marco, you don't know what's going on, and you other three know we're chasing stolen antiquities, but you don't know what I'm about to tell you. George Gaskill is not dead."

Four shocked faces stared back at me.

"George Gaskill is, in fact, Nigel Endicott. I know this because I've been studying the pictures in the photo shop and, unless you can believe that both men, one with a goatee, cut themselves shaving at the same time, in the same exact spot, and that both tried to stop the bleeding by sticking identical bits of tissue on their faces, you must agree. I told all of you last night I'd seen Kathryn and Nigel together, in Nigel's room. In each other's arms. You see? Kathryn was actually in the arms of her own husband."

"Impossible. They look nothing alike," said Bondurant.

"Have you ever seen George Gaskill?"

"Well, no."

"Have any of you seen both George Gaskill and Nigel Endicott?"

Silence. None of them had.

"I have, and I'm telling you the only difference between the two men is the goatee and the glasses and the hairline. And the hairstyle." I visualized each man as I went on. "Nigel always wears an earring in his left ear, but George's ear may have been pierced, who knows? George's front teeth were more prominent than Nigel's, but that could have been a plate. He lisped, probably because he wasn't used to it."

"Endicott has a tattoo on his arm," Bondurant said.

"Gaskill wore long sleeves," I pointed out. "And we know he wore a hairpiece. You have it in an evidence bag. I tell you, Nigel Endicott is George Gaskill without the hairpiece, the teeth, or the goatee."

My four friends sat and stared, as if they were putting all this together in their heads. Marco reached over and took my hand but said nothing. Luc looked at Sophie, who didn't lift her gaze from the floor. Bondurant cleared his throat, and turned toward the starboard windows, as if he wished he were somewhere other than here.

I waited for what seemed like fifteen minutes, then broke the silence myself. "Somebody say something."

"It defies all reason."

"Maybe there was a speck of something on the camera lens."

"If both men were really the same man, it would mean Kathryn Gaskill knew all about it and said nothing."

"What about the watch they found in Brittany's closet?" Sophie asked. "Are you saying Nigel Endicott left it there?"

The look on her face made it plain she didn't believe me and I saw no support for my idea on the faces of either Girard or Bondurant. I looked at Marco. He looked as if he was embarrassed for me. I felt his hand go slack.

"Kathryn could have done it," I suggested.

"It's too fantastic, Dotsy." Luc Girard wouldn't look me straight in the eye. "As one involved in research, you must know the Principle of Occam's Razor. It says the simplest solution is almost always the right one. What you've proposed is too incredibly twisted to possibly be right."

I fought back. "If you're going to cite Occam's Razor, cite the whole thing! It says, when faced with several possible solutions, the simplest one, no matter how improbable it is, is the right one. My solution is improbable, I'll grant you, but it's a hell of a lot simpler than anything you guys have come up with to explain why a man's blood is all over a deck, why his watch turns up in the closet of the girl he was once accused of raping, and why a tourist in a 'hey-look-at-me' shirt pops into a knife shop on a remote island in the Aegean Sea, buys a knife, and then uses it to carve up a photographer!"

Embarrassed silence all around. I thought about what I'd just said and only regretted the little hula dance I'd done to illustrate the shirt. This hurt. Not that they didn't believe me but that they felt sorry for me. I could feel it.

Bondurant said, "Nigel Endicott has a passport. George Gaskill had a passport. You can't enter Greece or any other country and hand the immigration officer two passports. It's one per customer. Nigel Endicott's passport indicates he flew from the U.S. to Turkey the same day George Gaskill flew from the U.S. to Athens and each of those flights takes at least nine hours. It's impossible for all that to have been done by one man." He paused long enough for that to sink in, then went on in a soft, condescending voice. "The FBI has run a check on both Endicott and Gaskill. Both men have jobs, Social Security numbers, credit cards, phone numbers, addresses, even wives…except that Endicott is a widower. His wife died some five years ago."

"Excuse me." I stood up and made a dash for the other side of the cabin where I'd seen a door with the universal "Women's" sign. I couldn't let them see me cry. The door was locked, so I found a space nearby where I could stand and keep my back to my four turncoat companions. I waited. I heard rustling noises that told me the toilet was occupied, but someone was taking a long time.

The tender was fully loaded now and had pulled away from the *Aegean Queen*. Through the short breezeway flanked by the bathroom doors, I glimpsed the horizon, and as the boat swung around to enter the caldera along whose rim the town of Fira nestled, I saw great strips of red rock, black rock, and tan rock, running more or less horizontally along the crater wall, like layers in one of those sand pictures with shifting sands between two layers of glass. The various colors were from different eruptions, I guessed. I played with that idea for a while to get my mind off the fool I'd made of myself. I still thought I was right, although I had to admit I didn't have enough evidence to make a convincing case.

Whoever was in the bathroom was taking an impossibly long time. I found a shred of tissue in my pocket, wiped my eyes, blew my nose, and returned to my seat.

All eyes were on Marco and no one seemed to notice I was back. Marco, his eyes glittering, slapped himself on the forehead and shouted, "That is right! Now that I think about it, there was something very familiar about the man. Of course, I was looking down on him from the promenade. He was standing on the lower deck of the tender, so I was looking down on the top of his head. But

I have seen pictures of Robert Segal in the files of the Carabinieri. In fact, I was looking at his photograph only two days ago, when I was in Milano."

Robert Segal? Brittany's boyfriend? Was he here?

"What about the box? What did it look like?" Bondurant ad dressed this question to Marco, then turned to me to explain. "Captain Quattrocchi remembers seeing a man with a large box standing on the lower deck of the tender that took the first load of passengers. We think it may have been Miss Benson's boyfriend."

"I wish I had looked at the box more, but I did not know it would be important. It was dark, I remember. Possibly wood or metal painted black. It was more than a meter long, and at least a half-meter wide and deep." Marco showed us with his hands. "He carried it by a handle, like a guitar case, you know?"

"More than a meter long? Then it would have been large enough to hold the amphora," Luc said.

"Did he appear to be with Miss Benson?"

"No, he was on the lower deck. Miss Benson was sitting on the top deck with the potted plant beside her. You are right, Dotsy. I did not even look at the pot. I only noticed the very tall plant."

"He probably used some ruse or other to get onto the ship and pick up the box," Luc said. "Probably told them he was picking up a cello or something for repairs. Oh, he is a clever one!"

With a big clunk, the tender shifted into neutral and a young man in coveralls dashed past us to the stern rail and grabbed a dock line. Almost time to disembark. There was confusion all around the cabin as passengers grabbed their belongings and their children. Bondurant suggested we move to the rail on the outside deck and remove ourselves from the hubbub so we could talk.

Once we were all gathered around him again, Bondurant began talking slowly and deliberately as if weighing each word. "On Santorini we may lose them because there's an airport, not to mention a dozen small towns where they could hide. In Fira, the town on the cliff overlooking the harbor, the streets are all pedestrianized. Only foot traffic and donkeys. But behind that part, the picturesque part, you've got the town's main square with a bus terminal and roads leading out in all directions. One road goes to the local airport. If either Segal—if that's who he is—or Miss Benson suspects we're after them and they get as far as that square, we've as good as lost them."

It seemed odd to me that an American would know so much about Santorini until I recalled Bondurant was stationed at our embassy in Athens. He may have lived in Greece for years and made any number of trips to the island.

"There are three ways to go from this dock to the town. You've got the cable cars." He pointed somewhere to his left but, as the boat was still shifting in its berth, we couldn't actually see the cable cars. "And the winding path you can see up there." He pointed a bit more to the right and we all turned to look.

"Omigod!" I said. I saw a portion of the path zigzagging, switching back and forth up the craggy face of the caldera. From where we stood it appeared to be miles long and bounded by nothing much to keep the climber from tumbling to his death if he slipped. With my fear of heights, I knew I couldn't handle that on foot or on donkey.

"I think we can assume, with their heavy loads, both Segal and Miss Benson will take a cable car. Now, we do have an ally. Dimitris Villas is already here because he's supposed to be keeping an eye on Nigel Endicott. Villas has a cell phone with him so I'll call him in a minute and find out if he's in Fira, on the way up, or still down below.

Sometimes there's a long line for the cable car. We have to take both Benson and Segal into custody, but we must do it without letting the things they're carrying get broken. Both the amphora and the krater are extremely breakable and irreplaceable.

"Here's what I suggest. I want Dr. Girard and Captain Quattrocchi to grab a cable car as fast as they can. Break in line, guys. Whoever you piss off, we'll settle with them later. Meanwhile, I'll call Villas and find out where he is. If he's already up top, I'll get him to start hunting. Keep an eye on Endicott, of course, but look for the other two. I'm going to stay down here because, if our suspects find out we're after them, they might catch the next cable car going down.

"Now, Mrs. Lamb and Miss—oh, hell—Dotsy and Sophie. You need to stand in line like good citizens, scanning the line ahead of you for our suspects, of course, and take a cable car to the top. Then split up. One of you should stay at the cable car exit and the other should locate the top end of the donkey path. Watch to make sure neither of them tries to escape by either route. When I know for sure that they're up there, I'll come up and we'll have six people looking for two. But it's a maze of tiny streets up there. Even with six of us, it won't be easy."

I had to interrupt. "I don't know what Segal looks like. How would I know if he's sneaking away down the donkey path or not?"

Bondurant sighed. "If he's carrying a black suitcase about the size of a refrigerator, that might be a clue." His tone was blatantly sarcastic.

Marco said, "I think he was wearing dark clothing. Dark trousers, dark shirt. But he has blond hair. That might help."

"One more thing," I said. "Ollie and Lettie Osgood are also up there. If we run into them, they'll help us."

"Be a bit strange, getting a suspect in one case to help you catch suspects in another case. But, sure. We may need all the help we can get." Bondurant stopped and took a deep breath. "Now, who has a cell phone with them?"

Luc and Marco both pulled phones out of their pockets.

"Good. Let's input each other's numbers and get moving."

I looked around and realized we were the last folks left on the boat.

TWENTY-SEVEN

DAVID BONDURANT GROANED when he saw the line for the cable cars. It snaked along the shoreline from the entrance at the ticket booth all the way back to the dock. What he couldn't see was that, inside the building at the base of the cable, the line continued, winding through a labyrinth of halls. Another hundred or so folks inched along inside, sweltering in the heat from the tropical sun beating down on the roof and the sweat of a hundred bodies, a hundred pairs of lungs sucking out whatever oxygen remained. Marco and Luc had quickly disappeared into the entrance and beyond his line of sight. Dotsy and Sophie had taken their place at the end of the line, as he told them to do.

The foot path snaked up the cliff to the right of the cable. From his vantage point Bondurant could see some stretches of the path but not others. Donkeys wound their doleful way both up and down, outnumbering the humans who plodded along on foot. People walking down seemed to be evenly divided between those walking alone and those who were riding or leading a riderless donkey down to pick up another tourist. In places the path switched back and disappeared behind jutting rocks.

Bondurant flipped open his phone and punched Villas's number on his speed dial.

"Bondurant here. I'm at the ferry dock. Where are you?"

Villas answered in his heavily accented English, "I'm in a cable car halfway up the mountain. It took me nearly an hour to get through the line, and now the damn thing has stopped."

From where Bondurant stood, he could see six cable cars, like pearls on a string, partway up the mountain and another cluster of six on the descending part of the loop. "Where's Endicott?"

"He's two cars ahead of me."

"Look. We've got a situation here. We're chasing two folks who're trying to abscond with stolen artifacts from the ship. Nothing to do with the murders, we think, but we need your help. Have you seen Brittany Benson? She'd be carrying a very large potted plant. And a man dressed in black—blond hair—carrying a huge black case?"

"Yes, I have. Miss Benson and her plant were on the tender with me coming over…"

There was a pause. Bondurant said, "What's that? Hello?"

"Sorry. We started moving again and it surprised me. The man with the suitcase. He's about four cars ahead of me."

"Right now? He's on his way up right now?"

"Yes, and we'll all be there in about one minute."

"Listen carefully, Villas. Here's what I want you to do."

MARCO AND LUC, both dripping with sweat, bullied their way past two hundred people and to the front of the line. There, Marco turned and shouted to the sea of scowling faces behind them. "We are sorry! We are policemen and we are trying to catch someones. Thank you for your patience!"

His cell phone jangled. "*Pronto.* Quattrocchi."

"How's it going, Captain?" Bondurant said.

"We are at the top of the line. We will be on the next cars going up."

"Did you pass Miss Benson on your way?"

"No."

"Anyone else you recognized?"

"No. No one."

"Our man with the box, and Endicott and Villas as well, are on the lift now."

"Are they all in the same car?"

"No, three different cars. Now, look. When you and Girard get off up top, find Villas. Try to cover the area between the lift and the city square as well as between the lift and the donkey path."

"Right."

I COULD HARDLY STAND the thought of waiting in the interminable line at the back of which Sophie and I found ourselves. The sun beat down and the line was barely moving. Yanking off her sling, Sophie tried to blow air into her arm cast. We'd both worn shorts and our four legs, with their antiseptic-gold and bruise-purple splotches, were attracting stares and comments. For the first time since breakfast, I thought about my cracked collarbone and how much it hurt. I had intended to wear the clavicle brace today, but I hadn't had a chance to go back to my room after breakfast. Sophie squinted up the hill toward the donkey path as if she was getting ready to suggest going that route. If she did, I had news for her. My aging legs would not make that trip and the last time I tried to climb a cliff like it, I'd had a panic attack. I'd scooted on my butt down a half-mile of trail, clinging to every sapling along the way.

"Dotsy, look! It's Brittany!"

It took a minute to see where she pointed, but she was right. On the trail above us, a white donkey trotted along, a girl with tousled auburn curls and a large potted plant on his back. *We'll never catch her,* I thought. Sophie, however, had already taken off toward the path.

At the foot of the path, a row of donkeys awaiting riders stood tethered to a rail. The path itself, I noted, was divided into broad, flat steps made of cemented cobblestones speckled with donkey poop. Hundreds and hundreds of piles of donkey poop. There was a retaining wall along the outside side of the trail but it wasn't nearly high enough to assuage my acrophobia. I had no choice, though, did I? I looked around and couldn't see Sophie anywhere.

"How much for a donkey?" I asked a man, and then realized I had no money with me. I'd have to walk, but I knew I'd never catch her that way. I considered stealing the one at the end of the row. The one that looked like Eeyore.

Like an angel, Sophie reappeared behind me. "I paid the man for two donkeys, Dotsy. Let's go." She had a bit of trouble swinging with only one arm into the saddle, but when she looked fairly settled, I put the reins in her good hand.

An attendant already had my donkey untethered and ready. I mounted, nudged the little animal with my foot, and together we took off up the side of the caldera. I passed Sophie almost immediately. She didn't look as if she knew much about riding, but I, having grown up on farmland in the Shenandoah Valley of Virginia, was in my element. This animal and I understood each other. If only we weren't clopping up the side of a sheer cliff. I steered my steed to the inside of the trail and he responded by scraping my right leg against the red pumice rock. As pain shot up through my leg, my right arm caught the full impact of the next protruding boulder.

I couldn't tell how far ahead Brittany was, because, as we rounded a sharp bend, we found ourselves at the back of a four-donkey caravan. I kicked my long-eared friend out into the passing lane, although the path, no more than ten feet wide, scarcely allowed room for two donkeys with riders to pass. My little guy loved it. It was as if he said to himself, "Finally! A rider who knows what she's doing, and she wants me to haul ass! Watch this." We passed the whole line in a flash, taking the next stretch at a virtual gallop.

I forced myself not to think about the hundreds of feet of open air between me and the sea below, or to think about our chances of slipping on a pile of donkey poop and my donkey's hooves flying out from under him. The woman on the last donkey we had to pass was Kathryn Gaskill. I turned abruptly and looked over my shoulder. I'd certainly have missed seeing her if I hadn't been determinedly not looking out to sea. Kathryn was talking on her cell phone as her donkey plodded upward.

Before rounding the next bend, a hairpin turn, I looked up and saw Brittany some twenty feet above me. Unfortunately, she also saw me, removing all hope I might sneak up on her. She nudged her donkey to hurry. I looked down the path behind me and caught a glimpse of Sophie, some thirty yards back and weaving dangerously in her saddle.

"Go!" I kicked my donkey into high gear and we flew around the hairpin turn so quickly I had Brittany's donkey by the reins before he even had a chance to respond to his rider's command. "I need that krater, Brittany."

She tried to jump off the right side of her donkey because I was close on its left but there wasn't room. She'd have hit the caldera wall. Sliding off the rear end, she hit the ground hard, wobbled, and the krater in her arms swayed forward. The tips of the snake plant's tall spikes grazed my cheek. I hopped off and tried to grab both her and the krater, desperate to stabilize the careening spikes, but to no avail. The krater, snake plant and all, flew out of her hands and over the side of the retaining wall. I felt sick. After all this, the krater was gone, smashed to bits, and it was my fault. If I hadn't forced her off her donkey, it wouldn't have happened.

"Efharisto!"

I jerked around and looked downward in the nick of time to witness Sophie Fumblefingers, Sophie Stumblebunny, her feet firmly set in the stirrups, rise off her saddle and pluck the flying krater from the air with one hand. The snake plant flopped out and onto the path, but the krater snuggled against her chest, encircled by the arc of her one good arm.

Brittany, having no choice but to continue on to the top, remounted and left. I didn't need to escort her, only keep an eye on her. I waited until a very shaken and shaking Sophie rounded the bend and caught up with me. I took the krater from her and congratulated her on the most spectacular catch I'd ever seen.

Rounding the next-to-last turn before reaching the top, I looked up ahead and saw Brittany. She was on her cell phone. "Oh, no," I said to Sophie. "She's telling her boyfriend we're onto them."

VILLAS HOPPED OUT OF his cable car as soon as its automatic door swung open. All the cars in the six-car cluster opened simultaneously, and all their passengers stepped out onto stairs leading up and out into the town. Since both Segal and Endicott were in cars ahead of his, he expected to simply follow them out but, from there, they'd probably head off in different directions and he'd have a decision to make.

But as soon as Segal and his big suitcase hit the stairs, he bolted, taking the stairs two at a time. When Endicott stepped out, he glanced briefly down toward the car on the end, and then took off, pushing the other off-loading passengers aside as he flew up the stairs and around a corner.

"BRITTANY, WE HAVE A BUNCH of men out looking for your boyfriend," I said, "so why don't you make things easier for both of you? Tell me where he is, and we can wrap this thing up."

"I don't know what you're talking about."

We found a taverna with outdoor seating near the top of the donkey path, where it widened out into a small plaza. I set the krater under one of its tables so Sophie could guard it with her legs while she sat and ordered a drink. Meanwhile, keeping Brittany with me, I turned in the three donkeys. "Your boyfriend, Rob Segal. We know he's here on the island and he has the amphora from the ship with him."

"Oh, that's right. You know all about my love life from snooping through my room, don't you?"

"I wouldn't have known what your boyfriend looked like, though. For that, we needed Captain Quattrocchi of the Italian Carabinieri, who spotted him and recognized him as an international antiquities smuggler. Small world, isn't it?" I patted my dear little donkey friend on the neck and thanked him for his help.

"Hey, maybe he's the one who planted George Gaskill's watch in my room. Or could that have been you?" Brittany's cute little turned-up nose turned up a bit higher.

"Not me."

I looked over Brittany's shoulder and glimpsed Kathryn Gaskill hurrying by, now on foot. There was something odd about the way she hurried by. She had no reason not to say hi to me and she couldn't have failed to see me standing there. No reason unless she knew I was onto her. But how could she know that? Her walk was a little too casual, though, and her head turned a little too much toward a perfectly ordinary stone wall. She sped up just a tiny bit after she passed me, and I knew. I knew she knew.

I had to catch her.

Could I leave Brittany in Sophie's care? I thought not. Sophie, with only one usable arm, had enough to do guarding the krater. Brittany might even be of some help to me. "Look, Brittany. You and your boyfriend are caught. There's nothing you can do about that. We've got four big, beefy men on his trail, but I need to catch Kathryn Gaskill, who is currently heading down the alley ahead of us, and I need to find the man who's going by the name of Nigel Endicott. If you help me, I'm pretty sure I can get you off the hook in the Gaskill murder. Are you interested?"

"What are you talking about?"

"I'll explain later. Come on." Kathryn had considerately worn an orange shirt today so tracking her would be easy. If I could keep her from finding out we were following her, I knew she would lead us to Endicott. "Stay back. We don't want Kathryn to know we're after her."

At the end of the alley, Kathryn turned onto a narrow street lined with shops. I stayed well back, pretending to window-shop whenever Kathryn, about a block ahead of us, did likewise. People walking in both directions, stopping, chatting, kids darting in and out, made for enough confusion between us and Kathryn that I didn't think she'd spot us unless she was looking for us. She slipped into a jewelry store.

Brittany and I waited at the window of a leather goods shop for Kathryn to reappear.

"Now, can you explain what this is all about?" Brittany asked.

"Let's just say I've reason to believe George Gaskill wasn't murdered at all, and if he wasn't murdered, you can't be charged with murdering him."

Kathryn reappeared and crossed to the other side of the street, but she glanced ever so quickly in our direction, then turned, heading up the street away from us. Had she spotted us? Did she know we were behind her when she went into the store? I looked around to make sure Brittany was still with me, and collided with a baby in a stroller. I apologized to the mother, cooed something to the baby, who looked startled but unharmed, and resumed my pursuit.

In that short time, no more than an instant, Kathryn had disappeared.

"Where did she go?"

But Brittany was exchanging admiring glances with a couple of continental-type hunks lounging suavely outside a sweet shop. She shrugged and said, "Who? Oh! I don't know. I missed it."

In this little cliffside town, every street no wider than an alley, every alley running either uphill or down, every slope offset by jutting buildings and overhanging terraces spilling bougainvillea over their sides, a person could get lost in five seconds. My only chance was to keep moving forward and look for orange shirts. We went up a street and down a winding alley, down a spiral stairway, across a tiny plaza, and up another street. At the next intersection, salvation!

"Dotsy! Yoo-hoo!" Lettie called from up ahead.

Dragging Brittany by the arm, I ran to Lettie, keeping an eye on Ollie's bald head sticking up above the crowd. "Kathryn Gaskill. Have you seen her?" I spluttered out between gasps.

"Hello, Brittany," Ollie said, smiling. Just like a man, to ignore my desperate plea and smile at the pretty girl.

Dear, observant Lettie came through for me. "Kathryn? She went that-a-way." Lettie pointed up a long, winding alley on my right. "She went into the last door up there on the left-hand side."

It turned out to be a restaurant. Lettie was certain this was where Kathryn had gone, but I could see a maître d' lurking, menus in hand, inside the door. This wasn't the sort of place where they'd let you come in and look around. They'd expect you to eat. "Anybody hungry?" I asked. "I'm about to die of thirst. Who'd like to buy me a drink? I'm temporarily embarrassed by a shortage of funds." Put that way, they could hardly refuse.

The maître d' had no trouble finding us a table for four, as there were few patrons. I looked around for Kathryn but she wasn't there. There was, however, a table set for one with a small bowl of tsatziki and chips and one glass of water, and it was vacant. A napkin lay across the seat of a chair that had been pulled back recently because it was in the waiter's way. He pushed the chair forward and laid the napkin on the tablecloth as he walked by.

He explained the menu to us and took our orders for water, beer, and coffee.

"Lettie, I think Kathryn's in the bathroom," I said. "I'm going to check." The ladies' room was down a short hall that also led to the kitchen and to a back entrance. I opened the bathroom door and peeked in. Mirror, sink, towel dispenser, two rather nice marble-slab stalls, a vase of fresh flowers on the vanity. No Kathryn. "Damn!" I said out loud. I looked under the stall doors and saw one pair of feet but they couldn't have been Kathryn's because they were shod in red platform wedges.

I stood on tiptoes and peered out the window over the towel dispenser. Outside, a tiny alley with garbage cans and a couple of cats. No Kathryn. "Damn, damn, damn!"

A toilet flushed, the stall door opened, and a delicate little lavender-scented woman stepped out. "Are you looking for someone?" she asked in a voice I pegged as coming from Boston. "I couldn't help hearing your damns."

"I'm looking for a friend of mine. She's short with dark hair and she's wearing an orange shirt. I thought she came in here."

"She's gone to the Archaeology Museum. The one near the cable car."

I could only stare at her.

The woman laughed and dodged around me to the sink.

"She was here a minute ago, when I came in. She was on the phone, and I heard her say, 'How am I supposed to find the Archaeology Museum?' and 'Across from the cable car exit?' Whoever was on the other end apparently explained how to find it and she dashed out."

"Thank you so much," I said. "I don't know how anybody ever finds anything in this place. So confusing." Back in the hallway, I slipped down to the other end and opened the door onto the alley. It wasn't locked, so Kathryn could have gone out this way instead of returning to her table. I knew she hadn't gone out the front door and now, it would seem, she had seen us, called Endicott, and split.

Back at our table, I caught Brittany trying to make a phone call. She looked up, saw me, and meekly closed the little device. Obviously, she'd been trying to call Segal. I chided myself for not warning Ollie and Lettie of that possibility before I went to the ladies' room. When I explained what I'd learned in the bathroom, Ollie cancelled his sandwich order and paid for the drinks. Meanwhile, I grabbed Brittany by the wrist, gave her my most intimidating motherly glare, and said, "The Archaeology Museum by the cable car station. We need to get there fast, and you'd better lead us straight to it. No detours, no phone calls. Do you think you can handle that?"

DASHING OUT OF the cable car station, Luc Girard and Marco heard Villas call to them from somewhere above their heads. They spied him, standing at the rail of a hotel terrace on top of a cliff north of the cable, from which vantage point he commanded a wide view. They located a winding stairway that led up to the terrace and joined the frustrated policeman from Mykonos now charged with the responsibility of following two men who, unfortunately, had run off in different directions. Of the three, only Girard was familiar with the layout of the town. Villas pointed out the directions he thought his quarry had fled—Segal to the east, roughly the direction of the main square, Endicott to the north. "I don't know why either man ran. Why did Endicott run away? He's used to being followed. And why did the other man run? He doesn't even know who I am."

"Segal is probably headed for the bus station or the taxi stand," Girard said. "I don't know where Endicott is, but since you're supposed to be following him, I'd suggest you go north. Marco and I will try to find Segal. I know the layout of the town and Marco knows what Segal looks like."

Villas said, "You can't miss him even if you don't know his face. He's carrying a huge black case."

"We need to know your mobile number," Marco said. Villas pulled out his phone and exchanged his number with those of Marco and Girard.

THE ARCHAEOLOGY MUSEUM charged a three euro admission, which Ollie had to pay for all four of us. Inside, we split up. *It would be easy for us to check out the whole place,* I thought, because it was a small building. I described Kathryn and Nigel to the woman at the front desk and learned the woman with the orange shirt had, indeed, come in a few minutes earlier. A man, not unlike my description of Nigel, had come in earlier but he might or might not have left already. She couldn't remember.

Taking my captive, Brittany, along with me, I made a sort of counter-clockwise circuit of the rooms while Ollie went the other way and Lettie stayed near the front door. There was no way Kathryn Gaskill could escape me now. But I ran into Ollie before I ran into Kathryn.

"Where can she be? She can't possibly have left," I said. "I know! The bathroom." I located the ladies' room, positive for the second time in less than a half-hour that I was about to face Kathryn Gaskill in the loo, but the loo was vacant. I moped back out, shaking my head.

Ollie said, "I'll bet she's in the men's room," and turned, heading for the door with the masculine icon. He walked in but held the door open while he checked around. Turning back to Brittany and me, he raised one finger to his lips and motioned for us to follow him in.

A urinal along one wall, a stall beside it, and a sink beside that. It appeared the room was empty, but Ollie pointed to the gap between the stall and the floor. I saw two feet wearing men's shoes, but rather than toes pointing toward the door, they were pointed in the opposite direction.

Ollie craned his neck to peer over the top of the door and said, "Mr. Endicott, I presume. And Mrs. Gaskill! Fancy meeting you here."

Nigel and Kathryn tried to bolt but, as soon as they saw Brittany and me, they were drawn up short. Ollie had both of them firmly by the collar.

TWENTY-EIGHT

To THE EAST THE LAND beneath the town of Fira rose, then crested at a broad, paved road running north—south and roughly dividing the tourist part of town from the part where the real people lived. Marco followed Luc Girard up dozens of steps. They stopped to catch their breath when they reached the top. Down the road to the right, they could see a white sugar-cube building with a sign on top that said TAXI in English, with the Greek equivalent in smaller letters.

"The bus station is beyond the taxi place," said Luc. From where they stood, the tops of two buses could be seen above the roof of the TAXI. "There is a bus that runs south, to the airport and to Akrotiri, every hour during the day. If Segal has taken a taxi, he may have already left, but if he's waiting for a bus, we may still catch him."

"What about Brittany? We know they were not together when he came up in the cable car. I think they will have to find each other before either of them goes anywhere. They may be planning to meet at the bus station."

"Good point. Let's go."

"Wait!" Marco threw up both hands, like a traffic cop. "What will we do with him, or them, when we find them?"

"Arrest them."

"We cannot do that. First of all, we do not have a warrant. Second, I do not have any authority in Santorini and neither do you. You are an archaeologist. Third, we do not have any handcuffs."

"I see," said Luc, stroking his goatee. "We could ask the local police to help us. Their station is somewhere nearby, I believe."

"The Fira police cannot arrest them. There is no warrant, no extradition papers, and they have not violated any local laws. They have stolen artifacts off a cruise ship that is owned by people from God knows where."

"Call Bondurant. Ask him what he suggests."

Marco called the number Bondurant had given him. "I am hearing the engaged signal. He is talking to someone." He rang off, stuffed his hands in his shorts pockets, and rocked back on his heels. "Come." He headed down the road toward the bus station but stopped well shy of it. There was no indoor waiting room here, only a small information kiosk and a few trees under which passengers could wait. There, on a bench beside the kiosk, sat a blond man. Beside him lay a big black case.

Marco grabbed Luc by the arm. "Wait a minute. I have an idea."

OFFICER VILLAS WAS on the phone with Bondurant.

"I was looking for Endicott in the north part of town when he passed me going south. He hasn't spotted me yet, but he sort of sneaked around past the cable car entrance and now he's gone into the Archaeology Museum."

"Very good. I suggest you stay with him now. Try to find out why he bolted like that. I'm on my way up the hill right now, so if you hear from Girard or Quattrocchi, tell them to call me."

"Right, sir."

"Seen Brittany Benson yet?"

"No, I haven't. Oh, there is an admission charge for the museum. I hope I have enough money to get in."

"Flash your badge, man!" Bondurant said with a deep sigh.

Luc walked casually up to the bench where Rob Segal sat and said, "Going to the airport?"

Rather than giving an answer, Segal looked up at him and squinted into the sun as if to say, "What's it to you?"

"I ask that because it's where I need to go and I just heard the next bus will not run. It'll be an hour before the next one."

Segal exhaled loudly. "Well, that's fine!" His accent was American. "I have a five o'clock flight and it's—what?—two-thirty already."

Luc pushed at the black case with his foot. "The last time I saw a man traveling with a suitcase that big, it turned out he had a mummy in it. You have a mummy in there?"

Segal shifted the case away from Luc's foot and glared at him. "No."

Luc bent as if he were preparing to sit on the case.

Segal shifted his body and patted the bench beside him. "Have a seat."

"Well, I think I'm going to take a cab to the airport. Costs more than the bus, but I hate the thought of waiting here for another hour." He turned toward the road behind him. "I don't know why they've canceled the bus, but I'd bet it has something to do with the smuggler they're after."

Segal's pale face flushed crimson. "What smuggler?"

"No idea. I walked by the police station on my way over here and there were a half-dozen cops out front. I heard them say something about a man trying to smuggle a pot out of the country." He waited for that to sink in. "Interested in sharing a ride to the airport?"

"Right. I don't feel like waiting here any longer, either. Not with a five o'clock flight." Segal grabbed the case and headed toward the taxi stand.

On the opposite side of the road, a man in a black cap

stood behind a cab. He was reading a newspaper. He looked up as Segal and Girard crossed the bus station parking area and shouted, "Taxi? You want to go to airport? Ten euros, I take you to airport!"

"Right."

The man in the black cap popped open the trunk by using the remote on his key ring, and grabbed Segal's case. At the same time, he opened one of the back doors and said, "Hop in."

Segal climbed into the back seat, which was separated from the front by a Plexiglas partition, and Girard, rather than climbing in behind him, slammed the door. The man in the black hat clicked all the doors locked, removed his hat, and peeked into the back seat at a dumbfounded Rob Segal.

"Thank you for the amphora, Mister Segal," Marco said. "And the next time you want to take a taxi, remember. Real cab drivers do not wear shorts."

THE TENDER TOOK a silent bunch back to the ship. Rob Segal and Brittany announced they were clamming up until they spoke to their lawyer, and the only thing Bondurant got out of them was the key to the black case. Ollie and Lettie, beyond their part in the museum caper, still didn't know what was going on. Villas followed Endicott around the boat because, in spite of everything, he still had no probable cause to handcuff or arrest him. Marco and I walked out on the stern deck and watched Santorini shrink toward the horizon.

"I didn't get to see Akrotiri today and yesterday I didn't get to see the Palace of Knossos. I'm going to have to do this cruise again sometime."

Marco slid one arm around my waist and squeezed. He kissed my temple, then turned his face back to the sea.

"I wish we had a few more days together. Could you fly with me to Florence tomorrow? I could show you places the tourists do not know about."

I paused a moment. I had to be sure I really meant the offer that was on the tip of my tongue. "Why don't you wait a couple of days before you fly back? Lettie and Ollie and I are staying in Athens until Thursday. We have rooms at the Grande Bretagne."

"I am impressed."

"They'll treat you like a king."

"I will call the caserma and ask if they can manage without me until Thursday."

I turned away from the rail and kissed him. "Do you believe me now? That Nigel Endicott is George Gaskill, reincarnated?" I could hardly believe it, but Marco didn't answer me. *What will it take to convince these blockheads?* "Come on, Marco! We found him in a bathroom stall with Kathryn! Kathryn was crouched on the rim of the potty in a fetal position and he was holding her to keep her from falling off. If that wasn't a husband and wife trying to avoid discovery, then it had to be a brand-new widow having a pretty bizarre rendezvous with a man she met four days ago. Which of those is more believable?"

Marco raised his eyebrows but said nothing.

"Even if you believe Kathryn has flown straight into the arms of a new lover, the bathroom stall thing still makes no sense. If they were that hot to be together, why didn't they stay on the boat where they have two lovely rooms? Or wait until they got back this afternoon?" I realized I was shouting and lowered my voice. "And, Marco, they were both fully dressed."

"There are still so many things that cannot be explained by saying, 'George Gaskill did not die. He turned himself into Nigel Endicott.' What about the blood? I am sure the

DNA test will tell us the blood was George Gaskill's, so what do you think he did? Go out on the deck, cut himself, smear the blood around to make it look like a fight, and then calmly walk back inside and turn himself into Nigel Endicott? Dotsy, there was at least a half liter of blood. If he had cut himself that badly, he would have had to get medical attention, or he would have bled to death. That blood was not from a little cut!"

A half-liter of blood. That part of Marco's tirade echoed through my head and I did a rough metric-to-English conversion. That would be about a pint of blood. A pint of blood. Give a pint of blood. Help to save a life.

"That's it! What if George had a pint—I mean a half-liter—of his own blood with him? Wasn't he scheduled for surgery right after this vacation? Heart surgery? People sometimes stockpile their own blood before surgery, for safety reasons. If he did that, who's to say he didn't bring a bag of his own blood with him? Oh, dear. Would they let you bring blood on a plane?"

"If you had authorization from a doctor, they would," Marco said. "*Va bene,* you may have an idea here."

"The EDTA your people found in the blood sample you gave them. Mightn't they use that to keep the blood from clotting in the bag? Didn't Mrs. Ziegler say it was a blood thinner?"

"You are too smart to be a woman." Marco hugged me, and I elected to let the sexist comment slide. "If Bondurant will fingerprint Nigel Endicott when we get back to the ship, he could fax the prints to the FBI and they can easily compare them to the prints of George Gaskill. The Pennsylvania police have Gaskill in their files. We might know the answer as early as tomorrow."

It felt as if the clouds of confusion were beginning to dissipate. The engines under our feet shifted to a low rumble as we pulled up alongside the *Aegean Queen*. Folks lined up at the rail of the promenade deck waved down to us, and I felt the general movement of the passengers around me toward the ramp.

"Luc Girard said he wished he had a video of the two of you trapping Rob Segal in the back of a cab."

"I must admit, I made a very good cab driver."

"I wish I had a video of Sophie catching the krater with one hand. She'd be drafted by the Steelers, immediately."

"What do you mean? Sophie would never steal."

When would I learn to avoid references to American sports when talking to Marco? Maybe I should have said "The Saints." No, that wouldn't do either.

TWENTY-NINE

BACK ABOARD SHIP, I snatched the photos of George and Nigel off the displays in the photo shop and dashed across to the security office. Bondurant answered my knock on the door. He and Chief Letsos were in conference, but I barged past Bondurant and plunked the pictures down on Letsos's desk.

"Look. Here's what I was telling you about. See the white, sort of triangular, piece of something in front of George Gaskill's ear? Now look at Nigel Endicott." I pointed to the second photo. "Identical piece of whatever, isn't it? Put this together with the fact that we found Kathryn Gaskill and Nigel together in a men's room stall on Santorini, and think about it."

Both men looked at the photos, and then Letsos picked up the one of George and looked at it closely. Bondurant did likewise with Nigel's. They exchanged photos and studied some more. Bondurant mumbled something I didn't catch. He dragged two passports across the desk and opened both of them to the first page.

"As a matter of fact, we were discussing these before you came in, so, you see, I did take your idea seriously." Bondurant looked sideways at me. "Look at this. George Gaskill's passport. He immigrated into Athens, Greece, on June fifteenth." I looked at the passport closely, as if I'd never seen it before. "And please note that this is the only stamp in the book. It's a recently issued passport."

Bondurant flipped forward several pages and back to the photo page, handed it to me, then picked up the second passport.

Letsos, meanwhile, sat hunched forward in his swivel chair, chewing an already shredded toothpick.

Bondurant turned to the first visa/entry page in Nigel's passport. "Endicott's is also recently issued and has only two stamps. The first says he entered Istanbul, Turkey, on June fifteenth. Entering Turkey requires a visa. That's what this sticker is for." He pointed to the visa sticker. "And the second one says he entered Athens, Greece, on June seventeenth. That's it." He handed me that passport as well.

He was right. Of course, I already knew what the passports had in them but Bondurant didn't know I'd sneaked a peek at both of these when they were still in the safe. "Wait! I see how it could have been done!" I found myself telling Bondurant and Letsos an idea at the same moment it was forming in my mind. "Suppose George and Kathryn flew from the U.S. to Athens and George shows his own passport to the agent, but he has another one—this one—in another pocket." I held up Nigel's document.

"He takes the next flight from Athens to Istanbul and shows Nigel's passport to the Turkish agent. The stamp says he entered Turkey, but it doesn't say *from where*. The passport tells us he's an American citizen but it doesn't say he was on a flight from America. So he stays in Istanbul a day or so, then catches another flight back to Athens, gets the second stamp, and rejoins his wife before they head for the ship."

Bondurant looked as if he'd been slapped.

"And another thing. When we all boarded that first day, Lettie Osgood noticed a man in a brightly colored shirt going the wrong direction down the gangway toward the security gate. We even started calling him the wrong-way man. So what if George and Kathryn came aboard like a normal couple, got their picture taken, went to their room where George quickly zipped off his false goatee, his hairpiece, changed shirts…took out his contacts and put on regular glasses…" It was all coming to me so fast it scared me. "He gelled up his real hair, took out his fake front teeth…but forgot about the little piece of tissue he'd stuck on earlier when he'd cut himself shaving! All he had to do then was to go back down the gangway, slip around the metal-detector gate, pick up the backpack he'd stashed somewhere in the terminal building, and come back through. Get his picture taken again."

Bondurant didn't say anything.

Letsos finally growled out, "Security doesn't let people go back through the checkpoint after they've already boarded."

"Would they even notice? They're concentrating on people getting on. They have no reason to care who gets off."

Bondurant cleared his throat. "Let's get Endicott in here. Right now."

IT WAS THE LAST MORNING of our cruise. Ollie, Lettie, Marco, and I sat drinking coffee at the same table on the Poseidon deck where we'd sat that first day. In a few hours the *Aegean Queen* would dock once again in Piraeus Harbor. Marco had told his office not to expect him before Friday and he'd promised to see the National Museum and the Acropolis with me. I'd promised to do a night on the town with him.

Ollie raised his hat, ran his hand over his bald head,

and replaced the hat. He'd learned, the hard way, to protect his vulnerable dome from the strong Greek sun. "I talked to Stone and Leclercq last evening. They were happy to hear the three of us are no longer suspects. The very idea! To think any of us would have killed a man over a poker game. It all sounds stupid, now."

"It was those shifty eyes of yours, Ollie," Lettie said.

"I still have questions, though, especially about Malcolm Stone," I said. "He's been up to something because everywhere we've stopped, he's either picked up something, or else I've seen him sneaking around…furtively."

Lettie wiggled her fingers spookily at me. "Oooh! Furtive sneaking!"

David Bondurant and Dimitris Villas came to our table and asked if they could join us. They pulled up two extra chairs. Bondurant sat, leaned back, and stretched his legs out in front of him. He was more relaxed than I'd ever seen him. "Two birds with one stone. How sweet it is!"

"What do you mean?"

"I mean we solved both murders at the same time. We got those two birds in the office last night and they sang like canaries." Bondurant paused as if he was surprised by his own wit. "And, Dotsy, I have to hand it to you. You nailed it. The little switcheroo Gaskill pulled with the passports was exactly like you guessed."

"Who said I was guessing?"

"There is no Nigel Endicott. Anymore. George Gaskill stole his identity after he died a couple of years ago. There was a real Nigel Endicott but the man who'd been posing, periodically, as Endicott was Gaskill. He bought the farm in Vermont, got to know a few folks in that area, established credit, bank accounts, driver's license, all that stuff, in his Endicott guise."

"So they had been planning this for a long time," Marco said.

"Yes. Seems Gaskill's whole life was well and truly ruined after he became a convicted child molester. He and Kathryn, over the years, built up such a hatred for Brittany Benson, they wanted revenge. They decided George had to get a new identity, start fresh without the cloud of 'registered sex offender' following him everywhere he went. Best way to do that was to make it look like he was dead.

"They knew about the law that says unless you have a dead body, a person can't be declared dead until he's been missing for seven years, but they read about a man who fell off a cruise ship and was quickly declared dead. The premise being that a human can't swim all that far, so if he's not on board and there were no other vessels in the area to pick him up, he's a goner. So the Gaskills took out a big life insurance policy on George and began establishing his new identity. He got some fake teeth that fit over his regular ones, grew a goatee, started wearing a hairpiece to work and to church. He'd been doing this for some months so people had got used to him looking like that. A couple of weeks ago, he shaved off the goatee and started wearing a false one."

"Why?" I asked.

"Because if he appeared on the ship with a newly-shaven face, the difference between the tan on his cheeks and his chin would have been noticeable."

Marco stroked his own newly-shaven chin and grinned at me.

"And then, from old friends back in Pennsylvania, they learned Brittany Benson was working as a dancer on a cruise ship and—ta da!—let's get Brittany blamed for George's death. That would be a final justice. Let the girl who'd ruined his life learn what it feels like to get convicted of something you didn't do."

"I have a confession," I said. "I emailed my son back home. He's a high school principal like George was and he knows educators from Pennsylvania. So I asked him to find out about the Gaskill-Benson trial." Five pairs of eyes looked at me as if I'd told them I was a hacker. "He found that virtually everyone thought the charges were trumped up by Brittany and her friends, but the local political climate at the time was such that neither judge nor jury dared let the man go scot-free."

"But to convict him of a sexual offense against a child?" Lettie interjected, scowling.

"That's not as serious as the actual rape of a child."

Bondurant took over again. "Once the Gaskills started talking last night, we couldn't shut them up. They got it all off their chests. It seems that when George was going ashore in Mykonos, dressed as Endicott and wearing the sort of bright, splashy shirt conservative old George Gaskill would never wear, Papadakos was on the dock taking pictures and recognized him as Gaskill. He'd probably already looked at the embarkation pictures he took the day before and noticed the similarity. He may have noticed the little piece of tissue that Dotsy did, who knows? At any rate, Gaskill says Papadakos yelled out, "'Hey, who are you? You came aboard with a wife, and then you came aboard without a wife. Where is your wife?'"

"So George had to kill him."

"George had to kill him, and he had to kill him fast. He couldn't wait for Papadakos to blab that around the ship. It was too late for them to abandon their plan because they'd already done the bloody deck thing and three law enforcement groups were working on it.

"He told us he bought the knife in one store, bought one of those thin, disposable rain coats in another store, and tracked Papadakos down. Followed him, shoved him into an alley when he saw his chance. And killed him."

"But fifteen stab wounds?" Marco frowned. "Why did he stab him so many times? He was not angry at the man, he just wanted him dead."

"He didn't know what he was doing," Bondurant said. "This was his first murder and he made a royal mess of it."

"I have another question," I said. "Yesterday when I passed Kathryn on donkey back, she was on her cell phone. George would've been in the cable car at that time. Looking back on it now, I think she must have been informing George I was onto them. But how did she know?"

Bondurant winked and touched his temple. "Aha. She told us that, too. She was on the tender we were on going over to the island and was standing outside the cabin when you were telling the rest of us Nigel was actually George and George wasn't dead. She heard that through the open window, and hid out in the ladies' room until we docked. She slipped past us while we were huddled up discussing our plans, ran ashore, and grabbed a donkey. She assumed none of us would choose that path when we could take the cable car instead."

"And as soon as Brittany got away from me, after Sophie and I snatched the krater, she called Rob Segal."

"Poor Dimitris," Marco said, punching Villas on the shoulder. "When you hopped out, both of your suspects ran away."

We all had to laugh.

"What about the watch?" Lettie asked. "Who actually put it in Brittany's closet?"

"Kathryn Gaskill. She made up some story and got a cabin boy to open the room for her. She told us she really felt bad when they started accusing Ollie and the other two men in the poker game, so she planted the watch to throw suspicion back on Brittany."

"How cruel," I said.

"Not as cruel as it would've been to let me hang for it," Ollie said, and he looked dead serious.

I FOLLOWED LETTIE and Ollie to their room while Marco slipped away to his own room to finish packing. Lettie shifted one suitcase from the middle of the floor to clear a path between me and the sofa. Ollie walked into their bathroom and emerged with a double handful of bottles and brushes.

"As you can see, we aren't quite packed up yet," Lettie said.

"We have a bit more stuff than we came with." She pursed her mouth and squinted at Ollie. "I've squished four big vacuum bags flat. They're all full of sponges."

"Really, Ollie," I said. "Do you think you'll need all those sponges?"

There was a knock at the door. It was Luc and Sophie. "Dotsy, Sophie and I want to thank you for introducing us to each other. It's hard to believe we've been on the same boat for weeks and it took a total stranger to bring us together." He had his arm around her waist. "And I'm grateful to both you and Mrs. Osgood for discovering the stolen artifacts that had been right under my nose all along."

"Are they all recovered?"

"All but the bracelet. We found the bull head wrapped in a towel inside the amphora."

Another knock at the door, this time it was Dimitris Villas. He was in uniform now—badge, holster, revolver, and all. The sight of the gun startled me a bit, since police in these islands didn't normally walk around armed. In fact, the only gun I'd seen recently was the one Goatman fired at me.

Villas must have noticed the look on my face because he patted the gun and said, "I have to escort Mr. Gaskill to Mykonos. With a murder charge waiting for him, we can't be too sure what he might try between here and there. Can't be too careful, you know."

Sophie shivered. "That looks like the gun that nearly killed Dotsy and me two days ago."

"No, that gun was a pistol," I said, bending over to get a better look at the holstered weapon. "This is a revolver."

Villas took the gun out and showed Sophie the rotating cylinder.

"May I see?" Sophie took the gun from Villas's hand. Villas looked edgy. I felt certain he wasn't supposed to let anyone handle his gun, and he seemed to be forming a diplomatic way of asking her to give it back.

Luc made a little motion toward her as if he, too, didn't like the idea of the one-armed Sophie Fumblefingers with a gun.

It was too late. The gun bobbled in her hand, she clutched, and it went off. The bullet pierced a closet door.

The shot was followed by a strange rumbling noise. The closet door banged open and out flew bushels and bushels of damp sponges. The bullet, having ruptured all the vacuum bags, released the little puffballs from their confinement, hurling them outward toward all of us at warp speed. Ducking and weaving, we all screamed, Sophie dropped the gun, and Luc pulled it out from beneath the sponges that now covered the entire floor. He handed it back to Villas.

"Awfully sorry about that," he said.

"Don't be too sorry, Dr. Girard," Lettie said. "I think we just discovered where Brittany hid the bracelet!"

I recalled Brittany Benson had made two strange and rather unnecessary visits to the Osgoods' room a few days ago. We all watched as Lettie climbed over the sponges on the bed and plucked the gold serpent bracelet, circa third century B.C., off the telephone.

* * * * *

REQUEST YOUR FREE BOOKS!

2 FREE NOVELS
PLUS 2 FREE GIFTS!

WORLDWIDE LIBRARY®

Your Partner in Crime